Blurb

**He's cold as stone,
but she'll melt him from the inside.**

I couldn't believe it when my friend called to tell me she knew
someone who needed a nanny.

Jobless, broke, and with a landlord who hated me, I had to take it.

Turns out it was too good to be true.

Rex Sloane is cold, hard, and impenetrable. I'm not convinced he's
even human. Oh, and he's a dick.

I should've walked my over-qualified legs right out of his
penthouse the moment he screamed at me for wearing a tutu with
his daughter, but *stupid me*, I didn't.

His daughter captivated me with her sweet eyes and silent voice,
and I couldn't walk away.

Rex is clearly an ass and it's a mistake to stay.

Yet ... I have to.

For both of them.

KETLEY ALLISON

CHAPTER 1

Rex

SHE'S LATE.

I file that flaw under my *Not Good Enough* mental checklist, a list that's taking up major real estate in my brain, and I haven't even met Harper Mei yet.

But if this girl can't hack the simple concept of time, it's better I cause her to run for the city skyscrapers than waste even one second of meeting her—never mind allowing her to come within feet of my daughter.

"Time check?" I growl at Patrice, who doesn't flinch in the face of Cranky Rex. Nor has she ever made a T-Rex joke, and I respect her for it.

Patrice straightens the hem of her coral skirt, shoving it past her knees. Her brown hair is pulled back into a low ponytail and she's devoid of make-up, yet still looks fresh despite dealing with a puke-geyser of a kid. Man, I'm going to miss her.

"Miss Mei is about twenty minutes behind her interview time," she says. "But there's some kind of problem in the subway because of the rain. Could be why."

"I don't care." I relax into a white leather sofa chair in the middle of my expansive living room, with floor-to-ceiling windows spanning a Hudson River view. All three bridges and the Brooklyn skyline sit with us on this summer evening, the river misting underneath from the splattering rain.

"Is Stella still asleep?" I ask Patrice.

Patrice glances at the monitor on the side table where a black-and-white screen shows my five-year-old slumbering, butt in the air. Stella's kicked the daily nap, but when she's sick, we ignore all tantrum-infused defiance. Patrice is better at getting Stella to listen than I am, though. *Holy hell.*

"Off like a light switch," Patrice confirms.

"Good." I sigh, rubbing my eyes.

It was a long day with Stella and the stomach flu, capped off with the afternoon grind of a final rehearsal for my band's gig in the city tonight. After that, we board a plane to Canada for three nights and I haven't broken the news to Stella yet.

I haven't confessed that she's getting a new nanny, either.

The poor girl will throw up on me *again* for all this shit.

A knock on the door draws me out of my storm-fueled grumble, and I lift out of my chair to answer it, gesturing at Patrice to sit tight.

Another, more furtive knock sounds as I stride into the foyer.

"Oh, now *your* time is valuable?" I ask loudly. "Hang on a damn second."

I swing the door open, and a child greets me.

Her earthy gray eyes rise to meet mine.

"This isn't the season for girl scout cookies," I say.

Those same eyes narrow. "Wow, a short joke. I never get those."

"You look old enough to be someone's prom date."

"And you look like you should be an extra on the set of the *Aquaman* movie." She blinks. "I guess we both missed our calling."

I frown. My hair's down and I'm considered a large, tall man, but...

"I'd argue I'm more Tarzan-ish than ocean man-fish," I say.

"And I'd argue that my height makes me spry and able to corner toddlers under tables," she quips.

I say with an unintentional smile, "I'm guessing you're Harper Mei."

"That's me."

I angle my head. "You're wet."

Harper licks her dampened lips, and the movement causes the water droplets to sparkle against her cheeks. Her short black hair is as sleek and shiny as a seal pup, and her basic leather jacket shimmers and squeaks as she breathes. Her lavender t-shirt is open to a V at her collarbone, framing the alluring peak of her hardened nipples.

"Forgot my umbrella," she says, her words drawing my gaze back to hers.

I clear my throat and step aside to let her in.

Harper doesn't move. Despite resembling a barnacle that's washed up on the East River's shore, her posture shouts confidence and a complete lack of embarrassment. Even as a stray raindrop falls from her hairline and slides down to the tip of her nose, she doesn't blink or brush it away. Her chin remains stubbornly jutted out.

She's caught my notice, and not because she was recommended by my drummer Easton and his fiancé, Taryn. Of the five girls I've interviewed today alone, Harper Mei is the only one who hasn't tittered at the door in damp, see-through sundresses, asking to use my bathroom to "freshen up."

And then pilfer through my shit, searching for souvenirs.

"Come on in," I say.

Her shoes *slurp* with sound as she steps over the threshold.

"Rex." Patrice's voice comes from the living area, where she's still sitting. "Get her a towel, maybe?"

I give a curt nod, turn to the half-bath I have somewhere in this hallway, and grab a hand towel.

Harper takes it without complaint the minute my mind thinks maybe a hand towel after a storm is about as good as a washcloth after a jump in the pool.

"Can I get you something bigger?" I ask as Harper wipes her face and scrunches her hair in the small towel.

She shakes her head. "Not if you don't mind a giant wet spot on your couch."

Is she joking? I can't tell if she's joking.

I motion her into the main room and remind myself that she's in my territory and there's no explicable reason for the strange, invisible vibrations hanging between us.

"This is Patrice," I say as we hit the open area and Patrice comes into view. "Stella's current nanny. She'll be leaving us in a week."

Harper nods at Patrice, shaking off her jacket and hanging it on the arm of my couch, making me wonder if I should've taken it from her at the entrance and hung it up, like a true gentleman would. I'm no good at chivalry.

"Um..." Patrice blinks hard, then pays particular attention to the floor. I glance at Harper, wondering what...

Oh.

Harper's breasts are in full, damp, molded effect. I blink too, but a lot slower.

Patrice jumps up, considering I've lost what little powers of communication I had. "You must be chilly, Harper. Let me get you a blanket to wrap yourself up in."

"It's okay," Harper says, brushing her hair back from her face, a succulent, small breast lifting with the movement. "I'm—"

Harper's eyes stray to mine, and the tendons in my neck go hard once she's figured out where I'm looking.

"Oh God." She crosses her arms, a peachy, scarlet flush flowing into her rain-cooled porcelain cheeks.

"Apologies." I stare at anything but the girl and eat up hardwood as I find my seat. "Please. Sit while we wait for Patrice to come back."

Harper drags her jacket from the arm of the couch over her

chest as she sits, clutching the garment like a teddy bear. "To think I was worried about the blood stains on my shirt."

My brows turn into rods of thunder. "Excuse me?"

Now that she's drawn attention to it, I notice the splotches of red on her arms, made into a blurred macabre watercolor by the storm, and the black marks on her bare legs.

The flush in her cheeks depletes to white. "I mean—no, not real blood. I was helping Jamie with a school project. You know Jamie, right? Jamie Maddox? Easton and Taryn's son? He's eleven, and we're creating a diorama of *Pet Sematary* for school." She chews on her lower lip, then says, "I'm blabbering. Sorry. I didn't just come from a murder scene. I swear."

My expression doesn't change. "An eleven-year-old still needs a nanny?"

Hell, when I was eleven I was busy boosting bicycle tires and trying beer for the first time. In retrospect, maybe I could've bene-fited from a Patrice.

Harper crosses her legs, droplets sheening against the smooth, hairless skin. Her cut-off shorts curve up her ass cheek with the movement.

I sure as fuck wouldn't have benefited from a Harper. I would've had a hard-on for her.

Harper replies, "He's growing out of my company. Hence why I'm here."

She's young, this girl, and I may be a brute for picturing her curves and the parts of her body that bloom rose-like and sweet. Yet, I was a poet before I ever became a lyricist, and I can't help but appreciate a woman, even one who damns herself into a grave within five seconds of meeting her.

I'm almost thirty. I can't be eyeing a girl barely over the legal drinking age who could be my kid's nanny.

Except I am.

"Here you are." Patrice saves the moment by striding in with one of my cashmere blankets and places it over Harper's shoulders.

"Thank you," Harper says. "Today was laundry day and I... well. Forgot to save a bra before sending my stuff out to be washed."

"Happens to the best of us," Patrice says politely, stepping around Harper's legs and taking a seat opposite.

I glance at Patrice, who keeps ledgers for my pantry, categorizes Stella's toys and playdates, and alphabetizes bathroom supplies. I doubt she's ever forgotten to wear so much as an undershirt.

Unless I remember that one time...

Damn it, man, shake yourself out of it.

I let out a low growl in frustration and Harper's attention cuts to me, eyelids flaring, which I ignore.

"You come highly recommended from my boy East," I say, leaning back while splaying my palms on my thighs. It has the added benefit of adjusting my half-chub without being obvious. "You've been with Jamie for how long?"

"Eons," Harper says. "I took one look at the kid and fell in love."

She answers like the mere remembrance of her first meeting with Jamie is a pleasant shine to an otherwise shitty, storm-filled day.

I say, "He's affectionately referred to as Little Shit when he attends our rehearsals. So, if you're about to rave about that so-called sweet little angel and how lucky you were to nanny him—"

"Hell, no," Harper cuts in. "He blackmails more than he gives out hugs. Jamie's smart, cutthroat, and knows how to take advantage of anyone who considers him to have low IQ or special needs. He *also* knows how to get what he wants from anyone who feels sorry for him." Harper raises her brows. "How do you think he learned to be such a badass?"

The skin under my right eye twitches.

"Are you saying you taught the boy how to be a swindler?" I ask.

"No. I taught him to be strong. How to not take shit from assholes." Harper glances at Patrice, who's gone bone white. "Sorry for the cursing."

I scratch under my chin. "Would you consider yourself more of a protector than a nanny?"

"I think I'm both," Harper answers. "Jamie's the first long-term nanny job I've had, and he came with a lot of positive traits and independence already, but I like to think, after six years with him, I've groomed him to be the Little Shit he is today." Harper grins.

Patrice chokes on nothing.

After an amused glance at Patrice, I say, "I have to admit, this isn't the interview I predicted. What with Taryn's reputation..."

Harper arches a brow. "You thought you'd get a schoolmarm?"

"Well. Yes."

"I first met Taryn by cornering her when she was moving into our apartment complex," Harper says. "She was desperate for a babysitter, since to keep her Big Corporate Job, she had to start work right away. I said I was CPR-certified, and that was enough to take her kid, I guess."

Patrice lets out a squeak of disbelief.

I make a low sound in my throat, then say, "Patrice, do you have questions?"

"A few," she grits out, then straightens in her seat and picks up her notebook from the side table.

Patrice poises her pen over the paper. "Tell me, Harper..."

"Sure, what's up?" Harper asks.

"How did Jamie not *die* while in your care?"

CHAPTER 2

Harper

"Pure, dumb luck," I answer.

Patrice's lips thin at my response and she scribbles in her note-book, something to the effect of, *Never ever EVER will this girl come near Rex's child.*

"I'm kidding," I tell Patrice. "I *am* CPR-certified and have worked in daycares all throughout high school as a part-time job. Then I went full time for a while, after getting my Norland degree, obviously."

Norland College is an elite nanny school in the UK whose most notable pupils are nannies for the royal family. At its mention, Patrice's eyes grow small, wondering whether I'm fucking with her.

I'm totally fucking with her.

"Do you have a resume?" she asks.

This woman thinks I'm half-chewed gum, but I'm forced to admit that she's not far off. I'm a hot, wet mess. Couple that with my irresistible urge to rile up my potential future employer, who is otherwise sitting like a block of concrete, and this interview is on the fast track to Hell.

But Rex Sloane is just as god-like in person, his hair the color of a burnished gold coin and a body cut and molded by an Ancient

Greek sculptor. His eyes are blue-tinted glass, glistening and flawless, and whenever they're pinned on me, most of my internal organs screech to get closer.

I say *most*, because my heart's holding back. Despite his gorgeous veneer, I see what hides within his description, and how everything used to describe him is … cold.

"Yes. I have the resume right here."

I dig my hand into one pocket of my leather jacket, searching for the folded piece of paper.

When my fingers clamp around it, I groan.

It's a soaking, sodden disaster.

Much like yourself.

After a swallow, I pull it out and attempt to peel back the damp folds. "I really should invest in a raincoat."

"Rex," Patrice says. "Can I talk to you privately for a moment?"

I slouch against the hard, uncomfortable couch, rubbing my lips with the acknowledgment that yeah, I've screwed this up royally.

Rex clamps his hands on the arms of his chair and rises. As he stands, his thick lashes lower, but the ocean of his irises cuts through, crashing right into mine.

The connection sends shivers unrelated to the cold down my chest. Even my lips tingle.

Beneath the cascading depths of his gaze, however, there is a hard, granular bottom. I'm looking at a very closed off man—or a guarded soul. Either way, despite how my body reacts, I have full confidence I'm never going to know the man. I'll only come to know the Rock God.

Rex follows Patrice and her impossibly silent feet into a small hallway, turning into another room and shutting the door.

I use the alone time to study my surroundings. Rex's penthouse duplex screams money, and with that comes a lot of open space. There aren't many walls in his 5,000 square foot apartment. The large, top-of-the-line kitchen feeds into the living room, hence their need to find a hallway and hide.

I don't mind. I sit there, gnawing on my lower lip for a while, before I do exactly what I predicted I'd do.

Popping up from the chair, I tip-toe into the hallway with my sloshing, heavy, fake Army boots, and hold an ear up to the door.

"... under-qualified, frighteningly obtuse, and will probably be responsible for Stella's first serious injury."

To my surprise, it's not Patrice's voice I'm hearing. It's Rex's.

Frowning, I wait for Patrice's response, since she so obviously disapproved of me to my face. Unlike Rex Sloane, who low-key thinks I'll kill his child.

"... Jamie?" I catch the end-tail of Patrice's question. My ear aches the harder I press it against the closed door. Patrice continues. "... mastered sign language in less than a year. Managed a kid with special needs for close to six years ... not something to brush aside..."

She's defending me?

"You're defending her?" Rex asks, his low baritone easier to hear now that he's gotten louder. "I'd think a woman with a degree in child development would catch the *insane* under qualifications this girl has—"

"You can't teach a bond, Rex."

"The fuck's that supposed to mean?"

"Her connection with Jamie," Patrice clarifies. "Someone could have all the training in the world and still not connect with a child. I think Harper should meet Stella. Once that happens, you should decide."

"My opinion is my own. And I say no."

"This is the twenty-third interview you've said no to, Rex."

"Good. No."

"Your *best friend* recommended this woman—"

"It's suspiciously appearing to be a prank to me at this point."

I reel back. Rex thinks I'm a *joke*?

Patrice says something else and I hurry to resume my position against the door, my palms pressing hard on the wood.

"... and I'd think," Patrice argues, "that *my* opinion would matter more than your immediate dismissal. Especially after last night, when we—"

"Are you spying?" a high voice asks.

I freeze, then turn around, my cheeks betraying my sin by turning into two overripe tomatoes. With my pale, half-Taiwanese skin, embarrassment acts as a lantern for my lies. And the last thing I need is an eyewitness to my eavesdropping. Especially a kid witness. Children are the biggest narcs I've ever come across.

A little girl stands in the entrance to the hallway, holding a tattered, faded pink blanket. Her straw-colored curls are askew on one side of her head and flattened on the other. Her face is blotchy, but not from embarrassment. More like from awakening from a decent nap.

"No. Hi," I say, leaning oh-so-casual against the wall.

The girl—Stella, I assume—angles her head. "Are you my new mommy?"

I choke on my saliva but muffle it by coughing into my hand. "Um—no."

Her large, liquid gold eyes shimmer with lost puppy effectiveness. "Do you know where my mommy is?"

There are many things I could do right now. I could bend down to her level, tuck a stray hair behind her ear and whisper that wherever her mommy is, she probably misses her very much. Or, I could use this opportunity to scoot the child aside and leave—it's obvious I'm not getting this job. But children deserve honesty, especially when they've been around deceptive adults. And this one looks like she has.

I answer, "I don't. Sorry."

After a beat where I'm convinced Stella's waiting for me to crumble under her damp, beguiling gaze, Stella blinks away the fake tears. "You're the first lady to tell the truth."

I push off the wall. "Am I?"

Stella nods. "Most ladies give me a sad look. Some ask if I understand what happened to my mommy. One lady hugged me way too hard. I make all of them uncomfortable."

I can't help replying with a half-smile of my own. "On purpose, I'm guessing."

This time, Stella's eyes betray her mischief. "My therapist says I'm not good with people. Come on. I want to show you my ponies."

Stella spins on one heel and scampers into the main room, her blanket tucked under one arm like a football.

"Wait!" I throw a furtive look at the closed door where the voices of Patrice and Rex continue to clash.

Should I bang on the door? Tell them Stella's loose? That she's headed for some kind of pony stable in the apartment?

The smack of Stella's bare feet on hardwood fades, and my mind turns to what traps and trip hazards this expansive apartment harbors. It's a fancy homestead that has a garage, for sure. Which, when you live in a skyscraper, means an elevator for your car.

Oh, God. A five-year-old trapped in an elevator garage.

"Stella!" I whisper fiercely, then thud after her in my waterlogged boots.

CHAPTER 3

Rex

NO. Just no.

Harper Mei, while a beautiful smartass, is not the nanny for my Stella.

I need someone like Patrice, a fairy godmother type with Mary Poppins-like playdates and the discipline of a prep school nun.

Stella, while fiery and sweet, is also the most manipulative child to ever cross my threshold. She'd eat that unschooled, unkempt, un*prepared* Harper as a delectable dessert during one of her many tea parties.

And then save the leftovers for me.

"Rex? Are you even listening?" Patrice asks, hands on her hips as we continue to battle in the rarely used guest room.

"Yes, but it's not changing my answer." I gesture to the closed door. "You can let her down gently."

About as gentle as my palms would be as they scrape across her pale skin.

Patrice's lips thin in the shadows. "I'm leaving in a week. *One week.* If you don't choose someone soon, I won't be around to train them before I begin my teaching job. I can't prepare Stella."

The mention of my daughter's name grounds me. "All I'm thinking about is Stella."

"Don't I know it," Patrice blurts, before blinking hard and glancing to the side.

"Pats..." I try.

"Don't," she says. "Don't use my nickname with such a pitying undertone. Last night was hard enough to deal with."

My molars grind at the unwanted flashback, when Patrice snuck into my bedroom, clad in a thin, strappy pajama shirt. White. See-through. A shoe-string thong stretched over her hips and rode up the cleft of her ass as she climbed into my bed and grazed her fingers down my spine and into my briefs.

She's gorgeous, my Pats. And she tried, very hard, to remind me she could be more. She was more than willing to suck me and fuck me into oblivion whenever I wanted in addition to catering to the needs of my child. It was brazen, unexpected, and confusing—until it made sense. She'd put in her notice a few days ago. Patrice was giving the chance of us one last shot.

As a red-blooded male, it was difficult to pull her hand away. But as Stella's father, it's a no-brainer to explain to Patrice that she's not meant to be mine.

If only Patrice could understand that.

"I'm not what you need me to be," I say now, my voice going rough. I hate hurting the woman who has done so much for Stella. "I'm no full-time lover and I'm *especially* no boyfriend."

Patrice's nose scrunches like the very topic pains her.

She says, "If it weren't for that little girl, I'd be long gone, do you understand? Yesterday would've been *it* for me, and you'd be left alone to interview my replacement, without my input or pres-ence—though apparently that's what you'd prefer."

I throw my hands up. "You *really* think Harper's the one?"

"Her resume says it all," Patrice says. "What's left of it, anyway."

I shake my head. I didn't even bother to look over Harper's credentials. Interviewing her was a favor to Easton, who's a guilt-ridden pussy at letting his nanny go so abruptly.

"Harper's not perfect," Patrice allows, "But there's something there. She'll be able to handle Stella and if you give me this week to prepare them both, I'm sure I can leave here without regret."

She chokes on the last word.

My shoulders slope. I say, with a resigned mumble, "I'm shocked you're going to bat for her. Back in the living room, you were—"

"I'm tired, Rex," Patrice says, her eyes big, wide and wet. "And I want what's best for Stella and for you. Out of all the prospective nannies, Harper's been the only one to outlast your glacial stare as you oversee the interview."

I scoff, deep in my throat. "So she's not afraid of me. That's—"

"That's everything," Patrice cuts in. She levels a good, hard look at me as she passes by to get to the door. "Believe me on that."

"Pats—"

But Patrice, who has deemed herself no longer in my employ and therefore can be as cucumber cool as she likes, ignores my call and steps into the hallway.

I'm sorry last night didn't turn into what you wanted. I'm sorry I'm such an irredeemable asshole who will only ever give a shit about one woman, my daughter.

Stop trying to get caught up in my selfish storm.

But I say none of this as I follow her out.

Maybe I should've.

Harper isn't where we left her.

"What the—" I glance from the empty seat where Harper's damp body once perched. "Is she a kid I have to keep tabs on?"

Patrice sighs, disappointment etched into her features. "She left."

"Perhaps it was my glacial stare that made her run," I say.

Patrice gives me a sidelong look.

A mild *what a shame* enters my thoughts. I was looking forward to one last meeting with Harper. I wonder if her lashes were still dewy from the rain, her lips darkened like a rose in the cold.

That very line makes me itch for my notebook. My pencil. *My lyrics.*

Patrice cuts me another look, but says, "Then we're back to square one. I'll call another agency, get more interviews set up—"

Giggles and muffled bangs interrupt Patrice's planning, and we swing our attention to a second hallway on the opposite side of the room.

I ask, "Is that...?"

"Stella's awake," Patrice says, and takes a fast clip toward Stella's room.

I follow, Patrice enjoying every moment as I fall back on her heels, and the closer we come to Stella's door, engraved with large, rose gold, curlicue letters of her name, the clearer Stella's voice becomes.

As does another's.

I emit a low warning. "Is someone in there with her?"

Patrice turns her head before laying a hand on the knob. "It must be—"

"Oh. Hi!" a perky voice says.

Harper scrambles to a stand as Patrice swings Stella's door open and we both step over the threshold.

I register the tea party first.

And oh, it's a good thing I do, because it's what comes after that sends me into pure, unadulterated, barely contained rage.

CHAPTER 4

Harper

I NOTICE PATRICE'S STIFFENED, blank features first, which isn't a concern. Patrice is basically a Do-It-All Debbie doll come to life.

It's what looms behind her that causes my heart to fall, and fall, and *splatter* into a deep, dark cavern.

"Um..." I clear my throat in the resulting silence, straightening the pink tutu Stella insisted I shimmy into, since she blandly stated that her ponies only speak to ladies in ballet class.

By ponies, she meant figurines, and they surround us in a mini circle as we pour them pretend tea and Stella fixes her tiara. It's too big for her and slides down her forehead every time she leans forward.

I surreptitiously push Stella's tiara back into place as she stands at the sight of her father.

Stella's dad, the famous Rex Sloane, who right now looks like he ripped the head off a rather incorrigible raptor and now has to deal with the rest of the pack.

I gulp as he steps up beside Patrice, his irises turning ultraviolet blue as he takes in the scene in front of him, the box full of tutus and other ballet gear that Stella's dragged out into the open and the mess of plastic tea ware in the center of Stella's decked-out Princess room.

Not to mention the unmade bed and my wet leather jacket draped over the tangled duvet.

And we can't forget me, standing paint-stained and donning pink frills, wondering why the hell a kid's messy room is making Rex's face turn so purple.

"We were just..." I straighten my shoulders. Lift my chin. And say, with stronger emphasis, "Stella woke up and came into the main room. I didn't want to interrupt your meeting, so I thought I'd entertain her for a bit while you—"

"Stella," Rex says, barely audible through his teeth. "What have you done?"

"She told me we could, Daddy!" Stella says, and grabs my hand. I try not to jolt at the unexpected contact or the big fat lie she just told. "Harper wanted to play dress-up, and I told her we had stuff, but they were off-limits. She said those are the best kinds of costumes."

One corner of my mouth digs into my cheek. Did this kid just *play* me?

Rex's focus cuts to the plain brown box, overflowing with sequins and tulle and colorful fabrics. "Where did you find this?"

"In your closet," Stella says, then, too sweetly, adds, "Am I in trouble?"

I see the muscles of Rex's cheeks pulsing. It spurs me to get out of this tutu as fast as possible. Patrice notices and gives a minute nod of approval.

"I told you never to go in there," Rex says.

Stella asks, with the innocence of a child but the forethought of a fairy-tale villain, "Why's ballet stuff in your closet, Daddy?"

"Patrice," Rex says, and Patrice's shoulders straighten at the mention of her name.

Such a good little soldier, I think. Then I wonder, why do I have catty thoughts about Patrice? She's not the one standing in the middle of a set-up masterminded by a five-year-old.

Ugh, am I *jealous* amid being painted as the sole perpetrator of pilfering tutus?

"Collect these things and get them out of my sight," Rex says to Patrice.

Patrice shoots forward, stuffing the colorful, whimsical fabric back into the box and gesturing to Stella. "Come on, honey, it's time to take the costume off."

Stella's jaw locks, and in that moment, she looks identical to her father. "No."

"Stella, not now." Patrice glances at Rex, who maintains his imitation of a stone gargoyle in the doorway.

I also dare a peek at Rex, even though he's barely spared me a glance. *This* is the lead singer of Nocturne Court? The man who seduces his fans by singing to them, grabbing their hands at concerts, and kissing their palms? Signing breasts and belly buttons? Crowding in for selfies?

It can't be.

Who is *this* man?

"We were just playing," I say. "We weren't doing any harm."

Rex acts like I haven't spoken. Which is why I didn't bother to defend myself against a five-year-old. I'm already done for.

"Stella," he snaps.

Stella jerks at the whiplash of her father's voice, and her lower lip trembles. "But Daddy."

"I said *now*, Stella. You know the rules. And you broke them. You do not go into my closet. Ever. Do you hear me?"

"But Harper said…"

I'm about to deny saying any such thing, but Stella starts to cry softly and I don't see manipulation in her tears. She does as her father asks, and with Patrice's help, steps out of her tutu and hands over the tiara.

"They're such pretty things," I hear Stella whisper. "I don't know why you want to hide them away."

Me neither, I think in solidarity. This poor girl is being yelled at for reasons I can't fathom, and my pissiness at being blamed for something I didn't do transfers over to her dad for being so angry about ballet costumes he's stuffing away in his closet so his daughter can't use them.

No wonder the outfits smelled so musty when Stella gave them to me. That should've been my first clue. Glittering, over-the-top outfits like that are catnip for children. They would've smelled like candy and spilled milk if Stella had access to them. They should be stained with sweet, sticky fingerprints and ripped in places from overuse. The tiaras should have cracked diamonds and the pointe shoes shredded ribbons.

Yet they're too pristine. Too perfect.

Too preserved.

No wonder she lied to get to them.

The feeling that they should hang in Stella's closet, for whenever she wants them, grips me inexplicably.

When Patrice gestures for my pink tulle skirt, I school any rage I feel on Stella's behalf and pass it over. She stuffs it back into the box.

Not my business, I say as a mantra, and clamp my mouth shut, lest it act of its own accord and say something snarky to the asshole Rock God who harbors tutus in the dark recesses of his closet.

"And the crown," Rex says.

I tear my glare away from the box of ballet costumes. "What?"

"The crown. On your head." Rex can barely stand to look at me. "Take it off."

"Fine."

The tiara's combs catch in my hair as I fumble to slide it off, and a few ebony strands go with it as Patrice takes it from me and sets it on top. I don't wince, though. I fear if I do, Rex will sense weakness and devour me with his teeth.

My nether regions tingle and I frown. That thought shouldn't turn me on.

As Patrice wrestles the box shut, I direct my attention away from Rex's mouth to the strange scene unfolding in this room.

These must be precious heirlooms that Rex has hidden away. Either that or ... no. No way.

The very thought lifts my mouth into a traitorous grin, and that's the exact moment Rex notices me for more than a millisecond.

His eyes turn into an arctic freeze. "This is funny to you?"

"No." I search for words under the frost of his glare. "*No. I—I was only—*"

Stella smiles through the sheen of tears on her cheeks, and unless I'm hallucinating, it's colder than her father's as she watches me.

"You're dismissed," Rex says.

"Rex," Patrice hisses.

"Stella. Come with me," he says.

And with that, Rex leaves. Stella takes one last, longing study of the Ballet Box, then scurries after her father.

As soon as Rex's presence is no longer a tangible threat, I take a deep, needed inhale.

"I apologize for that," Patrice says, rising and brushing off her knees.

Now that the threat has disappeared, I can't resist the need to be candid. "What the hell *was* that?"

"There are some things Rex is very sensitive to. This is one of them."

"A child's dress-up game?"

"No." At last, Patrice releases her focus from where Rex once stood. "Not that."

I venture to ask, "... *His* dress-up game?"

Patrice snorts, then covers her mouth as she stifles her laughter. "No wonder you were grinning."

"I mean, with the way he reacted ... I had to ask," I say,

gesturing at the box. "Not that I judge. If that's his jam, good for him."

"It's nothing like that," Patrice says, then shakes her head as she collects herself. "He's a tough man to get a read on, but he's devoted to his daughter. What you saw ... that's rare for him. To yell at her like that."

"Is it rare for Stella, too?"

Patrice cocks her head, but no surprise registers in her features at the question. "What do you mean?"

"Her behavior."

"Oh."

Patrice doesn't elaborate, but I feel the need to in the way of establishing ... camaraderie? Rex may be cold, aloof and terrifying, but I don't have the same reservations with Stella's current nanny. "You must know what I'm referring to."

"Stella set you up." Patrice nods. "You're not the first prospective nanny to fall victim to her adorable lies. Or teacher. Or ... friend. She's doing that more and more. Withdrawing in class, lying or cheating to get her way."

"I don't know what's worse, that I fell for it or that Rex fell for it."

Patrice jolts at my frankness and I order my lips to sew themselves shut.

"There's a lot going on in his house, under all the pristine marble," Patrice says.

Honesty is not the response I expected, so I respond lamely, "Every family has their secrets, I guess."

"And Stella, well, she hasn't adjusted to life without her mother yet. That's why she's so sweet and sour with these nanny interviews. She thinks we're trying to replace Aesha."

Jeez. Even the name is beautiful. "Stella seems to have adjusted to you."

"To an extent. But I don't belong here." Patrice straightens the waistline of her skirt. "Not anymore."

I want to ask why but I've promised myself not to butt into anyone's business, lest they want to know my own.

"He's not the Rex Sloane I see at concerts, that's for sure," I say instead. I'm having so much trouble reconciling the famous persona with whatever just walked into this room. "I guess you can scratch me off the list."

Patrice's features grow serious. "Don't start shopping around your resume yet."

I arch a brow. "I'm pretty sure that's not my future employer. You know, the guy who just lifted his nose in the air and said *you're dismissed* after murdering me with his eyes."

"What happened in here was out of your control and not your fault. There's a lot Rex keeps to himself. A lot Stella needs to work through."

"What exactly happened in here?"

Patrice waves me off. She's doing that a lot. "Go home but wait for my call. I think I can still save this. Stella likes you. Even Rex can't ignore that fact."

Pretty sure that little girl hates me and is more than willing to frame me for more serious crimes.

I grab my jacket from the bed and slide it on, thinking at least I can leave here with little to no expectations.

We say nothing more as I get ready to leave, Patrice busying herself by sealing the box shut with some kind of twine she's pulled from her dress's pocket.

Man. This woman really is a modern day Nanny DoGood. I never stood a chance.

"Why are you doing this?" I ask.

Patrice looks up from her packing. "Excuse me?"

"This. Me." I place a hand on my chest. "Why are you fighting to get me hired? In the interview, you seemed..."

"Yes, well." Patrice rises back into a stand. "If I'm to be honest, we haven't had the best of luck with prospective nannies. If Rex hasn't rudely declined every application and person to date, then Stella has."

"Including me," I say.

"Including you," Patrice echoes. "Except with one small difference. Small, but notable."

"And that is?"

"He stayed for the entire interview. Even asked questions. That didn't happen with any of the others."

I gnaw on my lower lip. "He judges people that fast?"

"Rex's bullshit detector is spot on," Patrice says. "Same with his daughter."

Patrice may be on to something, but logic can't ignore the one, tiny hurdle that remains: There's no way Rex Sloane will *ever* hire me.

Muttering goodbye to Patrice, I show myself out, eager to leave this place as fast as my squeaky boots will allow.

I find the outside storm to be far more welcoming, especially now that I've been caught between the two eyes of an unexpected hurricane.

CHAPTER 5

Rex

SHE'S TOO hot to be Stella's nanny.

My cock does a little dance every time I see her.

She's right for Stella, but wrong for me.

Forbidden.

Harper is young, too-soon-to-be-plucked fruit.

Yeah, not things I can point out to Patrice, and therefore, she wins.

Harper Mei starts on Monday.

Patrice met my arguments against hiring her with unexpected curveballs and antagonism. For every one of my *nays*, Patrice mustered up a *yay*. She spent so many hours cajoling, badgering, and pointing out that no other potential nanny came close to maintaining my interest that I relented.

So long as Stella gets proper care, which, despite her multiple failings, Harper is capable of, I have little to argue against.

Four days from now, Harper begins as Stella's nanny on a trial basis, and it's during that week I plan to pick apart everything she does wrong and fire her.

The thought calms me, and I turn back to the music stand where I'm scribbling down lyrics and accompanying chords.

"Ready, Rex?"

I grunt and nod, lowering my pencil and adjusting my guitar strap. "Let's try this song on."

My bandmates, East, Wyn, and Mason, stand with me in our rented studio as we compose our latest album, set for release next year. We're only three songs in and I'm sensing the struggle to create a hit. So far, none of our new songs have caught the same viral steam, the similar fire, that our previous Billboard toppers possessed.

Writer's block happens. It gets worse when your main, black-hearted lyricist finds his happily ever after. Easton Mack is no longer morose, dark and secretive. Instead, he's happy as a lark and therefore no good to us. I can't strum chords and give a raw voice to *my dreams are alive and I'm waiting for you to arrive in a white dress.*

Well, I can, if I add *when I strip off your white but keep the lace, you'll become a sexy devil sitting on my face.*

East, unsurprisingly, doesn't support the changes.

"Spinner says we need more sex, more angst, more controversy," I say as I pass my recent pages around so the guys can glance over them.

Apart from East, I'm the only other lyricist in the group, and while not as good, I can still bring the shock-factor our manager is looking for.

"You're saying more rock and less lovey-dovey," Mason says, his brow smoothing as he reads my latest lyrics. "I like it."

"Guys, I can't help how I feel," East says.

"And we support you." Wyn smacks him on the back as he reads over Mase's shoulder. "Behind the scenes. Upfront, you gotta be the guy our Courtesans drool over. A mysterious, sexy loner who dissects his heart every night and puts it on paper."

"Like the rest of us single assholes," Mase says with a snort.

I add, "And any crooning about weddings and true loves needs to be directed at our fans, not our real girlfriends."

"Did Spin suggest that too?" East retorts.

My chin upticks at the sudden tone. "I'm only reiterating what's made us successful in the first place."

"Yeah, that's you, isn't it?" East says, grabbing the papers from Mase. "The stick-up-his-ass rule follower."

"Hey, man," Mase says to him.

"Be as pissy about it as you want," I say, then motion for the guys to get into position. "We're still doing it my way."

East mutters as he heads to his drum kit, "There he goes, our overlord, clarifying that if it weren't for him, we wouldn't be here."

I whirl from the microphone. "Say that to my face."

The snap of my tone has Mase and Wyn going stiff, but East doesn't react.

"Easton. Look at me," I say louder. And angrier.

Once he's seated on his stool, Easton deigns to glance up.

"I know you've been through a lot," I say. "And that happy ending you got? You deserve it. But this is our career, and we're no longer high school kids in Mase's mom's garage. There are professionals who look after us. People with stakes. Ones who need to get paid—including *us*. So, if you want to keep your happy ending, start paying attention to what I'm saying."

Easton's eyes go flat. "It's all clear to me, bro. Just because your happily ever after went up in flames, the rest of us better fall in line and write to the masses and basically give up any piece of individuality we ever had." He spans out his arms, each holding a drumstick. "Welcome to the mass market, folks! Rex Sloane here will be your tour guide."

I smack at the mike stand, sending it clattering to the floor. "East, what the fuck?"

"Guys..." Wyn tries. Mase doesn't even bother and rubs at his eyebrow while finding particular interest in testing out his guitar.

East continues, "Everyone here knows that if our roles were reversed and you were the one with the girl, we'd be writing nothing but love songs. But because it's not you and you continue to be a miserable son of a bitch, now the songs gotta be explicit. Heartless. Angry and—"

"Raw," I cut in. "Original. Emotionally fueled."

East bites at his lower lip in a half-snarl, half grimace. "Whatever you say, *boss*."

"Is this about the fucking nanny? Harper?" I ask.

I spit out the question before thinking it through, and to say it causes perplexed expressions in the room is putting it lightly.

"Say what?" Mase asks.

East's snarl-grimace turns into a lip-curl and a raised brow. "No, it's not about the fucking nanny, even though you treated Harper like crap, despite Taryn and me assuring you she's the best."

"It's about the fucking nanny," Wyn mutters, then motions to Mase for them to take five.

They leave the room, and neither East nor I stop them.

"Who says I treated her like shit? Did Harper say that to you?" I ask.

East's shoulders slump like I just asked the most disappointing question to date. "No. She's said nothing. Only came back to our place red-faced and silent, like she'd been crying."

"Crying?" *I made the girl cry?*

"Look, I don't know the details, but Taryn's given me enough to note that you were pretty unfair and disrespectful."

"Disre—" I cut myself off and take a deep breath. I fucking swear, this is why I keep my inner circle so limited. Adding new characters causes nothing but drama. "There was a misunderstanding at the end, but until that point I was nothing but cordial."

"Which means, in Rex-speak, you were a rude dickwad."

If he only knew. "What do you want from me, man?"

East rises and paces away from his drums. "You can be however you want with your nanny agencies or whoever you interview, but not with Harper. That girl has done more for Taryn and Jamie than I can list, and yeah, that doesn't mean she'd be an automatic great fit for you and Stella. I get that everyone has different requirements. But she deserved better than your curt dismissal."

"I fucking *hired* her, man!"

"Because you wanted to or because you felt compelled to?"

I don't let his question faze me. "Does it matter?"

"For Harper's sake—"

"It's not for her sake," I say. "Or hell, for mine. It's for my daughter's. And Stella likes Harper."

"Uh-huh."

It's like the dude can see through me and right into the inner workings of my dick. "That's *all*, East. Harper's qualified, too. With all her experience and shit."

"I'm aware."

"Fine. Then it's settled."

I'm not sure what we're settling. I just want East's eyes off me.

"Which leads me to my next point," East says.

I let out a long-suffering sigh.

"Treat her right." East stops in front of me, meeting eye-to-eye. "She may not be perfect and you may not be perfect, but Harper will be great with Stella. Give her a fair shot. And don't scare the shit out of her."

Something tells me I've already tested that theory, when I caught Harper and Stella dressing in those cast-off uniforms I'd forgotten were lying in my closet, collecting dust and dark thoughts. Harper hadn't balked at my all-consuming anger at their innocent discovery, so I doubt she scares easily.

Unless I made her cry afterwards, in private and alone.

Jesus, that thought doesn't sit well.

"Or fuck her," East adds.

"Christ, East. Lay off. I'm not going after the nanny."

"You better not."

My brows shoot up. "Have I screwed any others?"

East mulls this over for a second. "You've only had one."

"Yeah, and? Have I fucked her?"

"I've noticed Patrice when she's around you—"

"Whatever's in Patrice's head, that's where it stays," I say. And I leave no room for argument. "Can you back off now?"

"I'm fairly confident Harper's in good hands," East allows. "If you're nice to her."

I respond to Easton, "I'll work on it. All right?"

East searches my expression before answering. "Fine. You made the right decision, by the way. Maybe Harper will be a bright spot for Stella. I know she was for Jamie."

I clench my jaw. God knows Stella needs more light in her life, especially with a father growing more shadows by the year.

I ask, before East goes back to his drums, "You gonna cooperate with these songs, or what?"

East gives a one-shouldered shrug. "If it means that much to you."

I don't appreciate his tone, or the heavy cloud that's falling over this band the more successful we get, but it's too much to answer for at when we have three songs due by the end of this week.

I open the studio's door, calling Wyn and Mase back in.

We take our positions. East hits the first beats and I close my eyes, music collecting inside the empty recesses of my soul.

I'm where I belong. Where I'm destined.

When I open my mouth to sing, Stella sits in the back of my mind, an open space reserved just for her. It's a faded image of a little girl in someone else's ballet dress that I'm terrified I'll never make happy.

Out of nowhere, Harper walks into the image, dressed in pale pink leotard, her hair combed into a high bun, and takes Stella's hand.

Is this a bright spot, or a warning sign?

CHAPTER 6

Harper

"I've never had a man hate me so much that he's hired me," I say to Taryn after I sip—okay, gulp—my Moscow Mule. The acidic tang provides ironic relief to my overheated throat.

"I'm thinking that means he *doesn't* hate you," Taryn replies, idly stirring the straw in her rum and coke.

I scowl at her over the high-top table we grabbed in a crowded dive bar near her and Easton's apartment.

It's happy hour, I have a job, and my ex-employer turned best friend is hanging out to support me on a Thursday night. All signs point to Happy Harper, but I can't nudge the gnawing, annoying worry in my stomach to get out of the way.

"You didn't see the way he looked at me," I argue, this time forgoing the straw and drinking straight from the frosted, copper rim of the glass. I swallow. "It was like I found his forbidden treasure and he ordered me to walk the plank right out of the window of his high-rise penthouse, witnesses be damned."

"I can't picture Rex being that angry," Taryn says. "He keeps a lot to himself, sure, but the most I've seen out of that guy is strict adherence to rules, schedules, and deadlines. Any deviation and he gets pissed, but not deadly. You have nothing to worry about,

Harper. As long as you follow his calendar, he's as square as they come."

"Even squares have sharp edges," I mutter.

Taryn says, gentler, "I looked over the contract you emailed me earlier. Rex is paying you a nice sum."

"You're telling me."

I can't believe the salary Rex has written on paper, *and* he's giving me health insurance. And paid vacation days. And paid sick days. Such a contract in my line of work is unheard of, and no gnawing worry can keep me from scrawling my signature all over the damned thing.

"You saw there's also a trial period," Taryn says. She takes a drink then continues. "One week to see if you're the right fit. And if he hires you after that, your vacation and sick days don't start for another three months."

I nod. "That seems legit. Right?"

There's the lingering worry that either Rex or Patrice will use this next week to their sabotaging advantage, but it's an immature one. I'm hired. There's a more than fair contract in place.

So *why* do I keep sensing my ignorant stroll into a lion's den?

Rex's storm-blue eyes, filled with a silent roar, won't leave the back of my mind. Remembering his shaking, visible anger, having to be forcibly calmed as he turned away from Stella's door, still sends a shiver down my spine.

Rex is hiding a demon. And I don't know if I'm destined to be the poor soul about to meet it.

"Totally," Taryn answers, triggering me out of my tense fugue. "It makes the years I employed you seem slumlordy."

I laugh. "Those were some of the best years of my life. My favorite memories are of us, crammed in your tiny apartment, eating junk food in the dark when the power went out."

"Don't remind me." Taryn rolls her eyes, then signals the waitress for another round. I don't object. "God, times have changed, huh? Now I'm living in my boyfriend's two-story duplex with security up the yin-yang, and you're about to nanny for his bandmate, the lead singer of Nocturne Court and arguably the most famous out of the bunch." Taryn's brows draw together.

"What is it?" I ask after sipping up the dredges of my drink.

Her head angles, taking in the one bodyguard Easton insisted come with us when we agreed to meet for drinks. He stands obviously in the corner, not drinking, not smiling, and watching our every move. It's a "perk" gifted to Nocturne Court by their label after several restraining orders were brought against women and men tracking the guys and their families' homes and vehicles.

"I'm not worried about Rex's attitude toward you," Taryn says. "You can handle him just fine. It's this new life the band's gotten, it's ... it's taking some getting used to. And I will always wonder if you're okay."

"Aw." Warmth creeps into my veins as I find Taryn's hand and squeeze. "I'm not going far. Rex and East live ten blocks from each other."

"You know that's not what I mean."

I sober. "I'll be fine. And I'll make sure the adorable little girl with the scheming personality she *must* have gotten from her father will be safe, too. Didn't Jamie turn out all right?"

This time, Taryn laughs. "Save for all the near-death-experiences he gives me almost every day, sure. He's becoming a fine, upstanding man. One who hates all the attention that's coming down on him now that his stepdad will be Easton Mack."

"Jamie loves it," I say. "I witness that smirk on his face daily, and soon he'll be using it to his advantage to score points with chicks."

"Harper!" Taryn guffaws. "Don't give me those nightmares. My boy will die a virgin."

I choke with mirth but allow Taryn to have her dreams while she still can. "I'm really gonna miss that little asshole."

Taryn smiles. "He'll miss you, too."

"I'm only a text away," I say, more to assure myself than Jamie's mom. It's hard to believe I'll no longer be meeting Jamie after school or hanging out on the floor of his room helping with homework, or making dinner for our three-group crew on Taryn's barely operable stovetop. "And I'll visit all the time. Maybe Stella will enjoy *Fortnite* just as much as Jamie and we can cross-play—"

Taryn winces.

"Right. Schedule. Calendar. Rules." I nod once. "I'll await Mr. Sloane's instructions, but I assume no screen time is one of them."

Taryn can't contain her grin as she pats my hand. "This one-week trial will be just peachy for the both of you."

"*Drinks*," I demand. "Now."

The weekend refused to be slow and pleasant.

After Friday, my last afternoon and evening with Jamie, I trudge upstairs to my third-floor apartment while checking my phone. An email from Rex pops into my inbox.

I say "email," but really, it's a screenplay.

After a curt, **Please see attached for your expectations and requirements while being responsible for Stella's care - R.**, I open up the attachment, and a thirty-page document fills my screen.

It contains everything from Stella's likes and dislikes to her daily activity calendar, dietary restrictions and screen time limits, expectations and education, learning curves, quiet time, and other extensive details of a modern five-year-old's life.

No way did Rex write this. Most parents have similar one-page lists of do's and don'ts for caregivers, but it's usually not written by the caregiver herself—*ahem*, Patrice. Yet, that part doesn't bother me. It's the asterisk at the bottom that screams for my attention.

. . .

***You are expected to memorize this document upon your first day of work. Be prepared for random quizzing throughout the trial period. A single wrong answer will cause immediate and unpaid dismissal. No exceptions.**

Jesus.

No wonder Patrice is the only nanny ever to take care of Stella. No mere human could withstand such boundaries.

No one except me.

My lips draw firm as I unlock my apartment door, phone falling to my side as my purse slides from my shoulder and onto the floor.

Rex can't know it but challenging me is akin to dangling the latest cell phone in front of a preteen. I thrive on tests, feed off competitions, and live through winning.

I'll arrive on Monday prepared to knock his pants off.

Rex without pants.

No. I can't think of that—Rex's nakedness.

But, his body, combined with his wickedly handsome face, exposes itself to my imagination.

With an uncomfortable wince, I shake off the mirage, climb into comfy sweats, and prepare to hunker down for the rest of the weekend and study Stella's requirements until my eyes bleed.

Fast-track to Monday morning with my alarm screaming into my conscious and I rise onto my elbows, blow at the empty candy wrapper stuck to my face until it peels away, and get ready for my first day as the nanny to Rex Sloane's daughter.

Stella has pre-school in the morning, and according to Rex's schedule, I don't see her until pickup at 1 p.m. However, on this particular day, I'm expected to arrive at the Sloane residence at 9 a.m. sharp so he can go over some specifics.

I'm not sure what could be more specific than the novel of instructions he sent me, but he's the boss.

After a quick shower, I comb my damp hair into a short ponytail at my nape and change into simple black leggings and an oversized, pale gray blouse. The nanny dress code isn't too restrictive—nothing too casual and zero allowances on anything considered sexy—but I'm no fashion icon. Rex basically outlined my entire wardrobe without realizing it.

Snatching my purse from the floor where I left it, I head out, pleased to see the day is bright and blue in greeting, no storm warning in sight.

Yet.

CHAPTER 7

Rex

AT EXACTLY 9:01 A.M., Harper's face fills my security screen and I buzz her in.

There's no pacing through the foyer today, since Harper is on time. Patrice sits on one of the sofa chairs, but I need not look at her to know she's sporting a small smirk at the idea I've been prevented from prowling my house with impatience.

"She's coming up," I say unnecessarily.

Patrice sets down her coffee mug and uncrosses her legs, bare under a light orange sundress. "You sent her the relevant materials?"

"Of course," I growl, pleased to see that my moodiness still has somewhere to go. "I hope it scared her half to death."

Patrice smiles, like I'm supposed to understand what her grin means.

My former nanny is in sunny spirits this morning, despite Stella's meltdown a few hours ago over being unable to bring her *Moana* doll to school today. The child screamed bloody murder and cursed me out in every form her developing brain knew how until Patrice shut the front door behind them.

Never had Stella Sloane resembled her mother so accurately.

I avoided the comparison for as long as I could, but the sheer firelight in Stella's eyes had my blood running cold, all the way until her screams faded, then her cries, and the elevator dinged their final departure.

Swallowing against the memory, I turn back to Patrice. "If this morning's any clue, Stella will be in excellent spirits for her new caregiver this afternoon."

Patrice sighs, but says nothing more as the doorbell rings. She rises from her seat as I stalk back into the foyer and allow Harper inside.

"Hi," she says at the threshold, her chin tipping up to regard me.

I grunt. "Hello."

"Um, thanks for hiring me." Her scuffed, used-to-be-white Chucks cross the doorway and she's inside, transforming into a dull chameleon before my very eyes and becoming one with the staples of my home, also done up in muted creams, whites and grays.

Patrice pads over on bare feet, shoes being a definite no-no in my home with a young child. I'm waiting for Harper to realize this.

Any wrong moves, immediate dismissal.

As if sensing my warning, Harper angles toward me, and after a fast second of meeting my eyes, she kicks off her shoes.

Next to each other, the women are sunshine and clouds. Yet, it's not Patrice's breasts, cupped in the light corset of her dress, that I'm envisioning. It's Harper's hidden body, disguised in a gray potato sack, that gives me pause. Not simply because I've seen Patrice's breasts before—an unwilling shock to my brain and lightning rod to my dick—but I'm intrigued by what Harper doesn't want seen. Her skin is milk smooth with creamy swirls of beige and ivory. And I remember her nipples when they poked through her wet shirt, the color of two young roses in bloom...

Patrice holds out her hand. "Nice to see you again, Harper."

"You, too," Harper says, clutching her gigantic black purse with one hand and clasping Patrice's with her other. "Stella get to school all right?"

"Oh, yes. She's easy to put together in the mornings." Patrice refuses to look at me as she says this. "Come on, there's coffee waiting in the sitting room. The three of us will sit there and chat."

Chat. Like I enjoy idle conversation.

I follow the women into the all-encompassing main room, with wall-to-wall, two-story windows facing north and offering a picturesque, millionaire's view of upper Manhattan's most famous buildings. Chrysler. Empire. Rockefeller.

With stairs heading up to a loft-like balcony to my second floor, I get the view at sunrise or sunset whenever I step out of my bedroom.

I'm amazed I live here. Even more thrown I can afford it.

I wait for Patrice and Harper to take their seats before claiming my own, a chair off to the side. If it weren't morning, I'd be sitting in the city's shadow, my expression as worn and concrete as the buildings surrounding us.

Instead, I'm cast in glaring relief by the sun filtering through the windows, one of the many reasons I despise early meetings.

"I have to be at the studio in twenty minutes, so let's keep this brief," I say.

Harper leans forward to pour herself a cup of coffee from a silver carafe, unperturbed by my command. "Sure."

"You read through what I sent to you?" I ask. Patrice sits back, content I'm taking the lead.

Harper clears her throat after taking a small sip from her mug. "I did. You're very thorough, Mr. Sloane."

My eyes narrow at the use of the mandatory moniker. I should be happy she's following instructions. "I expect you to refer to me as Mr. Sloane, regardless of any circumstance. You're aware you have one week to show that you understand said instructions?"

"Yes." Harper leans back, meeting my stare in that unfiltered way of hers. Her eyes are bright with grays and blues. "I'm happy to prove to you that Stella will be in the safest of hands."

This isn't the girl we interviewed—the one who at the mere mention of her previous charge, Jamie, lit up with a passion fueled with defense and pride.

She has to be up to something.

"I'm only sorry I wasn't able to start this morning," Harper continues.

"You'll be expected to live-in with us when I'm on tours or out on publicity junkets," I say. I don't add that Patrice has been our live-in nanny since she started. I'm oddly reluctant to have Harper stay overnight while I'm here. "Otherwise, save for today, you're expected to arrive at—"

"Seven a.m. sharp," Harper says. "I have no problem with that. I'm an early riser."

I add, "Stella also has regular playdates, at parks and play-grounds with—"

"With pre-approved nannies and other parents, all of which you laid out in the summary. Yes," Harper says.

"Including the one—"

"Today at two. At Fort Greene Park," Harper finishes for me. Again.

My brows shadow my vision. "In one week—"

"You'll be starting your major tour for this year, beginning in the UK. By that time, if I'm hired, I'll be expected to move in temporarily and provide for all of Stella's needs, save for the part-time cook who arrives in the evenings to prepare dinner and weekly meals. And she's also the housekeeper. Her name is June, right?" Harper blinks innocently, then looks to Patrice. "Do I have that right?"

My lips turn down so forcefully, I'm creating caverns in my chin.

"Yes," I snap.

"Great." Harper smiles.

"Well. Mr. Sloane." Patrice's lips pull up like she's hiding a smile at that particular rule. "It appears we have it under control here. You can leave for the studio early, if you like."

That's my prerogative, not yours, I'm close to retorting.

Harper arrived equipped. Patrice will stay on and train Harper for the next seven days. Yet, I can't seem to get my ass out of this chair.

When I don't move, when I say nothing, Harper glances between Patrice and me and licks her lips. The sudden movement has me focusing on the pink satin of her tongue, and I reel in the animalistic craving to either bite or suck that piece of her until she moans for more. I don't ignore the poetic urge to write about the sheer, innocent seduction.

"I've heard some of your new songs," Harper says.

The surprising topic has me moving from her lips and back to the coastal fog of her eyes.

"Oh?"

"They're different," Harper adds.

I cock my head while maintaining her stare, noting that every single second that ticks by adds to the color in her cheeks. "How so?"

"The agony and the passion … using all the senses to punch that feeling into the listener. It's…"

I'm half-expecting her to take Easton's side on this, since that's the only way she could've heard the new material, so I answer for her. "Offensive? Off-putting?"

Harper blinks in surprise. "Not at all. I would say intense."

"Are you ready for the tour of the apartment, Harper?" Patrice asks, cupping her knees as if ready to stand.

Harper continues as if Patrice never spoke, keeping her attention on me. "Easton didn't write them."

"No." I offer a bitter smile. "He didn't."

"You did."

I lower my chin in acknowledgement. Harper searches my

expression in silent question, but I'm not about to give her anything. Anything at all.

"Patrice is right," I say. "You should see the place, get familiar." I stand at the same time Patrice pops up from her seat.

Harper takes her time, continuing her eerie study as she lifts off the chair.

It's pushing me off-balance. What does she think I hide in my lyrics?

"The singer, Rex Sloane, is a persona," I find myself explaining. "A guy I created for the audience who loves and fucks and litters hearts on the sidewalk so he has room to drive for more. He seduces about as well as he collects, but still waits for that one woman in the crowd who'll change him." I smile, but it's with cruel intention. "He's not real. Our Courtesans will believe to the death that he is, but the lyrics aren't true."

After a pause, Harper whispers, "I'm coming to realize that."

I refuse to pay her loaded response any mind or mull over the rampant insecurity that follows—that the real man she's met, the Rex Sloane of the every day, is a cruel disappointment.

"Good luck today," I say to her.

Patrice tosses me a perplexed eye-scrunch at my uncharacteristic farewell. I frown at her—at myself—and she schools her expression.

Pats, the dear girl, has already seen the true Rex and been carved up by him. Perhaps she'll communicate her sentiments to Harper, and Harper can get rid of whatever eager sunrise peeks through the mist of her eyes whenever she looks in my direction.

CHAPTER 8

Harper

WHY DID I SAY THAT?

Why did I have to bring up Rex's music?

It's like a fairy-sized Harper whispered in my ear that it was the right thing to say. When really, all that that mischievous, evil little sprite wants to do is stir shit up.

Everyone knows—at least, everyone on the inside—that Rex has taken the reins and is changing Nocturne Court's brand. It's controversial, maybe even taboo, but potentially epic and—

—not something a newly hired nanny *should bring up over coffee on her first freaking day.*

Thank God he left.

"Are you ready to see the home?"

I nod at Patrice's question. "Sure, since the map provided in the Dossier wasn't nearly as detailed as it should've been."

Patrice smiles at my sarcasm. "I admit, I'm not the best at Powerpoint."

I shake my head on a sigh. "I knew you must've written that textbook."

"Guilty." Patrice waves me forward down a hallway. "Subject to Rex's approvals and proofs."

I laugh. "Of course."

Rex. Not Mr. Sloane. Again, I wonder if something more happened between them. I *don't* give credit to the resulting twang in my gut at the thought.

Patrice takes me through the first floor, the relevant areas I'm already familiar with. Stella's room, her playroom, kitchen and large outdoor balcony. I balk at the clear glass barricades, a mere sliver of glass separating us from forty floors of falling death. I'm not afraid of heights, yet I still shudder at the abrasive wind and the drop of open air below our horizon as soon as we step out.

There's also a small pool out here—with, I'm relieved to see, a baby-safe pool fence installed. A few lounge chairs and a gorgeous teak table seating nine top off the outside entertainment.

Stella and me, if I ever gain the courage to play with her out here, will stick close to the apartment windows.

Patrice shows me her—I mean, *my*—quarters, just off Stella's room. Boxes are stacked in the corners and toiletry bags sit on tabletops.

"Furniture's included," is all she says, then directs me upstairs.

She then gives me an overview of the second floor but doesn't open Rex's bedroom door when she points and says, "That's his room. It goes without saying that it's off limits."

"Right." I want to ask, *have you ever stepped inside?*

There's a lot I want to ask Patrice, but I don't.

Can't.

Won't.

Not about him and what I want to know.

"Great," I say as we step back into the open kitchen and finish up. "Is there anything you'd like me to do these next few hours before I pick Stella up?"

"I'll show you where to make her snacks, the books we're reading and her favorite toys," Patrice says. "But I also have a favor to ask."

"Shoot," I say as Patrice pulls small cartons of berries from the fridge. Unable to resist, I pick out a ripe, red strawberry as she carries them to the counter.

"I have an appointment this afternoon that I can't get out of," she says. "I hoped to finish by the time we pick Stella up, but it's sort of out of my control, and—"

I finish chewing the strawberry and say, "No problem. I can pick up Stella and take her to the park."

"You're sure?"

"Totally. I'm familiar with Downtown Brooklyn and the surrounding neighborhoods. Stella and I will be fine."

Patrice bites her lower lip, which I'm sure has caused semi-chubs to many an unsuspecting man. "It's sort of against Rex's rules..."

"I didn't see it in the Dossier."

It's true. I didn't, and I've memorized that tomb sideways and backwards.

Patrice pauses in slicing a strawberry. "Really?"

"Mm-hmm." I steal another berry. "It says nothing about *your* time requirements. And if you're ten minutes late, I won't say anything."

Patrice frowns but doesn't object.

"I'm a former nanny," I reassure, "who's been in charge of Rex's—Mr. Sloane's—best friend's kid for six years. And Jamie is totally fine and untraumatized by my presence. I can handle an extra half hour alone with Stella. I'm meant to be her full-time nanny after all."

Patrice smiles. "If you're sure."

"No problem."

Patrice leaves Rex's apartment at around noon, after ensuring I have all her contact information. I use the spare hour alone to scroll through Stella's Dossier on my phone.

I'm nervous in the utter, cavernous quiet of this duplex, and as soon as it's time to leave, I hop out of my seat.

Throwing my tote strap over my shoulder, I step into the elevators, heading to the lobby. But when I hit the marble floors, I'm instantly accosted.

"Miss Mei! Hello there."

The ... bellboy? Lobby Man? Either way, a man wearing a suit approaches my path.

"Yes?" I answer.

"Your car is waiting. Miss Patrice En Vie notified ahead that it will be just you today using it."

My lips part with remembrance, and I think back to the Dossier.

Rule #157: No riding the subway when Stella is in tow, to protect her from paparazzi and the public eye.

"Great. Thank you," I follow him to the waiting vehicle outside the revolving doors.

Once I'm ensconced in the backseat, the driver introduces himself as Duncan and I nod hello. The leather is comforting and cool against my thighs and I lean back, thinking, *maybe being a nanny to the lead singer of a rock band won't be so bad.*

We arrive at Stella's school and I hop out, waiting for the children to exit with the other nannies and parents. It's a beautiful day and everyone is lingering and chatting outside. I don't know anybody, so I hang back, observe, and wait for Stella's slow gait.

She's one of the last kids to appear, dressed in a rainbow sundress and bright purple backpack, in complete contradiction to her solemn expression.

Stella searches the crowd with pale, blank eyes that gloss right over me.

"Stella." I raise my hand. "Hey. Hi!"

Her focus drifts back, then hardens when she spots her new nanny.

Taking her time, she clomps down the stairs, one hand holding on to the strap of her backpack. Her gaze doesn't find mine again, even as she sidles up next to me.

"Did you have a good day?" I ask, like a dumbass with nothing else to say to a kid who's allergic to small talk.

Stella shrugs, then looks to the curb. "Where's the car?"

"Over here." I offer to take her backpack, but she tightens her grip on it. "We have to make our playdate with ... Slate."

Another thing to get used to—the new generation of names, especially by celebrities and millionaires. I looked up the families of those named in Stella's Dossier, and this one is the daughter of some reality show producer.

Stella nods, the only sign that she's heard me.

"Um, this way," I say, and usher her to the car without touching her.

I have my work cut out for me. It's easy to believe Stella's the product of such a solemn man. But it's difficult to picture the woman who gave birth to her, Aesha. She's no longer in the picture, and it's for reasons the internet has yet to divulge.

The drive to Brooklyn is empty of traffic and we make it to the park with plenty of time to play. Stella sits in the backseat with me, clutching her backpack. I gave up trying to chat with her, giving her some space on our first day together. I sense they overcrowd this kid, all the time. With security, her dad's rules, a constant nanny presence. Maybe some peace and quiet is what she needs.

Duncan pulls up to the curb and Stella unclips the belt in her booster seat—*what the hell?*—aiming for the door handle before I can stop her.

"Stella, wait!" I say before she can get it open. Thank God Duncan has the child locks on.

I laugh, lessening the heart-pounding adrenaline at picturing

Stella flying out of the car and into a cyclist or oncoming traffic. "Wait for me to come around the other side and get you, okay?"

Expressionless, Stella turns to me. "I could've died, you know."

My brows jump. I'm still frozen halfway between my seat and my upper body drapes over the middle console. "What?"

"If I opened this door and fell out. I could've died."

Carefully, I close my mouth and swallow.

"And it would've been all your fault." Stella rolls her eyes. "You totally would've been fired."

My mouth falls back open as Duncan presses the auto-unlock button.

"Thanks, Duncan!" Stella says brightly and bounces out of the car.

"Stella, wait—fuck," I mutter, wrestling with my seatbelt.

"Don't let her get to you," Duncan says from the driver's seat. "She does this every damn time. But she's a good kid."

"In devil's clothing," I say under my breath, flicking the seatbelt away and jumping out of the car.

Stella's a few feet ahead on the sidewalk, but my legs are longer and more pissed off. When I reach her, I put a hand on her shoulder to turn her around.

"Stella, you can't—"

"*Don't touch me!*" she screeches, so loud she catches the attention of nearby parents and park-goers.

I throw my hands up. "I wasn't—I'm not about to hurt you, but you can't run away from me like that."

"Why not?"

Furious. That's the word that comes to mind as I regard this child with bright, angry eyes and a snarl too mature for a girl her age. Too sad.

"Because you could get hurt. Because you could get kidnapped or accosted or—" Shit. I probably shouldn't be saying this, since it risks giving her nightmares, but Jesus, this child.

Stella looks to the sky with all the weight of a teenager facing an annoying parent. "Okay, *Harper*."

I put a hand on my hip. "Why are you saying that like it's *allegedly* my name?"

"Because I will only say your name once. That's all the time I'll give you."

"Thanks for the vote of confidence."

Stella spins on her heel, dismissing me much in the same vein as her father. It gives me a grim outlook of how this nannying position will go.

"Are you Rex Sloane's new girlfriend?"

I half turn at the mention of Stella's father and wince when I see the lens before I register the person behind it. "Oh, for crying … this is a child. Get the camera out of her face."

The mouth below the large black lens grins. "You're not denying it."

"Get lost," I mutter, and turn my back on him, catching up to Stella.

Stella slows her pace as I come up beside her but says nothing and stares straight ahead. My gut sinks at the sight. At the awareness of this little girl, who clearly understands what's going on.

"What's your name?" the guy persists, heels clipping behind me.

"Get away from the playground," I warn over my shoulder. I move closer to Stella, but don't touch her as requested. I *will*, however, pounce on her if this guy dares to get any closer.

"The sidewalk in front of the park is fair game. Tell me who you are and I'll go on my merry way."

"I'm an undercover cop," I snap. "Now leave."

The man chuckles behind me, but a peek over my shoulder shows me he's lowered his camera. He's thin, with beak-like features and quite a few acne scars. "You know, the other nanny is way nicer than you. And hotter."

My shoulders stiffen, but I don't slow our walk to the park

entrance. I can't help but add one last parting shot. "If you know I'm the nanny, then you have your answer. Buh-bye."

The man stops in the middle of the sidewalk, letting us enter the park unhindered.

"I have my answer all right," he says.

I risk one last look back at him. He's wearing a smug smile, camera hanging by a strap against his chest. He winks. "Bye, Harper."

My upper lip twitches, but I give no further reaction other than to look down at Stella. "You okay?"

"Yeah."

I'm still staring at the man, though he's turned his back and wanders back to where he came from. "Does that happen to you often?"

Surprisingly, Stella answers. "Sometimes. Patrice says there are parts of the city where we can't hide from the cameras so we just gotta deal with them."

"And that includes your playground?"

Stella shrugs with one shoulder, but her attention's on her friends, clustered around the slide. "Patrice says if we just smile and wave, they'll leave us alone. She's not as mean as you." Stella grins, still staring ahead. "But I liked it."

Shit-stirrer. That's what this kid is.

"We shouldn't speak to them at all," I say. "That was my mistake. Go play. I'll be watching on the sidelines with the other grown-ups if you need me."

"Yeah, I'd say that's strike one for you."

Before I can open my mouth to reply, Stella heads to the swings, backpack flying into the grass, and a blonde-haired girl I assume is Slate greets Stella. There's a small sprinkler system set up nearby, with a surrounding circular dip in the concrete where the water pools into shallow puddles. Children in both swimsuits and school clothes dive in and out of the spray, splashing each other.

As I'm taking up position near the railings separating the playground from the rest of the park, I gain a better view of where Duncan dropped us off. There are plenty of open spaces closer to the entrance.

Why did he park so far away?

We were left vulnerable and exposed to any paparazzi waiting. For a hired driver accustomed to fame, I'm shocked that—

The scream rips through my thoughts, then my ear canals, and my heart's choking my airway by the time I glance back at the playground and see her, unconscious and on the ground.

CHAPTER 9

Rex

I STORM through the hospital's Emergency Room doors, furious they're automatic. I want to pry them open with my bare hands— strain against them until the glass shatters, roaring my arrival to the entire hospital staff and putting the fear of death into them until they bring me to my daughter.

WHERE IS SHE?

All those things, I keep simmering underneath my skin. Screaming and threats of torture will do me no good, though they're at the forefront of my itinerary if things don't go my way.

Laying my hands against the laminate reception counter, I say, with the threat of an incoming tornado, "Where is Stella Sloane?"

With a wry cock of her mouth, the nurse asks, "And you are?"

My lips peel back from my teeth. "I—"

I see Patrice's figure down the hall when a staff member pushes through an oversized wooden door to the right of the nurse's station, opening it wide before it starts closing. Pushing off the counter, I tear around the corner to get through the door before it locks. After a seasoned sigh at my departure, the nurse goes back to her phone.

"Patrice!" I call once I'm through the doors.

She jolts and freezes in the middle of the hallway.

"Where is she?" I call, readying to push anyone, *anyone*, out of my way.

Patrice holds up her hands. "She's—"

There. Her. Harper.

My attention darts away from Patrice to the figure sitting among a row of chairs in the hallway.

Harper sits beside something smaller. A child curled up against her side in the neighboring seat, snoozing against her shoulder, that gorgeous, cupid face calm and innocent in slumber.

Stella.

I resist the urge to fall to my knees, instead rushing to Harper and folding into the seat next to Stella.

I'm a blur in Harper's periphery, but she notices, and she's watchful and wary as I take up position beside them.

I'm afraid.

I'm afraid to touch my daughter. That I'll hurt her if I jostle her even slightly.

"Is she—" My goddamned throat seizes. "You did this."

Harper's eyes flare.

"Excuse me?" she whispers, so as not to wake Stella.

I emit a low, dangerous growl. "You are supposed to watch her at all times. Never take your eyes off her. How dare you let this happen? How dare you allow her the time to crack her head open? Where were you? What the fuck were you doing? You're fire—"

"Rex."

Patrice cuts in, laying a hand on my shoulder. I resist the urge to snarl. Harper remains thin-lipped and pale, but her chin trembles, like she's dying to argue her case.

"Can I talk to you a minute?" Patrice asks.

Jaw locked, I stand and lead Patrice to a quieter part of the hallway. An area where I can turn and still have a direct line of sight to my daughter.

"Stella is fine," Patrice says. She attempts eye contact, but I'm too busy assessing Stella from our vantage point. "It wasn't Stella that fell."

That last sentence has my gaze sliding to Patrice's, her features at last becoming clear through all the red in my vision.

"It wasn't Stella," she repeats. "Her friend, Slate, slipped in a sprinkler puddle and hit her head. She stopped breathing." Patrice licks her lips. "Harper gave her CPR."

One side of my mouth twitches. "Then what. The fuck. Was that phone call I received?"

Patrice sighs and shakes her head. "One of the other parents called you, maybe confusing Stella with Slate. Harper didn't contact you because she was, well … she reacted first. Out of everyone. I was walking up to the park when I saw her leap the fence and run over to the fountain, bending down beside a small child— oh God, I thought it was Stella, too. I thought it was Stella."

Patrice lays a hand on my forearm, her voice cracking. As she talks, my attention drifts from her to Harper to Stella, and it's when Patrice paints a vision of Harper running to a child that I meet Harper's gaze.

But once Patrice lays a hand on me, Harper's attention skitters away.

I step back, away from Patrice's touch, and say, "You're telling me I received the wrong information? I charged in here wondering who's neck I would break first."

Patrice turns her head to look at Harper, then back to me. She says in a low voice, "I'm sorry we weren't able to call you first. It all happened so fast. My first thought was to get to Harper and see what was wrong, I—"

My eyes flick to hers. "Why weren't you at Harper's side from the beginning?"

Patrice swallows.

Footsteps sound in the hallway and two individuals I recognize as Slate's parents turn the corner and go to Harper.

There's soft murmuring, a tearful mother, and a father who lays a hand on Harper's shoulder in gratitude.

Harper nods, a flush creeping along her cheekbones, but hangs onto Stella and doesn't move from her seat as she continues a murmured conversation with the parents.

After a moment, Slate's parents drift away from Harper and continue down the hallway, passing me and Patrice. The dad and I lock eyes and nod at one another. The universal sign of fear and thankfulness given from one father to another.

"Let's go home," I say to Patrice once they pass.

Harper stiffens as I come closer. A small part of me carries guilt at the way I snapped at her, but the larger part justifies that with the information I was given, of course I would damn well yell.

I stare down at her and ask, "Did the parents say she's all right?"

Harper clears her throat and continues to face ahead. "I assume you mean Slate's parents, and yes, the little girl will be fine."

"Then I see no need to stay here."

Harper gives a single, curt nod and stands to lift Stella in her arms. At Harper's height, Stella takes up more than half of Harper's real estate, but Harper doesn't fumble or complain as she adjusts Stella.

Nor does she pass her to me.

I allow it, since Stella is draped over Harper so comfortably. And, if I'm to be honest, Stella acts as a great buffer to the apology I'm certain Harper's waiting for.

I hold the door open for both ladies as we step into the waiting room, and then outside. I parked in the drop-off only zone and throw open both backseat doors.

When I reach toward Stella to put her in the car seat, Harper shakes her head.

"I've got it," she says.

I allow it, but only after rationalizing I should get the air-conditioning in the car running first.

Stella mutters as Harper shifts and settles her into the seat, but Stella's head droops, her chin dropping to her shoulder as she sleeps.

I round my tricked-out black Jeep and get into the driver's side. Harper slides in on the other side of Stella in the back and Patrice takes the front.

I'm disappointed Harper doesn't sit upfront but say nothing as I rev the engine and get us out of hospital traffic.

The ride is silent, and when I pull into my reserved parking space in the basement of my building, turning off the engine only makes the silence thicker.

Patrice speaks first. "Do you want me to stay a bit longer? Explain what happened?"

I shake my head, pocketing my keys before shouldering open the driver's door. "You wanted to see a few apartments tonight to lease. You should go do that."

"Yes, but I can reschedule—"

"Don't worry about it." I shut my door, cutting off any additional excuses.

As Harper opens hers, I hold it wider, offering my hand to help her out. I've customed out the wheels so the Jeep rides higher than normal, making it difficult for smaller individuals to get in and out.

Harper says, "I'm fine."

I pull back my hand. "If you say so."

Once her feet hit the ground, Harper looks back through the car opening at Stella, snoring. "According to the Dossier, my allotted time today is up. If you can handle her from here, I can leave, too."

One side of my mouth tics at the word she's used to describe Stella's schedule. "No."

I bite out the denial before thinking too hard on it.

She meets my eyes, albeit quizzically. "No?"

"We have things to discuss, you and I," I say. "I assume you know Stella's bedtime routine?"

"Yeah, I do."

"Then after that, you and I can have a meeting."

Harper's throat bobs. After a few seconds, she relents. "Sure. Okay."

I nod, then round the back of the vehicle and unbuckle Stella. Patrice lingers on the passenger side, biting her lower lip.

"I really can stay and help," she says as I lift Stella into my arms.

"You've moved on, Patrice," I say. "As evidenced by your failure to show up at the park in time today."

"Rex, I can explain."

"Your actions tell me enough," I say. "You've already distanced yourself from this job."

"That's not true." Patrice's tone turns pleading. "I love Stella."

"You're doing me a solid by staying on for Harper's trial period, and I appreciate that," I say, attempting a gentler tone. "And I'm not disputing that you care for my girl. But don't hold yourself back from the future you've chosen for yourself. Go. We'll be fine."

Patrice's gaze shutters, almost as if my words have caused some hurt.

"If that's what you want," she says, then adjusts the strap of her purse on her shoulder and walks to the exit. Her steps echo hollowly within the cavernous concrete.

I motion with my chin for Harper to follow me.

"Could've sworn you had an elevator garage," Harper says behind me.

I half turn with Stella in my arms as we head to the private elevator. "I hope you're not one of those people who likes to fill silences with nonsensical musings."

"Never mind," she mutters.

We ride up the rest of the way without talking. Usually, I regard the silence of my employees with respect. Small talk is one of my most hated forms of human communication.

Yet, despite my snide remark to Harper a few seconds earlier, I want to say something. Fill the quiet with useless words, if only to have her voice cut through the thick air. Not hearing her makes me realize I like the sound of her.

Harper crosses her arms, staring unseeingly at the mirrored elevator doors. When they open into my apartment, she steps out first, then holds out her hands for Stella.

"I'll give her a bath but make it nice and soothing," she says as I pass Stella over to her. "What she saw today terrified her."

Scared the fuck out of me, too.

Our fingers touch as we shift Stella from one warm body to another. The callouses on the inside of my palm should counteract any registering of another's delicate skin, but in this case, the rough, hardened ridges catch against Harper's satin, sending a ricochet of sparks down my arm.

I jerk my hand back like she's fire—Harper *is* dangerous—and cover up my horror by rubbing my palm against my jeans.

"Thank you," I say, hoarser than normal.

"No problem," she says, then turns with Stella and disappears into Stella's wing of the apartment.

I don't move until the elevator doors threaten to shut. I haven't even fucking exited the thing, too focused on the shape of Harper's ass as she strides away.

With a hard blink and a shove against the doors, I stride into my home, unsure what to do with myself while Harper's busy with Stella.

When it came to Patrice, it was easy. I'd head into my small private studio and write or make music. The hour would fly on instrumental notes until it was time to say goodnight to my daughter.

This time, all I can think of is Harper's presence, nearby but forbidden, caring for Stella. It conflicts with the events of today and the sheer fury at hearing my daughter was hurt under Harper's watch.

I can't be lusting after a girl when she screwed up my daughter's care.

Except, she didn't screw it up.

Harper took charge and helped to save Stella's friend's life. Moved when everyone else froze. Held a broken child while the rest gaped in horror. And in the afterglow, when everything turns out all right, and she received gratitude and thankfulness from Slate's parents, Harper acted like it was just another day in her life, wanting no credit, no undue gratefulness.

There's something to be said there. Patrice, in all her experience, would've basked in the attention, hugging Slate's mother and sobbing relieved tears along with her.

Visions of Harper in the hospital, clutching my daughter, score through my mind. The ghost of her sitting on my couch, damp with her shirt molded to her small curves, haunts the scene. My fingers itch, and I clench them to my sides.

Lyrics.

That's where I'll direct my restless energy. It's time to open my notebook and cull from the events of today. Put it into a song, a message, a distraction from Harper, whose fresh, rose-filled scent lingers in the air long after she left this room.

I spend the next hour hunkered over my artist's desk, penning sentences and humming structures until I'm satisfied Harper is out of my system and laid out on pen and paper instead.

Terror of falling
Facing the wind
You hold her, broken,
Until she blinks again.

Love makes you blind,

Fear makes you strong,
Hold her close, my friend,
Because you've lost her all along.

You want her.
You save her.
You think you do.
Until she comes to,
And you realize,
She's destroyed you.

The last sentence blurs and becomes an illegible smear of black ink in my vision, yet forms clear block letters in my mind.

She's destroyed you.

She hasn't destroyed me. Hasn't touched us. Not for years. I'll never allow it to be any different.

"Rex?"

I jolt, the pen dropping to the floor. I spin on my stool. Harper's standing in the doorway to my office. Stella stands beside her, blinking at me.

"Um, I mean, Mr. Sloane," she says. "Stella wanted to say good night. I know the rule is to have her in bed before you come and tuck her in, but she really wanted to see you, and considering—"

I bolt from my stool and have Stella in my arms so completely and abruptly that Harper falters back a few steps.

"Daddy?" Stella says. "You hug tight."

"I was scared today, too," I whisper roughly into her hair, then kiss her head. "I love you to pieces, sweets."

"You too, Daddy." Stella leans back, cupping the scruff of my cheeks and staring deep into my soul. "I was okay today."

"Yes," I say, and I lift my gaze above Stella's head to include Harper. "You were."

"Harper also yelled at a camera man."

My gaze drops back to Stella. "What?"

"Bed time!" Harper trills, and I set Stella down. "I'll be right back, Mr. Sloane. Say good night, Stella."

"Night," she says to me, her voice never going above a monotone.

I can't blame her lack of expression on today, or Harper, or shock. This is how Stella always is.

I wave, Stella's small, emotionless tone echoing in my ears long after they've left the hallway. It's been brought to my attention how isolated Stella is at school and the way she goes through tasks, never too excited but always tolerant. Teachers and therapists are reluctant to diagnose something that's not quite right, but not quite wrong, either.

My brows slash down as I wish I could do more with my talent than just sing. It's not like belting out notes to my child will fix her. She's not fucking broken.

Glancing over at my notes, I fist the loose paper off my desk, crumpling it and throwing it against the wall. It ricochets into the trash where it belongs.

I may be a puddle of uncertainty with my daughter, but with Harper, I'm twisted iron. Cold, yet in control of my shape, crafted and cut with deliberate sharp edges, and I hang onto that as I leave my creative space and prepare for our meeting.

To be anything else to that girl is an unacceptable weakness.

CHAPTER 10

Harper

ONE HOUR Earlier

Jamie was five when I started nannying him. He came with his own complications, but he was never a mini, fire-breathing dragon disguised in human form.

Half of me wonders if Stella orchestrated the events of this afternoon to get me into trouble. The other, more sensible part, reminds that she's five, she didn't plan any such thing, and the moment I suspect a child for my setbacks will be the day I need to sign up for some serious internal reflection.

Stella demands privacy while she bathes, but after her friend's slip and fall this afternoon, hell if I'll let her.

We compromise, Stella pulling the opaque pink shower curtain with metallic gold glitter all the way across so I have nothing but a silhouette to account for.

I sit on the closed lid of the toilet, scrolling through my phone while I listen to the splashing sounds with my ears perked. I peer around the curtain in every now and again to make sure everything's fine and am met with a glare each time.

"Privacy, please?" Stella asks through her teeth, appearing

more put out than the teenagers crowding the bus stop near my apartment.

"All done!" Stella calls, suspiciously happy, and I stand to hand her a towel. But as I reach around the curtain, I notice all the suds remaining in Stella's hair.

"Stella, um…" I say, then chastise myself for tip-toeing around a kindergartner. It's like my high school years zoom forward and I'm standing in front of the popular girl who has just been made my lab partner.

She is not your enemy. Nor will she throw chewed bubble gum in your hair.

"Your hair isn't washed," I say.

Stella shrugs. "I like how the bubbles pop in my ears."

There she is. There's the child I've been looking for.

I bend to my knees. "C'mon. Let me help you rinse them out."

"What if I don't want to?"

"Then you'll stay in here until you're nothing but a dried-up prune, since there's no way I'm letting you lie in bed with sudsy, crusty hair."

Stella pouts. "You don't get to order me around."

"Actually, I do, and right now you're going to sit your butt back down in the bath and let me wash your hair, or else I'll get your father in here to do it for me."

That has her splashing back into a sitting position.

Stella's brows remain low and pissed-off, but she lets me douse her head with a plastic cup and I run my hands through the wet strands, soft and straight as silk—so different from her wayward curls when her hair's dry.

"Ow. You're hurting me."

"No, I'm not," I mumble. It's like this kid looks for every excuse to find an inadequacy, and I'm not falling for it anymore.

"Patrice isn't this mean."

"Honey, I'm only finger-combing so we don't have to wrestle with your tangles later."

"Don't call me honey."

My lips tighten. "Fair enough. It'll only be Stella from now on."

"Good. Don't drown me, either."

I pause in my pouring and combing. "Why would I *ever* want to drown you?"

Stella moves with what is fast becoming her trademark response after making an uncomfortable statement. She shrugs.

I pull my hands away, covering what has become my trademark response to her. A sigh. "All set."

Stella stands and I throw a towel around her shoulders, helping her out of the tub and onto the bathmat, but let her dry herself off.

I'm observing Stella for signs of shock or trauma, but Stella shows nothing but frank routine as she shimmies into her pajamas, gets on her stepstool near the sink and gestures for her toothbrush as I wring out her hair with a hand towel. Save for the drowning comment, she seems her usual surly, quiet self.

"So, about this afternoon," I say as I hand her the yellow Disney Belle toothbrush from the countertop.

Stella applies the toothpaste with pert concentration, and at first, I think she's ignoring me.

"You doing okay?" I ask.

"Fine," Stella replies, then shoves the toothbrush in her mouth.

"It was a lot to see," I persist, but avoid staring at her in the mirror as I finish combing her hair. "But you know Slate's okay, right? She won't be in school the next few days, but she'll be just fine."

"Yeah. Daddy told me in the car."

She says it with the same bland, unaffected tone she possessed when she witnessed the events surrounding Slate's fall. I was the first to crawl onto my knees beside Slate, unconscious and bleeding, but I kept a careful peripheral watch on my charge as I checked Slate's vitals and administered CPR until the EMTs came. Stella didn't move from her spot a few feet away. She just stared, and stared, and stared at her friend.

Bland, unaffected.

Until the EMTs took over, and I ran over to Stella, held her shoulders, and reassured her that Slate would be okay, even though I had no freaking clue if that child was all right.

Stella shrugged. I squeezed her shoulders and pulled her into my stomach. She didn't fight me.

I don't know Stella. I don't know this family.

But I'm worried about her.

"Time for bed," I say with the type of tone where I'm some godmother or fairy ready to skirt my child off to dreamland.

"I want to see Daddy."

Bringing Stella into Rex's study isn't in the Dossier, but after a day like today, I'm hoping Mr. Sloane will bend the rules. I'm not about to deny a child her need to see her father, and as Stella hops off her stepstool near the sink and we exit the bathroom, an inkling inside of me reminds, *Stella is not you. Don't impute your needs onto her.*

We reach the open doorway where Rex sits, hunched over what looks like a cartoonist's drawing board, large, rectangular, and high off the ground. His feet are hooked in the stool's footrest, his t-shirt stretched tight over his broad, expansive back. Rex has thrown his hair up in a loose bun, strands curling at the back of his neck.

The urge to brush the loose hair aside and kiss the exposed skin, to feel his pulse beat underneath my lips is so strong that I gasp, horrified, and take a step back.

Stella glances up suspiciously but stays silent.

On a quenching inhale that I hope calms my heart, I knock on the frame on the doorframe.

"Rex?" I say.

He spins around, his expression thunderous.

Shit. "Um. I mean, Mr. Sloane. Stella wanted to say good night. I know the rule is to have her in bed before you come and tuck her in, but she really wanted to see you, and considering—"

Rex spans the space between us in less time than an apex

predator would, and I jump back as he hooks his daughter under her arms and presses her to his chest. All thunder dissipates, and what's left are cracks of light.

They share a moment, one I don't want to disturb. Stella holds her father's face with an openness to hers I had yet to witness before now.

Rex glances above Stella's curls, saying something, but I don't catch it because our eyes meet, his a hypnotizing blue, and my mouth goes dry at the unexpected *sound* it makes inside my head. Like a single, resounding drumbeat as soon as our eyes lock.

But then Stella breaks the moment by going back to the dark side and throws me under the bus with the cameraman.

"Bedtime!" I say, and Rex sets Stella down. "I'll be right back, Mr. Sloane. Say good night, Stella."

When they say their goodnights, I follow Stella back down the hallway and downstairs.

Once we make it to Stella's room, she says, "I can tuck myself in."

"I know," I say as I walk in behind her. "Do you want to read a book or anything? Listen to a song before you go to sleep?"

Stella pauses by her bed, playing with the loose hem of her pajama top. "You'll let me listen to music?"

"Sure, if that helps you fall asleep."

"No one's ever asked what I wanted to do before bed."

I don't know why that tiny fact breaks my heart. "We're still getting to know each other, but part of *my* bedtime routine is listening to my favorite song before falling asleep. And it helps a lot. So if that's what you'd like to do tonight…"

Stella grimaces. "I didn't ask what *you* did at bedtime."

I ignore the jibe. "What song are you thinking you'd like to listen to?"

"That's easy." Stella turns back to her bed. "My Dad's song. *'Heartfall.'*"

"Excellent choice." I take my phone out of my pocket and scroll through my playlists until I find it. I begin its sweet notes as she pulls back her covers, sliding into bed without argument, her attention trained on the phone in my hand.

Her hazel eyes are unblinking as I lay my phone on her nightstand and sit cross-legged on the floor by her bed, closing my eyes as the music plays over us.

With my words so empty, my soul so full
My body can't stop feeling magical
You reached for my heart, when I slipped through your wall
You're the one who caused my heart to fall.

Stella doesn't ask me to go. Doesn't screech for me to get out of her room and leave her alone.

She lays under her comforter, her eerie stare softening around the edges with slow, calming blinks as her father's haunting, beautiful voice, sinks into this room, until she drifts off and can't fight it anymore.

She sleeps.

With the silent, stealth-like movements I adopted when watching Jamie, since he registers every minor vibration, I straighten and pick my phone up once the song ends.

It's a loss when *'Heartfall'* finishes its cords. Rex's voice is unlike any rockstar I've heard, and *so* unlike the man it belongs to. It's an earlier song from when they were trying to gain fame, but it resonates in the same way Rex's presence rebounds through my chest. I can't shake the voice. I can't unscramble the man. It's a constant ache, this lack of understanding on how something so beautiful can come from a person so jagged.

And yet, Rex soothes his daughter to slumber, even when he thinks he can't.

I step out of Stella's room, leaving the door open with a three-inch crack, as written in her Dossier.

My socked feet pad throughout the first floor until I reach the stairs, and I make my ascent toward the man who sings of a falling heart, yet keeps his feet on solid, unbreakable ground.

CHAPTER 11

Rex

THE SIFTER of brandy sits to the right of my hand as I recline in my leather chair, one of two in the office, and take in the cityscape through the wide, apartment windows.

Night falls over Manhattan in the way I envision a woman throwing her skirt over her legs as she stands. Modest. Flippant. Ultimate protection against straying, prying eyes as she strides toward sunrise with confident, pristine steps.

All the while, sin bides its time. Succulent, sexual curves only temporarily cloaked until the right person comes along, lifts those layers, and strokes with his finger until he finds—

My song.

The notes hit my ears at the same time I blink myself out of the fantasy, half wondering what I was picturing—a certain woman, or the city?

An unnecessary distinction, since the reasons I'm hearing '*Heartfall*' has yet to be explained.

"Hey," Harper says.

Rubbing my temples, I say without turning from the window, "Did Stella go down okay?"

Harper steps into the dim lamplight by my chair, the only illumination in the space. The city lights outside provide more than enough radiance.

"She went to sleep without issue."

Harper doesn't sit. She crosses her arms and glances around at anything but me.

"Why did I hear my band's song?" I ask.

"Oh." Harper's gaze clashes with mine, then scrapes away. "Stella requested it. She wanted to listen to music before she fell asleep—"

"That's not on the list of instructions I gave you."

"No. It's not. But I assumed—"

"Never assume."

"I *thought*," Harper amends, "that it wouldn't be a problem. She needed soothing after the events of today, and when she requested 'Heartfall', I didn't see a problem. It's one of your most G-Rated songs, if that's what you're worried about."

"I'm not worried. I'm annoyed."

"That your daughter likes your songs?"

She bites her lips at my resultant glare but doesn't stand down.

"I like to keep Stella separate from my job," I say into the silence. "Not that I should have to explain it to you. My work and my daughter are on the opposite spectrums of my life, for reasons I'm sure are obvious. Fame, hungry fans, inappropriate lyrics, the list goes on. Stella knows what I do, but I don't want her to get to where she understands just how precarious it could be for her. How much her life is shadowed by mine. She's to be protected at all costs. My songs she *likes*, included."

A line forms between Harper's brows, made clear with the play of light and shadow along the planes of her face. Sharp angles, almond eyes, a Cupid's bow of a mouth, all pronounced by the outside lights cast in this room.

"Understood," she whispers. "It won't happen again."

"Strike two."

Harper's chin jerks up. "What?"

"That's the second strike I've logged against you. The first was allowing Patrice to leave you on your first day of training."

"Are you kidding? That wasn't even my—"

"It was the catalyst to the string of unfortunate events that happened today. My daughter could've been hurt on your watch. You should've known better than to think you could handle her on your own, without Patrice's counsel, at least for the first few days."

Harper's eyes flare, the only sign she's pissed. "I'll admit, your daughter is slippery and wily and I underestimated how fast she can run. But at no point was she in danger."

"And the photographer?" I angle my head.

"The..." Her expression clears. "Oh."

"I'm not a betting man and even if I was, I wouldn't bet on the bullshit of finding my daughter's picture on a rag magazine's website, with you at her side, yet there it is. All of which would *never* have happened if Patrice were with you. She knows exactly where to go to avoid such confrontations."

"I-I'm sorry." Harper rubs at her cheek, like she has a toothache, as she stares past my shoulder and out the window. "You're right. I should've been with Patrice."

I wait for her to explain herself further, but she doesn't. It's a stark difference between the Harper the cameraman caught with his lens—snarling, protective, hand curled to raise a finger—with the docile, chastised woman in front of me.

I wonder which one is the fake.

"You're lucky he only got a shot of the back of Stella's head," I say. I won't admit it's because of her, Harper's instinctual response to angle Stella away from the shot, that blocked Stella from view. Harper's arm shaded Stella's face as she pulled her away, her oversized gray blouse providing a buffer as they turned their backs on the photographer.

I *want* to fire Harper. I'm desperate to find reasons to get her out of here, for reasons I can't ... justify.

But I will. I always do.

"From now on, I won't deviate from anything you outlined." Harper adds, "Mr. Sloane."

I respond with an approving grunt, lifting my drink to my lips. I want her to leave, but I enjoy the play of light across her body, the skinny leggings and blouse, made romantically see-through from the single bulb of light, the silhouette of her curves on shadowed display through the fabric.

"Stella talks a lot about death, you know," Harper says.

It's enough to sink any heated tide rising beneath my skin. "Come again?"

Harper crosses her arms again, blocking any further appreciative views. "Today, before getting to the park, she talked about being hit by a car. And during the bath just now, she asked if I was going to drown her."

I swallow the brandy stuck in my mouth. The alcohol, warmed by settling on my tongue too long, burns. "I was hoping she was over that phase."

"A phase?"

I shake my head, setting down the brandy. "I took her to a therapist right after her mother ... left. The doctor assured me it's like any milestone a child goes through. She's at an age when she's realizing people can't live forever, including her."

I'm noting Harper's reaction to my explanation. The drop of her lower lip, the squinting of her eyes. Like she can't believe I'm talking about my daughter's psyche with the interest level of whether I prefer chocolate or vanilla.

"I don't know you, Harper."

Harper's lashes flicker at the use of her name. I'm shocked at the way it feels on my lips. A ripened taste I'd like to savor again.

"So, Harper, I will not justify the way I talk about my daughter," I finish.

Or the nights spent holding her in my arms as she screamed. The days of anguish when I hired Patrice, unsure if I was forcing a substitute mother on Stella or a saving grace. The mix of terror and pride when I'm forced to step back as her father and see how strong Stella is, yet how she crumbles when I'm around. Like the nights I held Stella through her constant nightmares, screaming her mother's name.

And how I'm screwing up every single fucking thing about her, because whenever I look at Stella, I worry so much it hurts.

"That's not at all what I was thinking," Harper says.

Liar.

"I'm aware of Stella's current focus. I'm working on it. That's all you need to know," I say.

And I'm clueless how to stop it.

Harper nods, and I notice the way she's wringing her index finger, playing with three stacked, slim silver rings.

"If you—" I clear my throat at the sudden clog. "If you have any ways to deal with it, you know, suggestions or activities to help Stella through this, you may do so."

Harper softens. "I'll do my best, R—Mr. Sloane."

"Thank you."

The gratitude is thick and foreign on my tongue. I banish it with the familiar taste of brandy.

"I'll see you tomorrow, then." Harper turns, tucking her hair behind her ear as she departs, her silver rings flashing.

I don't appreciate her form as she leaves. Or the way she walks. I don't linger on the shape of her.

Instead, I turn back to the windows, where the city's night attire is as close as I'll come to stroking a woman's curves tonight.

CHAPTER 12

Harper

"THANKS SO MUCH FOR DOING THIS," Taryn says as she opens her door wider for me to step in. "This last-minute filing can't be done at home. I have to do it at the office and make sure the junior associates don't shoot us all in the foot. And Easton's off in some coffee shop refusing to come home until he pens out at least two songs."

"No problem." I plop my purse on my usual armchair, glancing around for Jamie. "I just finished getting face-blasted by fire, so this will be a nice reprieve."

"Oh no." Taryn pauses in slipping on her jacket. "It's that bad with Rex?"

"It's not good." I perch on the armchair, rubbing my hands against my thighs. "It's just ... every criticism Rex has is on point. I screwed up. But I feel like I'm being set up to fail. Like I can't win."

Taryn arches a brow. "That's not the usual Harper I'm hearing. You love a challenge."

"Not when it comes with both a five-year-old and a twenty-nine-year-old intent on my destruction."

Taryn laughs. "Rex needs a nanny, especially with Nocturne Court going on tour in a week. His old nanny is leaving for a teaching job, no matter how much he tries to ignore it. He *needs* you."

"Beg to differ." I pick at invisible lint on my blouse, mulling over Taryn's opinion that Rex wants Patrice to stay. I wish I was only thinking he wants her to stay because she's a great nanny to Stella.

The thought leads me to a worse one. I venture to ask, "Hey, do you know anything about Stella's mom?"

Taryn freezes with one hand on the doorknob. "Only through what Easton's said."

"And what's his opinion on it all?"

"Well." Taryn turns, leans her back against the closed door, and crosses her arms. "East is tight-lipped about it, Rex even more so. Only that they met in their early twenties, that Stella was unexpected, and it didn't work out."

"Huh." I rub my lips together. "And her name is ... Aesha?"

"See, I didn't even know that much." Taryn pushes off the door. She asks, "Why do you want to know? Trying to gain deeper knowledge of Rex Sloane?"

I huff out a laugh. "Kind of."

"He's tough." Taryn walks over and places a hand on my shoulder. "But underneath, there's a heart of gold. I promise. Stay the course, because even if Rex doesn't realize it yet, you're the best thing he's ever had."

I smile. "Can you email him a reminder of that?"

"You got this, Harp." Taryn pats my shoulder. "I gotta go, but Jamie's in his room on his computer. He has a nasty habit of sneaking out at night to meet up with his friends in front of a bodega and pop wheelies on their bikes. You're here to stop any such stealth maneuvers."

I give Taryn a salute. "Grabbing teenagers by the ankles as they attempt to slide out windows is my specialty."

"See?" Taryn laughs. "Rex doesn't know what he's talking about. Just wait until Stella turns six."

"I remember those years." I roll my eyes at the utter chaos Jamie wrought at six years old. Mostly involving a Sharpie and other people's walls.

Taryn waves as she shuts the front door behind her, and before I know it, I'm left alone in the silence, with the ice cream I know this family stacks in their fridge.

Before eating my feelings, I pop my head around the doorframe to Jamie's room, pressing the button outfitted on the outside hallway a few times so the specialty lights flash by his bed.

Jamie glances over his shoulder with an annoyed glaze to his expression.

I smile and sign with my hands, *Want to split some ice cream?*

He shakes his head and turns back to his video controls.

Not today, James Maddox, I think as I invite myself in and tap him on the shoulder.

Fine, I sign once I get his attention again. *But I'm coming back in here and I'm playing* Fortnite *with you whether or not you like it. I've had a day and you're going to help me make it better. Got it?*

One side of Jamie's mouth quirks, forming lines on cheeks that have thinned and angled with maturity. Even the cowlick at the top of his head is smoothing over.

Got it, he replies, albeit distractedly. I still call it a win.

After a curt nod, I scoop myself a triple serving of white chocolate brownie ice cream and head back into Jamie's room, where there's an extra gaming chair I make myself comfortable in.

After a few satisfying bites, my brain freezes and I grab his spare controls.

Let me in, I sign after elbowing him.

Jamie nods, and my avatar pops up on screen.

You're babysitting for Rex now?

Jamie's hand movements cause my gaze to slide from the screen.

Sure am, I reply. *Since you're too cool for a babysitter now.*

Jamie smiles. *Rex is my favorite, out of all of them. Besides Easton, I mean.*

I nod, but my lips turn down.

Why do you like him? I ask, making sure my expression remains serene.

Jamie shrugs. It's not with the heaviness that Stella seems to carry, but with a carefree attitude. *He's got the best voice.*

I roll my eyes. *Jamie was born deaf. Ha ha, Jamie.*

Jamie grins, then signs, *But he's cool. He doesn't take shit from anybody. I wish I could be like him.*

Softening, I squeeze his shoulder, then sign, *You're the strongest kid I know.*

But still a kid, he responds, with a wry expression.

You and he are alike. You both have a ton of attitude, I sign.

Jamie's smile splits wide.

We go back to playing the game, but when we're at an impasse and Jamie stops for a drink of his coke, he signs, *I think he got his heart broken.*

I pause with my spoon of ice cream halfway to my mouth, set it down, and ask, *Who, Rex?*

Jamie nods. *It changed him. That's why he can be such a Scrooge. Why so many people take his attitude the wrong way.*

You're too old for your years, Jamie, I sign, but my face feels pinched in thought. I'm not sure why I'm thinking so hard on the fact Rex was in love with someone.

Of course he was. Look at him. He's no shrinking violet.

Nah, Jamie signs. *Easton mentioned it when he thought I wasn't around. I read his lips when he spoke to Mom.*

So Taryn knew something crucial about Stella's mom and Rex.

I wonder why she didn't tell me?

Jamie and I play another hour of *Fortnite* before I sign that it's time for him to get ready for bed.

As predicted, Jamie's full of denial and eye rolls, and I relent only by signing, *If you're not tired, then at least crawl into bed and crack open a book.*

This is why I'm too old for a babysitter, he says.

And this is why I'm going back to hanging out with five-year-olds, I retort, then hold out a warning finger before stepping out of his room and giving him privacy as he changes clothes.

Taryn's warning remains bright in my mind, so I slide down to the floor in the hallway by his door, planning to hang out there until I either hear the scrape of shoes heading to a window, or the gentle snores of a kid who insists he's not tired.

My phone acts as both a conduit to the outside world and a reading tablet as I chew my lips and bounce between social media and my current romance read. I hone my ears to the tiniest of noises, and soon enough, I catch Jamie's snores, and poke my head around his door to make sure he's in bed and not using some fancy recording app and pillows as a fake-out.

Jamie's profile is shaded by the foggy moonlight from his window and a book is open and face down on his chest. Pretty sure he didn't even get through a sentence.

My phone vibrates in my hand, shifting my attention. I place it to my ear before absorbing who's on the other end.

"Hello?" I ask.

"Harper. Hey."

Rex's voice fills my head, low, husky, sexy and … tired.

"Mr. Sloane." I try to maintain the blasé tone he always conveys when he's around me. My back straightens. "Everything okay?"

"I'm sorry to call so late."

"That's okay. I'm at Easton and Taryn's watching Jamie."

"Oh. You're busy."

"Uh, not really. Taryn's meant to be home any minute. Is Stella okay?"

"Actually, she's not. The ... whatever happened today, it's affecting her."

I get to my feet and head to the living room, the phone pressed hard into my ear. "How so?"

"She can't—or won't—sleep. She's screaming a lot and I'm trying to do everything I can for her, but it's ... I'm not the best at calming her down, I—Patrice handles this, but I gave her the night off."

I've never heard Rex like this. Unsure and perplexed and just plain confused.

"Harper, I'm sorry to ask this of you, but I don't know what else to do. If you could please come..."

Stella's hoarse cries sound in the background.

"Sure. I'll be there."

Rex sighs into the phone. "Thank you."

"I'll text Taryn, see how far out she is. Then I'll come right over."

I say it without hesitation. Without thought that maybe Stella doesn't even *want* me there.

I hang up with Rex and text Taryn, my brows so low against my eyes, they ache.

I can't ignore the pained howls of Stella. The ragged calls for her Momma, over and over until the word is nothing but a garbled, devastated mess.

I know all too well what it's like to scream for a parent into an empty room.

CHAPTER 13

Rex

WITHIN THE HOUR, Harper returns to the duplex.

I open the door to let her in. She looks exactly the same as when we last spoke, so I don't know why I feel a spike of ... something ... when I see her again.

A vibration in my throat.

A kick-start to my heart.

Veins and arteries throbbing with my pulse.

Cock ... following suit.

"Come in," I say after clearing my throat.

She steps in, shedding her leather jacket and purse. The late August nights have become cool. "Where's Stella?"

"In the den." I grimace. "Watching TV."

If Harper wants to lecture me that it's two a.m. and there is no viable reason a kindergartner should have screen time, she doesn't. I'm thankful for that.

"She's quiet for now?" Harper asks.

Harper strides into my kitchen and I follow her, bemused by her sense of purpose.

"Kind of," I reply. "Clutching her blanket like it's a lifeline and her lack of eye blinks are a little worrying."

Harper nods as she reaches up to a cupboard her tiptoes and

pulls out three mugs. "She's afraid of the dark. I knew it. I frickin' *knew* she wasn't okay with what happened to Slate as soon as I put her to bed, but I left anyway. I'm sorry, Mr. Sloane."

There's no way Harper can beat herself up as much as I have these past few hours. "Don't be. I'm her father. I should know these things."

Harper bends down to the cupboard under the stove, pulling out a pot, but peers over her shoulder at my statement. "Just because you're her father doesn't mean you should have the innate ability to understand your kid. You're a parent. Sometimes you miss the mark. Nothing to be ashamed of."

I jolt at her frankness.

She notices, and as she straightens, she says, softer, "Societal pressures really piss me off. It's hard enough raising a child not to be an asshole."

Surprisingly, I smile. Harper meets my eyes and we stay there for a second too long, invisible steam curling between us, before I break the connection and glance at the stovetop. "Can I ask what you're doing?"

Harper rubs the back of her neck with her free hand, and I want the action to be because of me. Because I make her nervous.

"Uh, warm milk with a dash of green tea and honey," she says. "My grandfather always made it for me when I was upset."

"That's very kind of you." And I take that small nugget of Harper's history, the glimpse into her past, and keep it close. "But we don't have any tea in this house."

"I know. I stopped off at my favorite bodega before coming here."

Harper spins out of the kitchen, back to her large purse, but she has to pass me to get to it.

I should move to let her through.

I don't.

"Can I get by?" Harper gestures with her hand but won't meet my gaze.

I've lowered my chin so I can get a good look at her. Feel her warmth this close, see the sheen of her black hair against my floodlights, the spots of pink on her cheeks.

My mouth parts.

I want to taste you.

I step to the side, ashamed and sickened that I want to take advantage of this girl when she's come this late at night to help. To *assist* as my nanny, nothing more.

"Apologies," I mutter, but I doubt she hears it, since she's scurrying to her purse like I've put a cattle prod to her ass.

She finds what she's looking for, what seems to be a box of tea, milk, and a bottle of honey. As she balances everything in her arms and comes back, I say, "We have milk."

Harper doesn't react to my sharper than intended tone. "I didn't want to assume."

I open my mouth to—

"To address your concerns about caffeine content, it's only a splash of green tea. For flavor. It'll be less than what you find in hot chocolate."

"I wasn't going to ask about that," I lie.

Harper smiles dotingly. I frown at it.

"I have it handled in here," she says. "You can go sit with Stella."

"Oh." The thought occurred to me, but the shame got there first.

I'm afraid to sit beside my daughter. For her to push me away again, screaming I'm not her mom.

How much Stella wants her mom.

I don't know how to tell my daughter her mother's never coming back.

"If you give me instructions, I can make the ... concoction and you can go sit with her," I say.

Again, Harper smiles. I'm noticing tonight that her smiles reach her eyes. "It's a trick of the trade. You won't be able to make it as well as I do." She laughs, but sadness coats the sound. "Even I can't make it the way my ah gong did."

"Ah … gong?"

"My grandfather. He was from Taiwan."

"Was. I'm sorry."

She shrugs, and it's an awful lot like my daughter's brush-asides. "He lived a good life."

"Did he raise you?"

Harper's back stiffens as she works near the stove.

"I apologize. I didn't mean to intrude," I say.

"It's okay." But Harper doesn't turn around. "Like I said, check on Stella. I'll be there shortly."

I give a gruff nod, realize she can't see me, and say, "All right, then."

It isn't until I reach the threshold of the den that I figure out I've been dismissed in my own kitchen.

Stella draws my attention, so small and pale on the leather couch, taking up the least amount of space she can as the blue glow of the television outlines her drawn face.

When I move forward, she doesn't react, her fingers still buried in the soft down of her blanket—one of the last gifts of Aesha's.

My chest rips at the sight, but there's nothing I can do other than be amazed at how steadfast and fixed a toddler's memory is. I thought Stella wouldn't remember much of her mother, seeming how she left when Stella was two.

Stella did. She has.

"Harper's here," I say in an attempt to engage.

Stella doesn't react.

I don't push it and take up position at the far end of the couch, watching her with crunched brows. Blinking moisture into my eyes when they seem too dry. Telling myself that Stella is vivacious, and beautiful, and loved. She hasn't been left behind.

Yet, her posture, curved, bowed and devastated, tells me differently.

"Hey, Stella."

Harper's soft voice enters the room before she does, and she carries three mugs on a tray. Stella blinks, but that's about it.

I'm worried my daughter's gone comatose. And I'm the idiot who brought her to this state.

As she passes me, Harper hands me a mug which I take with both hands, noting it's not too hot. Just warm enough.

She sets the tray on the coffee table and perches next to Stella.

"I made you a drink," Harper says, her tone remaining soft. Harper picks up the smaller mug and cradles it against Stella's arm. "See? Nice and warm. I even used one of your favorite teacups. I bet you and your blankie will really enjoy it."

Stella blinks and I swear, my heart plummets in relief.

"It's not anything you've tried, ever in your life," Harper continues, unruffled by Stella's lack of response. "It's a special, secret drink. Meant only for fairies. But my grandfather made a deal with one of them, when they became trapped under his cottage window. He said he'd let the fairy go if the fairy told him of their secret potion, a brew that was said to heal sadness. If you drink it, it'll wrap around all your sad parts, like a warm blanket, and stay there for as long as you need it."

Cute story, though I doubt my daughter will buy it.

Stella breaks out of her fugue to side-eye Harper. "That's the dumbest thing I ever heard."

I'm elated my daughter has spoken again, but not so impressed at her rudeness. That kind of talk is reserved only for me. But through my elated annoyance, I notice Harper grinning.

"Is it?" she asks, unruffled by Stella's reaction to what sounded like a very personal childhood story. "Why don't you try it and find out?"

Stella squints at the teacup, still held aloft by Harper, and bites the inside of her cheek. I take the quiet moment to test my own.

Cloyingly sweet but coating my throat like the soft fleece blanket Harper promised. And there's an exotic, earthy taste, similar to the fairyland Harper swears it comes from, that brings me back for more, despite my demand for black coffee and black tea—all things black. Sugar isn't usually welcome.

Stella sees me tipping my mug to my lips, and curiosity drives her to take the teacup from Harper and perch it against her own mouth, daring a tiny, barely bubbling sip.

The same bemused expression crosses her face, and she goes back for more.

"It's good," she says, "But I doubt fairies made it, since they don't exist."

"You're right," Harper says, to my surprise. "But it got you to speak to me, didn't it?"

Stella's upper lip curls, like she hates that she was bested by the new nanny, and Harper's resulting smile mirrors my own.

Harper settles in next to Stella, allowing my daughter the time to sip and mull over whatever she needs to, without pressure or coddling or urging to go to bed.

I allow it, since Stella's eyes are getting heavier the more she dives into that drink, her head lolling the side.

"Stella," Harper whispers. "How about we go to bed?"

Stella jerks awake, the lukewarm remnants in her teacup sloshing. "No."

Harper extricates the cup from Stella's small hand, placing it on the coffee table. "Aren't you tired?"

"Yes." Stella rubs her eyes, but the break in her voice tells me she's gearing up not for sleep, but for another cry. *Shit, not again.* "But I don't want to dream."

My heart cracks in places where I thought it couldn't break anymore.

Harper shifts so she can face Stella better. "Why don't you want to dream?"

"Because the bad things come."

"What bad things?"

"The things that hurt Slate. The monsters that took my mom."

My thighs tense, ready to jump across the ottoman, to fly over the *Earth*, just to hold my daughter, but I've tried it a thousand times before. And each time, she doesn't want me. Each time, she wishes it were me that left and not her mother.

"I'm here to make sure that doesn't happen," Harper says.

I make a large, audible swallow, but I can't move. Can't stop watching this play out.

"Those monsters won't get you. I promise," Harper continues.

"How do you know?" Stella asks, so tiny and fragile against my leather couch. *Christ, she's so vulnerable.*

Harper's throat bobs. "Because the monsters have tried to get me, too. But I won't let them have me. No matter what."

Stella's chin dives into her blanket, but she looks up at Harper. "How do you fight them?"

Harper licks her lips. Glances at me, as if for permission, but I have no idea what she's asking. I nod anyway, because I'm at a loss. Hell, if Harper has a solution, Harper can say whatever she damn well pleases.

"I sing," Harper says.

Stella frowns, the fleece from her blanket tickling her nose, and she pats the stray fabric down. "How can that work?"

"Monsters hate light. They despise anything good. Singing, music, makes everyone feel good. It makes you forget the bad. And where there's no room for sorrow, there's no room for monsters."

"I don't know if I believe that," Stella says.

Me neither, sweets. And singing is my job.

"Let's test the theory, shall we?" Harper stands and holds out her hand. "Let's all go into your room. I'll tuck you into bed and your dad can sing you a song."

"I can what?" I blurt.

Harper levels me with a look. "You can sing to her. She loves your music. Loves your voice. If anything can get her to sleep at three in the morning, it's your lyrics."

My growl curves in tone, it's so low to the ground and menacing. "I thought I told you, Harper—"

"Please, Daddy?"

The tremulous, pleading question stops all threat from exiting my throat. I glance at my daughter, those too-bright eyes in such a dim room aiming straight for my utter weakness—my heart.

"Please?" she asks again, and this time it's nothing but a whisper.

I stand in surrender. I was a goner from the first moment Stella said the word *Daddy*. This time is no different.

"All right," I say. "One song."

"'Heartfall'?" Stella asks.

"Don't push it," I grumble, but follow Harper and Stella out of the room.

I SETTLE Stella into her bed, conscious of the looming shadow behind us.

Rex waits until Stella is comfortable before taking up residence in the rocking chair in the corner, likely left over from when Stella was a baby.

He can barely fit in it. Rex's thick thighs, already restricted by tight, ripped denim, spread wide, his ropey arms spanning over the chair's arms by at least a foot. He leans forward, elbows on his knees.

Picturing him rocking a newborn Stella to sleep in that chair, his arms akimbo with nowhere to put his legs, is an adorable image that leaps into my head.

I smile, glad he can't witness it in the dark.

There's a small reading nook in Stella's room near her window, and I perch on the built-in bench, settling a throw pillow against the windowpane behind me and leaning back.

There's the possibility I should give these two privacy, but neither has asked me to leave. And I'm desperate to hear Rex's singing voice. In person. Alone. With a private audience of two.

It's a privilege I don't believe Rex realizes he's gifting, and I'm not about to remind him I've gotten a free backstage pass. My stomach twists in anticipation.

"Okay," Rex says. Stella's nightlight is the sole illumination in this room, adding a slumberous, whispery effect that no one wants to ruin by using a normal voice. "I know you want *'Heartfall'*, Stell, but can I sing you something I've been working on?"

My ears perk up. A new song?

Stella pulls the comforter up to her chin, the atmosphere doing its job of relaxation. "I guess."

I see Rex's half-smile in the gloom. "Thanks, sweets."

He clears his throat and I become still as a cat, afraid that the tiniest twitch will distract him and he'll ask me to leave.

I don't want to go.

I want to be here with this little family tonight—an incorrigible little girl with a gloomy, brooding dad—and nowhere else. The realization terrifies me, since I have no experience playing house.

Rex clears his throat, glancing at his daughter, then at me.

I shrink back the tiniest amount at the eye contact, but the reminder that I'm in the room doesn't deter him.

Rex turns back to his daughter and sings, his legs rocking in tune to his song.

"I've had my share of pain-filled memories,
My heart anchored to the ground,
But then a lady came to shore,
And asked me to come around.

I thought she would take my soul,
But instead she left a gift,
She pulled at the weight,
Held on as she lifted,
And set me free to fate.

She's my one and only,
My sole source of light,
I love her deeply,
She's part of me,
She's my flesh, my soul, my daylight."

Rex croons, so softly and eloquently, that I don't know when the verse ends and the chorus begins. I sway in time to his words, wanting to close my eyes to the music, but needing to see him, to watch him and the way his lips part, curling and curving over his lyrics. His lashes are dark crescents against the slant of his cheeks, his long hair brushed away from his face, tucked behind his ears, and I swear he fills the room with his soul.

When Rex's voice tapers off and he sings the final notes, at last I blink. I look to Stella, sound asleep in her bed, her tiny chest rising and falling beneath the covers.

Rex stands and I follow suit, tiptoeing around Stella's bed and slipping through the door Rex holds open for me. I duck under his arm but wait for him in the hallway.

"That was beautiful," I say once Rex shuts Stella's door behind him.

He rubs at his jaw. "I've never done that before. Sang to her like that."

I risk asking, "How did it feel?"

"Good?" Rex says it like a question. "I don't know. I ... I never thought I wrote music my daughter could listen to."

"I've heard most of your songs." I rush to add, "Through nannying Easton's future stepson, Jamie. I mean, you know who I'm talking about." I attempt to lean against the wall, but I'm too far in the middle of the hallway and stumble against air.

"Are you okay?"

"Yes. Sure." I smile, wishing my awkward antics could come another day. Another *moment.* "What I'm trying to say is, you have songs she can listen to. Stella knows you're a singer and wants to become a fan. And if your voice relaxes her, especially on a night like this…"

"You think I should make a habit of it." His lips pull taut.

"I'm not trying to tell you what to do. I'm just here to notice things, and part of that is Stella's nighttime routine. She needed you tonight, and you did well."

My teeth clamp together around the same time my brain scolds my mouth to *Shut. Up.* Like Rex would ever need a compliment from me. Or an observation.

"Thank you," he says, and when he says it, he's looking into my eyes.

I blink. Swallow. Refuse to become awkward because I've drawn a gorgeous man's attention.

He's cranky.

He's mean.

He scares the crap out of me a lot.

All reasons *not* to fall victim to his oceanic stare.

"What's the song called?" I ask. My lame attempt at distraction.

"The working title is '*Stella*'." This time, his answering smile is more relaxed.

It never occurred to me that the lyrics could be about his daughter. I assumed it was a lost love, Stella's mom probably, someone who impacted Rex but who ultimately walked away.

"Really?" I say, before my brain collects better sense. "But it's so … sad."

Rex cocks his head. "Why do you say that?"

Damn it. "I-I'm not trying to criticize. I loved it. It's beautiful and rings so true, only … I thought it was about someone you lost."

I laugh through his uncomfortable, answering silence.

"But what do I know?" I say. "I just happened to be around. I'm not your target audience."

"Actually, you are."

That face of his, so angular and shadowed, refuses to move

from my horizon. Rex pins me in place, shivers coursing down my arms, throughout my legs, and he doesn't even realize it.

"I, um." I low-key clench my hands, trying to keep it together under his unsettling, heated gaze. "The lyrics were happy, yes. Gorgeous even. But the tune, I don't know, the tune was melancholy. Bittersweet. It's a dichotomy in the most beautiful way—I don't know how else to describe it."

At last, I'm able to break eye contact and lower my attention to the ground. I feel dumb even saying this stuff, especially to a seasoned rockstar who has people in the highest of pay grades to give him this kind of advice.

"I wouldn't think such heartache applies to your daughter," I continue. I can't seem to stop myself. "I see you with her and all I see is happiness. Nothing sad."

I hear Rex's swallow and I'm afraid to look up. To witness what kind of anger I might've ignited.

You barely know us, I picture him yelling. *You have no right to talk about my family this way.*

"Stella is my everything." Rex's voice, soft and uneven, hits my ears. "And as a result, that terrifies me. When it became me and her, when I turned into the person responsible for raising her, for teaching her morality and humanity, I broke. I broke in half, and one section of me went into my child. I'm left incomplete, but complete, since I have her by my side. And I keep hoping the better half of me is in her, that I haven't—that I won't—screw her up. She's a gift of light that I'm terrified I'll snuff out." Rex scratches at his chin, no longer directing his weighted gaze on me. "Anyway. Maybe that answers your question."

He moves past, but I'm seized by the need to reach out, and I do. I touch his arm. "Mr. Sloane."

Rex pauses, half-turning with his profile, his lidded eyes. He's not focusing on me anymore.

His lashes flicker. His brows twitch. And he draws his arm away from my hand.

I feel the loss, but I'm confident he doesn't feel a thing.

"I haven't brought that song to the band yet," he says. "As for tonight, it's late. Please stay the night. Patrice has moved her things out of the nanny's wing and there are fresh sheets laid out."

I nod. The mere mention of a bed as my eyelids drawing closed, but I want to keep Rex talking. I want to *know* him, almost more than I've ever wanted to know anyone.

"I'll see you in the morning, Harper."

"Um—"

At the sound of my voice, Rex stops mid-turn.

"I have nothing to wear. To bed," I say, and gesture down my body. "I'd rather not sleep in a blouse, so maybe I'll call a car—"

"Don't worry about it. I have some clothes for you. I'll bring one of my shirts and some shorts to Patrice's—to your room in a few minutes. That okay?"

I nod, unsure how to handle wearing Rex's clothes. They'll smell like him. They'll be soft and pliable from *his* use.

And my body will be warmed by them.

Rex continues down the hall, his steps heavy, yet I'm unable to move from my vantage point as I watch him leave.

Such sadness. And he has such longing attached to a beautiful, healthy daughter.

I wonder what causes such turmoil in Rex. How such a beautiful, healthy man can be so confident he'll destroy his child.

How much damage did Aesha invoke?

I'm so, so curious, but I'm also no fool. I'm determined to keep this job.

And, as it's turning out, I'm wanting it for more than just a paycheck.

CHAPTER 15

Rex

I'M NOT sure where to look, other than at her.

Harper and Stella are hanging out the next morning amicably enough. Harper's with Stella at the kitchen table, enticing Stella to eat pancakes with some syrup she warmed on the stove.

What's enticing to me is the way Harper's pulled back her short hair. The elastic can't contain it. Strands wisp into her face so she's constantly tucking them behind her ear. Especially when she bends close to my daughter with a big smile and a plate of pancakes, despite Stella's pinched expression.

I should remind Harper we've hired a cook to do these things.

I should absolutely tell her that Stella does not get such extravagant breakfasts on weekdays.

I should confess to her how gorgeous her legs look in my athletic shorts.

Yet I don't.

With confident strides I don't feel—*why the fuck did I tell her about my fear for my daughter last night*—I stalk to the table and pull out a chair. It scrapes loudly, obnoxiously, and both girls jump at the sound.

"Daddy?" Stella asks, breaking out of her disdain enough to register shock at my arrival.

"Thought I'd join you," I say as I sit down. I still don't glance Harper.

"But you never come for breakfast," Stella says.

I push my brows up and act interested in the layout of pancakes. Using tongs, I place a few on Stella's empty plate that I then slide in front of me.

"Hey—" Stella starts, then shuts her mouth. She probably realizes that by showing distress, it'll prove to Harper that Stella really wants pancakes.

"I happened to pass by the kitchen and saw the excellent spread Harper made for you. A treat you're never supposed to have on weekdays, I might add."

Out of my periphery, I notice Harper cringe.

I cut into a pancake and take a huge mouthful, saying out the side of my mouth, "And you're not even enjoying it."

Stella sits straighter and stares sidelong at Harper. "Because I know the rules, and I didn't want to break them, Daddy."

Swallowing and dabbing at the crumbs sticking to my scruff with a napkin, I say, "Maybe just this once."

Stella crosses her arms. "I don't like pancakes."

I respond, "That is a lie, it's your favorite meal aside from grilled cheese, and you're going to eat some." I shove her plate back in front of her. "Don't be rude to Harper. I taught you better than that."

Stella's tongue pokes out of one corner of her lips. Yep, she's about to say something snarky. "You're not around enough to teach me anything, Dad."

Harper says nothing, leaving for the stove to grab more syrup out of the pot.

I grit my teeth. "I'm here now, aren't I?"

"Probably just to see my new nanny," Stella says. "I'm not stupid. If she's my new mom then I—"

My fist comes down on the table with a *slam*. Harper drops the pot at the sudden noise, spilling syrup all over the gas burners. Luckily, they're turned off.

"Stella, that's *enough*."

I immediately regret my actions. Stella's lower lip trembles, her shoulders quaking as she slides off her chair.

After a deep inhale, I offer as gentle a tone as I can. "Sweets, I'm sorry. I didn't mean to yell."

"You didn't scare me," Stella says, though her voice shakes. "Your angry noise tells me all I need to know."

"Stella—"

I lift my hand as if to stop her from leaving, but I don't get out of my seat. Outbursts like this are happening more and more often, the older she gets.

After a few seconds, the slam of her bedroom door rings out.

"I'm sorry about that," I say to Harper, who's busied herself cleaning up the syrup.

She stops wiping and turns. "Don't apologize. She's going through a lot."

I sigh, dragging Stella's plate back over. "Still. She shouldn't have said that. I hope you don't think—"

"No, not at all." Harper twists a rag in her hands like it's someone's neck. "It's probably my fault. Here I am, wearing your clothes. I explained to her that I didn't have pajamas and I slept in Patrice's old room, but she's—"

"More precocious than I give her credit for." I sigh again, throwing my napkin on the plate, but it feels as if I'm staring through it. "You know, Aesha left when Stella was barely two, and I thought because Stella was so young, it was almost a gift that she wouldn't remember much. But here we are, three years later, and missing her mom."

After a few seconds of silence, it's clear to me Harper won't respond. I'm annoyed I said as much as I did, so I go back to eating Stella's pancakes, to give myself something to do other than brood.

Then, I hear, "Stella doesn't have to know her mom to miss her."

I stop chewing and refocus my gaze on Harper.

Harper's face is downcast, that rag still twisting, her lower lip caught between her teeth.

"She's at that age where school brings up a lot of crap," Harper says. "Maybe she's seeing other moms, or her peers are asking where her mom is. Or her friends are asking why her famous dad's single. It's bringing up a lot of feelings for her."

"You sound as if you've been through it."

Harper twists around, finding renewed interest in cleaning the stovetop. "Did Patrice do anything special when Stella got into these moods? I can try to do the same. Maybe it'll help Stella find her routine again."

I take the hint, drop the subject, and stand. "Not that I know of. But Patrice is a safe space. She's been there for Stella since Aesha— since Stella was two. Patrice is normal and expected. You..." My voice softens. "You're different. New. Unchartered territory. For both of us."

Harper's scrubbing slows. "I don't have to be."

I hear the murmur, but I can't decipher the meaning. *Don't have to be* as in, Harper can be more? Or *don't have to be* as in, give her a chance so she can prove she's as good as Patrice?

It has to be the latter. I'm a douchebag to think Harper wants something more. It's an inappropriate, foolish thought that must be reined in with constant, brutal reminders.

She's my kid's nanny. Harper's too young. A college dropout who's used her one semester in Computer Science to babysit rich people's kids. Her goals are all over the place, whereas mine are intact. Carved into stone.

My attention moves to the breakfast platter full of pancakes on the kitchen table.

This is strike three. I could fire her.

I've wanted to fire her since hiring her and it's only day two of her training.

Last night keeps replaying in my mind's eye. Harper's beauty cast in moonlight. Her ideas at calming my daughter. Her presence creating warmth in this otherwise cold and vast house.

She's good for Stella.

On a grunt, I shake myself out of it.

"This is your final warning." I point to the remnants of breakfast. "It's stated in the Summary. Fruit with oatmeal or Cheerios on weekday mornings."

"Yes, I know."

Harper's shoulders slump, but I refuse to feel bad about pointing out the obvious. My sharpness feels good. Right. Much better than reminiscing on *what if's* and *as in's*.

Harper says, remaining with her back to me, "She'd had a rough night. I thought maybe pancakes would cheer her up."

"You already got me to sing to her. That was enough of a bonus."

"I overstepped. Again. I'm—"

"Don't be sorry." My lips pull back from my teeth, but she can't see it. Harper doesn't fight me. She *never* fights me.

How much would it take to get her temper to rise? For angry color to cast over her cheeks?

"I allowed it," I say. "But I don't make allowances often. Remember that."

Harper nods, and I try not to cede to the snake that seems to be writhing in my gut at talking to her this way.

I step away from Harper right at the moment the cook walks through the front door.

June trills hello, adding the final break to the heavy spell cast between us.

Harper refuses to turn around, and I consider that a good thing. Her face haunts me enough when she's not nearby. She makes me want to write songs and pen lyrics constantly.

"I'll get ready," Harper says, just as I'm about to walk out of the kitchen, "then take Stella to school. After, if it's okay with you, I'll go home and change and be back in time to pick her up."

If there's sarcasm hidden in her *okay with you* comment, she's hidden it well. My eyes narrow.

"That's all fine," I say.

"Fine."

Harper drops the rag on the counter and brushes past me as she leaves the kitchen first.

And as she departs, I wonder if she decided that by leaving first, she got the last word.

A low rumble hits my throat.

Strike three.

Goddamnit. I can't fire her.

THE REST of the week goes by with no fireable incidents.

Patrice helps me through it, and by Day 7, I have Stella's routine down. I don't dare add pancakes to her breakfast roster. Nor do I give in to her requests to wear tutus to school—except for that one time when I *almost* believed the tiara she wore belonged to her friend and not that damned box she found again.

Stella's also responding to me with more than a sentence, which I consider a check in the *I Like Harper* column. So far, she tolerates me and notices Patrice's growing absence less and less.

If I didn't know any better, I'd say I had the job in the bag.

But.

My employer remains ominously missing. I barely see Rex these days. He leaves for the studio or rehearsals right when I arrive, leaving their part-time chef to oversee Stella's breakfast until I walk into the apartment not a minute past seven.

Despite his lack of presence, I act like Rex has got cameras on me at all times. Hell, maybe he does. Either way, I give Rex zero excuses to cut me out of his employ.

I've caught on to Stella's blank expression each time I ask if her father's around, so I've stopped bringing it up. The girl is lonely and aching for Rex's attention, but I don't dare mention it to Rex—not that I could, since I never see him.

If I didn't know any better, I'd say Rex is avoiding me. But that's true insanity. There's no reason for him to freeze me out or act like I'm not around. I've given him nothing to mull over nor have I been the reason for any overcast, demonic expressions on his face. Not lately, at least.

Maybe it's the strange, thick heat that's making him avoid me, curling in the space between us, a space that grows smaller and steamier the longer we linger together in the same room.

I force the thought to exit stage right and instead get back to wrangling Stella into her green leggings with sparkles she insists on wearing today. I'm certain they're too small for her, but Stella won't have it.

"You're all set for today?" Patrice asks as she perches on Stella's bed, her legs crossed at her ankles.

It's Day 8, but Patrice is hanging out this morning, prolonging her goodbye. She looks stunning, as usual, in a chambray sundress, her silky, brunette strands pulled back in a low ponytail. Meanwhile, I'm running around in exercise shorts and a tank top, forgetting it was laundry day.

"Yep," I grunt. After one final shove and yank, Stella is in her pants. I throw up my hands. "Success!"

Stella frowns. "They're tight on my tummy."

"No kidding." I push off the floor. "I told you they're too small."

"But they're my *favorite*," Stella whines.

Stella's voice never goes an octave above bored when I'm around. That she's used extra syllables with higher decibels gives me hope. "Maybe after the park today, I could take you shopping—"

I halt once I notice Patrice raising a finger to shut me up. "You know the rules, Harper."

The Dossier. I glance down at Stella, unwilling to be beat yet again by an encyclopedia written for a five-year-old. "How about I talk to your dad today, see if he'll let us get you some new clothes?"

Stella doesn't risk true emotion peeking through her careful mask. She falls back to her usual form of communication, but I notice the flash of eagerness before the shrug.

"I take that as a *yes Harper! I'm so excited!*" I say to Stella, then turn to Patrice. "I'll be fine. Since it's your last morning, if you need to go do other things, feel free. I'll text you if I need you or have questions."

Patrice has grown more comfortable with me and my handling of Stella. There's been no further paparazzi or traumatizing friend injuries since my trial period, so I'm not surprised when she agrees.

She pats Stella on the head as she passes, and Stella smiles up at her. A flare of jealousy hits my belly, but no sign of it shows on my face.

"I'm just going to say goodbye to Rex, then I'll be out of your hair," Patrice says.

My shoulders straighten. "Rex—Mr. Sloane—is here?"

Patrice has never appeared more blasé than at this moment. "Sure. I heard his shower going when I passed by his room earlier."

Shower. Rex, naked. Patrice "passing by" his room. Upstairs, where there's no real reason to be up there. Nothing Stella related, at least.

I can't for certain say that Patrice has hooked up with him, but I can't *not* say it, either. And, I'm ashamed to admit, I seem to fixate on the possibility that Rex hooks up with his nannies.

His wet body, hair slicked back from the shower's spray, keeps hovering at the back of my mind. That Patrice could join him, her lithe, lean body as exposed as his as she wraps her arms around his neck and captures his damp, shining lips with her own, comes next.

But then that woman morphs into *me.*

I'm claiming Rex in his shower.

I'm naked, jumping up and wrapping my thighs around his torso, feeling his shaft pressed up against my core...

"Harper? Are we leaving?" Stella asks.

I blink.

Patrice is long gone, taking her mysterious Rex connections with her. Stella's chin is tilted up, and she's regarding me like I'm one of her live-action dolls who's standing in the middle of her room.

"Yes, bug. We're leaving," I say while ushering her out of her bedroom.

"Bug?" Stella scrunches up her face. "I don't like that name. You promised to only call me Stella."

Dang. Sometimes, when I get comfortable, I fall back on the previous nicknames I had for kids Stella's age: bug, kiddo, munchkin, crazy-face.

And every time I do, Stella calls me out, either unfamiliar with it or annoyed that I won't use her actual name.

It's a precocious demand, but I have to give her props for it.

A small sigh escapes my lips, but I say, "You know what? I wouldn't want to be called a bug, either. Stella only from now on. Promise."

Turns out, my apology doesn't matter, since Stella's already on another topic.

"You know how you said we might go shopping later?" Stella asks as we head down the hallway.

"Sure do."

"Well, I think I also wanna do ballet."

I mull this over as I slow my steps to keep pace with her. "You do?"

"Yeah. Slate does it, and Kimberly, and Frances. I wanna do it, too." She glances up at me. "Do you think you could ask Daddy?"

Her gorgeous honey eyes are trained on mine. Hard. I'm unsure if this is another set-up or a pleading demand to be like her friends, and as always, I hope it's the latter. I only need to think of the box of hidden ballet clothes Stella's drawn to like a firefly to know she'd love to learn.

I move to squeeze her shoulder, but remember she doesn't like me touching her, so I say, "I'll ask him—"

"No need. That's a hard no."

My chin jerks up. Rex stands in the main room as we clear Stella's wing. His long hair is damp and tied back with a leather band, leaving the sculpted carving of his cheekbones on full display. He wears a plain blue tee and distressed jeans like he's in the middle of a photo shoot for the brand, and the sheer, charismatic force of him distracts me long enough for Stella to speak first.

"But Daddy!"

"I said no, Stella, as I've said no a thousand times before," Rex says. "I know what you're up to. Harper's new, but that doesn't mean she'll say yes to everything you ask."

"I just ... I really want to..." Stella's lower lip juts out.

"Oh no, Stella I forgot my purse in your room," I say. "Can you go find it for me?"

Stella's eyes, shining with unshed tears, darts between Rex and me, but she does as asked, trudging back down the hallway.

I cross my arms. "She's enrolled in soccer, isn't she?" I ask Rex. "Why can't she do dance class as well?"

Rex deigns to register my presence, and the instant, hard line of his mouth explains to perfection his current opinion of my opinions. "Because I'm her father and I don't want her to."

But you have a box of tutus. Stacks of tiaras. Why in the hell are you teasing her this way?

I don't voice any of these arguments for fear of repercussion, but Rex reads something on my face.

He adds, his tone curt, "She could get hurt."

I can't resist. "Stella could get hurt on the soccer field or from falling off a swing on the playground, yet you let her do those things. Why not ballet?"

Rex's upper lip curls, and as if unable to stop himself, he

ambles over to me. Hovering. Looking down. "You're walking a thin line, Harper. Don't question me on this."

He's trying to be intimidating. Those fueled bright eyes, the curved bow of his lips, the hard lines in his cheeks, all an overcast cloud against my vision, as if he can win this argument through overbearing force alone. Yet, all I register is his heat, pouring over the bare parts of my body, and the icicle mint of his breath casting frost over my lips.

I want to lick him, see if he tastes as peppermint cool as he believes he is.

"I've done nothing to make you question my nannying skills these past few days," I say, "And I'm only asking a question, since Stella seems so taken with dance. Your word is final and I'll respect it, but Stella keeps going to that box of yours, no matter where you hide it."

His upper lip rises with the beginnings of a snarl, but I press on.

"If you don't want her to be so desperate for ballet, why don't you just throw that stuff out? Clear the house of the very thing that tempts her?"

Rex's brow tics, but he doesn't step back. Refuses to clear the air between us. Instead, he stifles it. Dares it to become thicker.

"There are some things in this house," he begins, "you have no right to understand. That is one of them. Instead, focus on keeping my daughter healthy and happy. It's what I pay you for."

I see nothing past his face, his dark expression. He's encompassed my entire horizon. The apartment background, the whole environment, has disappeared, but for his threat.

My breath hitches, but not from fear. The boil between us is so tangible I could burn my fingers on it. We lock our eyes in battle with a simmering core beneath our chins, past our stomachs, and right at our centers.

Neither of us moves or gives ground to the other. I don't even try to blink. If I lift my chin the tiniest amount. If I part my lips ... will he...?

"Harper, your purse isn't there!"

Stella's heavy steps causes a fault between us, a silent crack that breaks Rex and me apart, and I fall back a few steps.

I hold my hands to my face. *Christ. My cheeks are so damned hot.*

"My bad, Stella!" I call, just as she comes into the room. "I didn't bring a purse today. I have my wallet in my shorts. Whoopsie!"

Stella puts her hands on her hips. "Then why waste my time?"

A laugh burbles out of me before I can stop it, cooling my over-heated body so that I'm sure steam is escaping out my ears. "My mistake. C'mon, we're going to be late."

"Because of *you*," Stella says to me, but as she passes her dad, she says, "Bye, Daddy."

Any remnants of disappointment are overshadowed by finding my nonexistent purse and getting to school, but I don't believe for a second Stella's wish to learn to dance won't come back. My glance towards Rex before we exit says as much.

After bending and kissing the top of his daughter's head, Rex answers me back with his usual, silent wrath of a stare.

What I say, goes, his glare all but says.

I yank the front door open, but my brain is in scheme-mode. Calculating and solving, figuring and stacking.

By the time I shut the door on Rex's deadly, warning gaze, I have the answer. All I need is a few more days, then he'll be on tour and farther than his glares can reach.

Stella and I head to the elevators, where besides walls, steel will also separate me from that man. Soon, it's floors.

Then a building.

Then street blocks.

But, no matter how far I get, the heat of him lingers within the goosebumps on my skin.

CHAPTER 17

Rex

THE NANNY GOT TO ME.

I'd been avoiding her this past week, knowing her schedule as I do. This morning was a mistake. I woke up late, showered later, and then assumed.

Assumptions, as I should know by now, are dangerous.

Stella and Harper should've been well on their way to school by the time I took the stairs, but some kind of preschooler issue held them up in Stella's room, whether it was outfit problems or hair combing or a standard Stella tantrum, I don't know.

And that's where my mistake lay.

When Harper appeared, I almost tripped on my own goddamned feet. It's amazing how such a tiny thing can have such high impact. But when she wears those shorts, and that billowy tank with nothing but a simple sports bra underneath ... I just fucking can't.

Her hair was all tossed, her cheeks flushed, and when we locked glares across the room, I swear her eyes smoked their gray.

A five-alarm fire, that's what's coming toward me if I don't staunch it, quick.

No surprise, but I don't heed the warning.

The first thing I should've noted: Harper was late getting Stella out the door. That's a strike three.

Strike four.

Strike fucking five.

Always a strike.

Yet, I never strike.

And *then*, the vixen has the gall to go toe-to-toe to me. Me, who towers over her and conducts thunderstorms about as well as I seduce audiences of thousands. I'm intimidating. Untouchable. Famous. And despite all that, this girl—my *nanny*—acts like I have no impact, when all she does is erode my stone.

Fuck. *Fuck.*

"Yo, Rex, get your head in this song or else I'll throw my bass at you."

I grit my teeth and swing my guitar from my back to my front. "I'm on it, Mason. Where were we?"

"Right after the time signature where you tell me what the fuck is going on."

My head does a slow loll sideways toward Mason. The guy's standing a little behind me, adjusting his mike, sweat gleaming on his forehead from the overhead studio lights. He's chosen a plaid shirt today that he's taken off and tied around his waist and baggy black denim pants with lots of pointless chains, capped off with motorcycle boots.

"Where's your shirt, fucker?" I ask.

"In your laundry. I expect it Wednesday." Mason strips off his bass guitar and leans it against the wall. "Dude, Wyn and East aren't here yet. We don't have to rehearse. Tell me what's on your mind."

"Nothing."

"Ah." Mase claps his hands once. "A chick."

"There's no woman." I point at his bass guitar. "Put that back on."

"No, *Dad.*"

Mase strides to the opposite side and pops open a Coke. He offers me one, which I accept with reluctance. I haven't sung a single verse today, yet my mouth feels Sahara dry.

We both gulp down half the cans before Mason speaks again. After he, then I, let out a nasty ass belch.

Hey, we're alone.

"You're distracted, Rex. That says something to me, since you're never fucking distracted."

"We're leaving for Europe in a few days. I'm not happy about being away from my daughter for so long. If I'm looking spaced-out, that's why. It's getting harder to leave her the older she gets. And understands."

Damn. I'm using my daughter as a crutch. I know it, Mase knows it. I'm limping over the real issue, but I ain't ever gonna say it out loud.

"I can respect that." Mason leans a forearm on top of my mike stand. "So, it's the nanny."

"It's not the fucking nanny, man."

Mason raises his hands, one still holding the Coke. "Hey, I've seen her 'round since she was sitting for Easton's boy. She's no wallflower. I can respect you wanting to make her yours, too."

"Jesus." I rub the heel of my palm against my eye. I sense a migraine coming on.

Mason claps me on the back. "I've known you since high school. No woman, save for a poisonous one, has made you get such pregnancy brain."

I stare out at him through my fingers. "Pregnancy brain?"

"You know. Spacey, forgetful, cranky as fuck."

"Are you calling me hormonal?"

"I call it as I see it."

"I don't know who should punch you first. Me, or women everywhere."

Mase smirks. "Get in line."

I use the opening in the exact way I should. "You wanna talk about my girl? Let's talk about yours."

Mason's expression closes off. "You don't get to do that."

"Turnabout's fair play, my man."

"I'm not trying to get to the heart of Aesha, for fuck's sake," Mason says. I stiffen. "I just wanna know if you're gonna bone the nanny is all." Mason shrugs. "Because if you're not, I'm gonna have me a go."

I snarl, more beast than man as my hands ball into fists, the Coke can crunching against my rage, aluminum cutting against my skin.

Mason's Cheshire grin tells me I played right into his stupid, fucking hands.

"You're going to miss Harper, too, huh?" Mase asks. "Not just Stelly-Belly."

My shoulders relax at the use of Mase's endearment for my girl. She and Mase have a special bond that not even Mase can make light of.

"It doesn't matter if I want to sleep with the nanny," I say. "I'm not about to do it."

"Why not?"

"Dude. She's my employee. My daughter's starting to like her. It's inappropriate." I flick a hand. "Should I keep going?"

"This is NYC, there are a million replacement nannies, and your daughter likes no one except for you, me, and Santa Claus."

"She liked Patrice."

Mason raises a brow at that one and considering I haven't explained my history with Patrice to anyone, including my best friend and bandmate, I'm not about to start now.

Mase says, "Stella liked the structure Patrice brought, sure, but I doubt she gives a fuck if Patrice sticks around or not." Mason uses his hands to add to his point. "Replace Patrice with Harper, and Stella won't blink."

My molars clench at the implications of Mason's point. At the inkling of fear that's forever remained since Stella was born into my arms. That her emotionless state could be permanent is an etched black nightmare at the back of my eyelids. Blinking doesn't make it go away, ever.

I grunt. "It's not that simple. I think Harper needs this job."

"Yo-ho-ho!" Mason hollers. "Not only do you want to sleep with her, do you *care* about her?"

The idea that I want more than sex from Harper gets me thinking about the night Harper spent with us, how she cajoled Stella into drinking milky tea, then convinced me to sing, the three of us sitting in the dark, my voice the only light carrying through the room.

Hell, if that's what "caring" means, then I am too far gone to consider finding that kind of illumination of the heart, ever again.

"Whatever." I busy myself tuning my guitar, which I don't need to do. "Can we get back to the music?"

Mason responds after a snort. "I guess."

Mason sidles back into position, picking up and adjusting his own guitar against his body.

Just as I relax, retreating into the pre-meditative state that centers my mind before I open my mouth to belt out lyrics and think of nothing else, I hear Mason say, "I bet she's great in bed."

I hurl the mike stand at him.

Operation Stella takes careful planning.

It can't be my idea. There can be no trace of my suggestions, opinions, or nudges, as I mention to the other nannies and parents in the park after school how great it would be to make some kind of day trip to catch a matinee and see a ballet with some of the kids.

I'd have to ask Rex's permission once a date was solidified. But it wouldn't be *my* idea, nor traced back to me, if all Stella's friends after school were going to a ballet and she wanted to go, too. The amount of FOMO Rex will give his daughter is likely a lot, but I doubt he'd resort to cruel.

At least, I'm banking that he won't.

"Girl, if your phone had feelings, you'd be ripping its guts out," Taryn says across the booth.

I realize I'm glaring at a blank screen and put the phone down on the table, my duffel sitting shotgun beside me. Rex and his band leave for their tour tonight, and I'm grabbing a quick lunch with Taryn, Jamie, and Easton before heading to Rex's apartment and spending the duration of the tour with Stella at the duplex. Jamie and Easton have yet to arrive.

It's somewhat of a goodbye party, since I'll no longer be

working for Taryn and Easton exclusively. I'm now officially in the employ of the Sloane household.

"You sure that's enough for two weeks?" Taryn asks, nodding toward my bag.

"I pack light," is all I'm willing to say before I sip from my straw.

"You nervous?"

I shake my head, but stare over the top of hers hoping to see Easton's scruff and Jamie's cowlick through the crowd so Taryn can stop assessing me. It's like she can *feel* when something's up, and I want her knowing nothing about my weird, tingly, sexual feelings for my new boss.

"Good," Taryn says, and she's so genuine that I return my attention to her. "I'm so glad it's worked out between you and Rex."

"We've come to a treaty where all I do is focus on Stella and all he does is focus on Stella and music, and it seems to work."

"Meaning..." Taryn scrunches her forehead. "You two barely talk to each other?"

"Exactly."

"That's—interesting." Taryn sips from her drink, but her gaze is steady on my face. "And you're happy with that?"

"Why wouldn't I be? He's a grump. And when he's not a grump, he's a drill sergeant. The less I see of him, the better."

"Uh-huh."

Crap. "Are you lawyering me, Taryn?"

Taryn laughs. "Am I what?"

"You know, doing that attorney thing where you ask open-ended questions hoping your witness will put their foot in their mouth with no prompting on your part?"

"You give me too much credit." Taryn smiles, but it's closed-mouthed. Strategic.

"Damn you," I say.

"I just want you to be happy," Taryn says, "And find a job you love."

"I have," I say, but it's after a hard swallow of carbonated sugar.

Stella's difficult, but not unbreakable. Rex is hard, but it's ancient, fragile stone. There are cracks in each of them that I've slipped into, giving me a preview into the real people underneath. I'm not sure what to do with it, or if I've earned the privilege of unfiltered access.

"Harper."

Taryn's hand on my own brings me back to the present.

"If you're feeling some type of way, maybe you shouldn't work for him," she says.

"What?" I scoff. "I feel nothing for Rex. This is about employment."

Taryn's focus narrows to where nothing escapes her notice. Not even the reddening tip of my nose. "Are you sure about that?"

"Hey, I see Jamie and Easton." I wave them over through the crowded pub.

Jamie catches my over-eager hand-flutters first, and they detour over to our table.

"This isn't over," Taryn says, but turns a mega-watt smile on her boys.

"Ladies," Easton says. He dips down to kiss Taryn, then ushers Jamie in next to her. East takes the seat next to me, my hip shoving into my duffel bag.

We all revert to sign language now that we're together and facing one another, and the conversation flows from our fingers. We talk about mundane things, funny memories, and that Easton's leaving tonight will be heavily felt by his family.

Sign language isn't the only form of silent communication at this table. It's gifted me with the cues and facial tics that I would never have noticed, including seconds-too-long looks, the constant "accidental" brushing of fingertips, the subtle curves at the corners of mouths.

Taryn and Easton do this to each other in multiples.

I catch it all. My heart swells at the sight. My small, shriveled, too-traumatized organ beats its life in my chest as these two people feel everything for each other.

It makes me think that *yes*, maybe mixing emotions could amount to happiness, when at the right time. At the very moment it's needed.

I look down at my hands, now on the table, my fingers curled and silent as Taryn and Easton express how much they'll miss each other.

At Jamie's nudge on my forearm, I smile, letting him know I'm fine, just tired.

I'm not so sure I deserve it, the peace Taryn and Easton have found.

And I'm 100% sure I won't find it with Rex.

I make it to Rex's apartment with minutes to spare. Stella's seated at the kitchen table, eating mac 'n cheese the part-time chef, June, left in the fridge in the late afternoon. Rex sits across from her and they're both attempting to list animals for each letter of the alphabet.

"Shoot. Am I late?" I ask as I drop my duffel near the kitchen entrance.

Rex holds up a finger, his attention remaining on his daughter. "What's X? I always get stuck on that one. How about I just go to Y. Yak."

"Because then you'll lose," Stella says after a giant mouthful of cheese and pasta. She says out the side of her mouth. "And you hate losing."

"True." Rex glowers as he picks at the remnants of his dinner.

"*Psst,*" I say as I busy myself opening kitchen cabinets and finding a clean bowl. Rex looks over as I pull open the silverware drawer, nearest to him.

"X-ray fish," I whisper.

Rex's lips twist. "Seriously? How is that not cheating? First off, it's a fish, not an animal, and second, it has the word 'x-ray' in it."

"Daddy!" Stella shouts, but it's an amused cry. "You can't let Harper help you. I win!"

I left a wry brow and lean into the counter. "Got any others?"

"No." He frowns over a forkful of pasta. "Because there's no animal that begins with X and my daughter set me up."

I fight off a smile. "Xerus."

"Now you're just screwing with me."

"Do you know how many daycares I've gone to that play this game?" I retort.

"Doesn't matter, I win, and now I get ice cream." Stella hops off her seat and scoots past me to the freezer.

"I can't beat you, Stella. You're too smart for your old man." Rex stands while wiping his hands on his napkin.

He sidles close to me—so close I can smell the hints of the spice of his cologne after it's settled on his skin—and a half-breath hitches in my throat.

"The ice cream is a diversion," he says to me in a low voice.

So low that it's filled with allure. He can talk about anything from diversionary tactics to how to strip the bra from my breasts and I'd be rapt. Held in rapture. Ready for his hands to follow his commands.

I clear the thickness from my throat. "Um. Yes. I figured."

"I'll sneak out while she's occupied," he continues, his lips close to my ear. Tickling the hairs there and sending shivers coursing down my neck.

My nipples pique. *You smell so good.*

Do it.

The devious whisper runs circles around my brain.

Stella's occupied by rummaging through the bottom drawer of the freezer for the boon of her winnings. She pays no attention to us.

Do it do it do it.

It's like my previous, instinctive, animalistic self has risen to the surface, goading me to take what I want, seize the opportunity.

"Understood?" Rex asks, his lips brushing the shell of my ear.

He wants it, too.

I shouldn't think that. Rex has given me nothing but instruction, only leaning close so his daughter doesn't catch on that he's leaving for two weeks. Fourteen days.

Hours and hours of not seeing him, and not because he's avoiding me. He'll be thousands of miles away. Somehow, that's different than Rex ignoring me nearby.

DO. IT.

"Harper."

His whisper isn't soft. It's deep and harsh. A command.

I do it.

I whip my head to the side, so quick that it could be a mistake, so fast that he doesn't fall back in time, and our lips touch by a hairsbreadth.

Rex jerks back as if jolted by lightning. Heck, I've been hit by the same strike. I can't catch my breath. My heart's hammering so loud, it's stretching its arteries up my throat, drumming into my ears. My vision's blurred with adrenaline and lust.

Blinking, I say, after licking my lips. "Oh—sorry. I forgot to grab a fork."

I'm holding a fork in my hands. Along with an empty bowl.

Rex doesn't notice. His attention is on my lips, those depthless blues trained on my every movement.

If I move, if I twitch, he'll take me down. I'm sure of it.

I want him to.

The sheer madness of desire in his eyes catches fire when he lifts them up to meet mine. His lips part, his chest heaving, his hands clenched.

Oh God. What have I done?

My chest moves with the same want, but I don't dare shift an inch.

"Chocolate double waffle crack! My favorite!"

I dart a look over to Stella as she dances with a pint of ice cream, then, when she notices what's in my hands, takes the bowl and climbs back up on her stool.

"Did she just refer to a street drug?" I ask Rex.

By the time I glance back, Rex is no longer standing there.

"Can you help me, Harper?" Stella asks in her regular, *you're here, so I guess I'll use you*, tone.

"Sure, Stella," I reply, amazed at the steadiness in my voice.

"Good." She glances at my other hand. "But I can't use a fork."

I pry my fingers off the utensil I've been clutching like a life preserver in torrential waters.

"Neither can I," I say to Stella as I lay it down on the counter and pull open the drawer for a spoon instead. With my back to her, my shoulders slumped with drifting adrenaline, I repeat, with added meaning, "Neither can I."

CHAPTER 19

Rex

I'M A GENIUS.

I write songs that cause the audience to stop breathing, play guitar riffs so on point, they send chills down shoulders and spines. I croon and sing in ways that send fans, women, people, into ecstatic, orgasmic puddles at my feet.

It's a job that pays in more than money. Singing feeds my ego, strokes my dick, and in any other world, I'd ride that bitch until she was exhausted—no, until *I* was sated.

Drugs fueled me for a good while. Cocaine especially, until it started killing my muse and made my lyrics sound more like they were doing the rounds on *Sesame Street*. Easton had to take over despite his own issues, writing lyrics, drumming beats, creating those orgasms and becoming God while I had to take the time to get my shit together. Raise a baby.

I let him have it for a while. I was too deep in self-wallowing to care. Too invested in my girl, in getting her better.

And somehow, despite our band's fuck-ups and secrets, we kept rising. We kept leading.

Having Stella changed all that. True, Nocturne Court rose to fame while Stella was still climbing newborn milestones, but now that we're here, now that I can have anything I want … I'm still away from her.

The feeling doesn't sit well. It's also been growing during this tour, becoming fuller, thicker, and taking on other forms—like Harper, and how she thinks Stella should be exposed to my music. Not my fame, she's quick to add, but the thing that fuels and drives me.

It's so much more than paying the bills when you get into this kind of business. Singing is like blue fire, beautiful, mesmerizing, hot to the touch, and deadly if you're not careful. Yet, if Stella knows nothing about it, how can she prepare for it when she's older? How will she understand that we have to live life differently from most? That instead of disappearing into New York City crowds, we stand out from it, just by moving through them?

Maybe Harper's not wrong.

Stella could see me play, just once. I'd edit the set, tell the boys to keep the cursing to a minimum, but … it's possible.

Back in the day, I was away from Stella enough that I could still be that asshole who fucks groupies and takes on any women our sponsoring companies hired to "meet any needs." Those chicks hang out in the front row. They're backstage. They're waiting in our VIP hotel suites.

At the moment, I'm finding that the only females I want to see in the crowd are my daughter and her nanny.

Nowadays, Mase and Wyn still take extra time sorting through their cash and women while on tour. Easton has no interest and uses his disability to strike pity in the hearts of the men in suits so they leave him alone—not because he believes he's disabled. The suits are too greedy to notice.

Me, I'm floating somewhere midline. A choppy purgatory where to be a good father, I don't fuck. That could mean many things: *I don't fuck it up* and *I don't fuck around* or, I straight up *don't fuck.* Especially as Stella gets older and stories could get back to her.

Or when the day comes that she asks for more info about her mom.

Our first show on our European tour went about as well as it should've. Having a constant case of blue balls has made me stricter than a Catholic school nun, and even though the guys whine non-stop about it, it gets us the crying fans, the sold-out concerts, the happy record label.

Despite our success, we still demand a shared backstage suite instead of each getting our own. Band bonding and all that shit. Mase and Wyn are sweat-soaked and somewhere in the hallway signing tits and taking selfies. Easton's in the corner on the phone —probably with Wifey, our new name for Taryn. I'm sucking on a secret cigarette on the opposite end, hidden by a pool table. Shirt off, sweat drying, ankle balanced on my opposite leg, my heavy-lidded eyes tracking the groupies that've snuck in, mixing with the women hired to keep our spank banks refreshed.

Spinner, our manager, is eager to please, hip cocked at the corner of the pool table, spinning the 8-Ball and praying the woman in the tight, hot pink dress is paid enough to keep him happy, too.

I can't stop thinking about Harper.

A sneer forms over the butt of my cigarette, and I take it out of my mouth and stub it out on the heel of my shoe, flicking it into the trash bin nearby.

It was so fast. The strike of a sea snake. One minute Harper was inches away, the next, she sliced through the air and her lips were brushing mine.

She claimed it was a mistake, but there was enough time to taste her. Sweet, like she'd just sucked on a hard cherry candy. I picture her tonguing the candy behind closed lips, coaxing it to melt within her satin heat until it dissolves into liquid sugar that courses down her throat.

My cock hardens in my pants and I adjust my hips. My hand twitches against the leather armchair, but not for another cigarette.

I want a notebook.

"Hey there, sexy."

A woman perches on my armchair, the curve of her ass bending into my forearm. It's Hot Pink Chick, who I'm guessing Spinner couldn't nail.

I don't glance at her face—or remember anything about her. It's tough to treat women as sex toys when you meet their eyes and think about what's behind them, what made them want to be paid to fuck celebrities. After Aesha, I couldn't help but pry. One woman mentioned she had a sick niece whose medical bills she was paying. Then there was another, who was putting her mom through school, since she always dreamed of getting a college degree.

And there was Aesha herself.

Too many women with stories. Too many chances to save. I'm done with all that.

"I ain't interested," I say, shifting to reach my back pocket for another secret cigarette. Hell, it's giving me something to do.

"Honey." She takes my free hand and presses it between her tits. "You ain't even tried."

She molds into my palm, hot and soft. I turn my head and make the mistake of looking up. "Damn it, I said—"

Her eyes widen as they clash with mine. I'm sure my face looks just as fucking stupefied.

"Mack?" I say. "McKenna?"

She straightens, adjusts her breasts and pulls up the straps of her dress. "I'm sorry. You must be mistaken."

"Uh, no I'm fucking—" She sprints to the other side of the room, ducking and weaving through the drunken crowd with ease, and disappears through our suite's door. "Not."

Well. Hell.

There's a blast from the past. And a fucking strange one, too.

No sooner is Mack—who I'm *sure* that is—out the door when

she's replaced by another tightly wrapped, sexy woman. This one's brunette.

I don't let her get a word in as I stand. "Not interested. I'm leaving."

"Yeah, they told me you were the asshole preacher of the group," she says.

Unable to deny any bait, I cock a brow. "Preacher, huh? As in, standing in front of my clergy spewing morals and shit?"

She gives a closed-lipped smile, but it reaches no other part of her expression. "The very one. They say your dick's so unspent, it's turned to concrete. Either that or you've undergone surgery to become a Eunuch."

"And who…" I curl a finger under her chin. She tips her head up. "The fuck is *they*?"

Her eyes should sparkle with mirth. She should at least be delighted with the banter. But, she remains blank. Eyes Dead. "Your band. Your manager."

"Mm." I release my finger and her chin drops as if she were relying on the stability. I walk away, but say to her glowering form over my shoulder, "Joke's on them."

In no way am I a castrated man. All I have to do is think back to those cherry lips, wisps of hair getting caught in the gloss before I smooth back her hair, cup her face, then turn feral. Licking and biting and taking until her soul is all written on paper, then matched to chords, made into music, and played to the world.

My employee.

My payroll.

My rules.

Mine.

Preacher, indeed.

It's easy to leave, since most people are pretty sauced and will stay that way until well after the sun breaks over the horizon. I wave to East who lifts his chin in acknowledgment. I figure I have a few hours, maybe, before we get on the tour bus and hit our next venue. Plenty of time to hole up in my hotel suite and get down the words that've been itching my brain since Harper stepped into my headspace, flicking on a long-dormant switch, thinking there'd be no consequences.

Little does my band know, I will make us millions by fantasy-fucking my nanny.

And I look forward to making her watch the show.

CHAPTER 20

Harper

STELLA CAN'T BELIEVE what I've done.

She's dancing, spinning and curving all over the place, barely clearing corners after I've told her the news that we're going to see a ballet recital. I feel exactly how parents must feel when they gift their kid with the perfect, most awesome present in the world and get to witness happiness morphing into tangible delight. All because of them.

Stella's showing emotion.

The urge to have Rex here to witness the moment is strong, and the follow-up sadness that he's not is expected. I send a bittersweet smile to Stella, anyway.

"Daddy says it's okay?" she asks as she twirls.

I answer with a brief, "Yep."

I stuff my phone in my back pocket with the surety that I'm not lying to her. Not exactly. I told Rex of the "field trip" to a theater show, which three or four of the park nannies were taking part in after naps in the afternoon. He texted back with a simple **fine,** which I took as utmost permission. I may mention that it was a ballet after-the-fact, but again, not my doing—totally the other nannies' idea.

As I'm packing up a backpack for Stella, including snacks,

drinks, and a change of clothes in case of a spill emergency, I have to dodge her hops, leaps, and various explanations to her stuffed animals that she's seeing a ballet for the first time in *ever*.

Part of me suspects the reason Rex is so averse to his daughter learning the dance has to do with Stella's mom. Same with the forbidden box. But I can't, for the life of me, understand the harm it would do to Stella to see a local recital.

Unless—Stella's mom is somehow involved in it.

So, being the amateur detective I am, I checked the list of dancers, and no one named Aesha is dancing today, nor do any of the previous or upcoming shows list her. Nor does she seem to be in the backstage crew or production team or ... anywhere. A Google search doesn't bring up anything about her.

Aesha is a unique enough first name. Perhaps it's because I don't have her last name and can't seem to find it with any variation of *Aesha ballet, Aesha dancer NYC company, Aesha girlfriend Rex Sloane.*

Whatever's happened between Rex and Aesha and her history remains locked in some very fancy, PR finagling vault that the likes of a somewhat obsessive, way too curious, amateur detective-nanny can't crack.

Thus, back to the no harm thing.

I've never seen Stella so happy and eager. *Never*, in the two and a half weeks I've been supervising her, almost two of those without Patrice. If Rex comes down hard on me once he figures out what I took Stella to see, I will look him in the eyes and say it was worth it.

Yes, I would.

A guilty lurch at my center has me wincing, but I keep stuffing things in Stella's pack like nothing's wrong.

As if staring Rex down wouldn't be a problem. Like I wouldn't drown in the arctic storm of his eyes or buckle under the stern line of his lips. Lips I touched, ever so briefly. Ever so sweetly.

The memory raises shivers at the back of my neck, but I rub them away.

Stupid.

My phone buzzes in my pocket, providing a thankful distraction. I answer it without checking the number.

"Harper speaking."

"Hey, Harper, it's Bobby."

Hmm. I have to go through the Rolodex of my mind to figure out who Bobby is, but it comes to me after a few seconds. Bobby Laurie, personal assistant to Rex Sloane and listed under the many contacts in Stella's Dossier. I've never met him.

I prop the phone between my ear and shoulder as I zip up Stella's bag. "Hi, Bobby. How's it going?"

"Tour's going well, Rex is doing fine. Stella okay?"

Stella's swinging a white stuffed rabbit around until it careens into a wall.

"Yeah, she's great," I say.

"Good. I'll let Rex know. Uh, hey, so I'm calling because Rex requested you two to come to one concert. We'll be in Philly tomorrow night, then ending at MSG the next day."

Now this, I have trouble Rolodexing. "MSG?"

"Sorry—I mean Madison Square Garden. He wants you and Stella to be there."

The phone almost slips from my ear. "Seriously? I thought you guys are still in Europe. And that he doesn't want Stella seeing his shows. She's too young."

"I hear ya, but what the boss says, goes, you know? Nocturne Court often ends their international tours with bonus shows on the East Coast. What can I say? They're rockstars."

Rex Sloane, what could you be up to?

I say, "Let me check Stella's schedule and get back to you."

"You could do that."

There's a high-pitched warning at the end of Bobby's sentence.

"What I mean to say." I pretend an amused laugh. "Is that we'll be there. Whatever Stella has going on, even if it's in Mr. Sloane's rulebook that I never digress or divert from her calendar without facing serious consequences, I will ignore and come straight to the concert hall with his daughter in hand."

"Great." Bobby doesn't get the joke. "I'll text you more details. Timing and whatnot."

"Sure," I say, with a dubious shake of my head.

We click off and I lift Stella's bag from the bed. "C'mon, Stella. Time to get going."

Stella pauses in the middle of her room, hands on her hips. "I've been ready since forever ago."

"Don't I know it." I hold out my hand. "Let's go see some dancing."

Stella drifts past me without taking my hand, and I follow her after a long-winded exhale.

I guess secret ballet tickets don't put me in the good books yet.

Once inside the auditorium, Stella and I take our seats near Slate and her nanny. As soon as Stella plops her butt down, she whispers and conspires with Slate.

Slate's nanny is on the opposite side of Slate, so I say to her over the two blonde-headed allies, "I'm so glad Slate's doing better."

The nanny nods and smiles kindly. She's older and French is her first language. She and I get by with polite, effusive comments and a lot of hand gestures.

Because we were stuck in mid-afternoon traffic, Stella and I arrived just before the show was due to start. The lights dim almost, and I sit back, hoping Stella doesn't spend the next few hours whispering with Slate instead of paying attention to something I sense could be important to her one day.

As soon as the orchestra begins and five or six female dancers glide out from the side of the stage, toned arms raised and chiseled legs spread and leaping, my fears turn unfounded.

Stella is rapt, whether it be because of the outfits I know she loves so much, the music, or the dancers themselves. She says nothing, doesn't move, for the entire first half. The whites of her eyes are obvious in the darkened theater, her hands clutching the armrests as she remains focused on the recital.

As the swan maidens fill the stage, the orchestra evoking emotion with mere strings, wood and brass, I find myself just as taken with the play as the stage lights mimic the dawn and the evil spell sends the princess back into the lake as a swan.

After the curtains draw closed, the theater lights blink a few times, signaling intermission. I dab at my eyes with a tissue before Stella can see, but she's twisted in her seat to chat with Slate about what they just saw.

"Hey. Stella." I nudge her to get her attention. She glances at me over her shoulder and I whisper, "Wanna take a peek backstage?"

Her eyes widen.

"But it has to be our secret," I say. "Just you and I are allowed back there."

Stella has no problem with this. "Be right back. I have to pee," she says to Slate, then slides off her chair.

Smiling, I collect our things and we steal down to the front, and then the side door, of the stage. An usher meets us there.

"Sorry darlin', no access beyond this point," he says.

I take a deep breath, readying myself. "I'm Nick Mei's daughter. I'm told I can access backstage whenever I want."

At the mention of the name I rarely, if ever, invoke, the usher sweeps aside. "Welcome, Miss Mei."

Stella remains ignorant of the exchange and follows me into the interior, neck cranking side to side as she takes everything in.

When we reach the shared dressing room with its door open, Stella can't help but point.

"There she is!" she says. "The princess!"

My hand hovers near the small of her back. "That's right. And I'm sure she'd be happy to meet you."

Stella's neck does one more crank as she stares at me, agog. "Really?"

I nod. "Go on."

With the carefulness that I often see in Stella, but containing newfound shyness, Stella approaches the dancer, her hands twined behind her back.

"Excuse me, Miss Princess?"

The dancer glances down from her seat in front of a mirror framed by bulbs. "Well hi there, sweetie."

"Hi," Stella says. I don't think I've ever seen her so taken with anything, or anyone.

"And what's your name?" the dancer asks.

"Stella."

"Beautiful name. I'm Ramona." The dancer holds out a slender hand, which Stella takes as if she might break it.

"My mom was like you," Stella says, with whispery awe.

My spine goes straight, and I know my face must look exactly like Stella's when she was watching the first and second act. Rapt.

"She was? And do you want to be just like her?" Ramona asks, her face sparkling and glistening with white powder and glitter. A feathered tiara crests the top of her head.

Stella nods. "My Daddy says I can't, but I wanna be."

"I'm sure your mom will be proud," Ramona says diplomatically. "Is she teaching you ballet?"

With a dejectedness reserved only for the saddest of orphans, Stella shakes her head, and I want to take her by the shoulders and hug her. "She can't."

"Oh, no? Are you taking a class then?"

"I can't." Stella gnaws on her lower lip. "I'm not allowed, in case I get hurt just like Mommy did."

"I'm so sorry to hear that, honey."

Ramona glances up and over at me, a clear signal for help. I step forward.

"Stella, let's get back to our seats. We should let the princess get back to her show. She needs to get out of the lake somehow, right?"

Stella scrunches her brows at me. "She's not in any lake. She's on a stage in a play."

Sometimes, Stella acts young enough to want to search for a hidden princess in a backstage theater. Other moments, she seems too mature to fall for the game of fairy tales.

"You're right. It's pretend, but we're still loving it." I wave her forward. "C'mon."

Stella gives a small curtsy to Ramona, softening me up again. "It was nice to meet you."

"You, too, sweetie. Enjoy the show. And here." Ramona pulls a feather from her tiara. "To remember your mom and what she loved to do."

Stella accepts the gift, staring at it as if her mother materialized right in front of her. To jolt her out of it, I say, "Stella, what do you say after getting such a nice gift?"

"Thank you," Stella whispers, then tucks the feather behind her ear.

We make our way back to our seats just as the theater lights dim again.

"Hey, what's that?" Slate asks, pointing to the white feather.

"I found it on the floor," Stella says with a shrug. She then glances at me as if we share a special secret, and *goddammit*, I'm delighted to be included in a five-year-old's clubhouse.

Stella makes it another hour, but by Act 4, she's asleep on my shoulder. I rouse her enough to see the final scene with all the dancers basking in the blue light of the stage as the Swan Princess and the Prince ascend to the heavens.

She's too tired to say much as we depart from the three other nannies who came with their charges and say goodbye to Slate. I'm tired, too, so I don't notice the cameraman idling outside the theater until it's too late.

Flash.

I hold up my palm against the light and pull Stella closer to me, despite her protests. "Screw off," I say.

"We meet again!"

I peer between my fingers, recognizing the voice.

"You again?" I say. "Don't you have anything better to do than lurk outside playgrounds and theater matinees?"

"Not really," he says, and gets another click in.

I shouldn't talk to him. I keep us moving toward our car, but I can't resist adding, "Does taking and selling pictures of other people's children really make you feel you're living your life well?"

"You'd be surprised how much people are willing to pay, honey," he says, clicking away at our backs. I shove the bag in front of Stella's face to protect it as I move her forward and into the back of the vehicle. I've never been so fast at clipping a kid into her booster seat.

"Fuck off," I mumble once I shut Stella's door and she's out of earshot.

"It's not like I'm here by chance," the dude says, though his camera is now at his hip. "Famous folks, they hire other people to sell information, sell *locations*, so the celebs can stay relevant in the public eye. I'm surprised you don't know this, being the nanny to an A-list singer."

"I know it," I say as I round to the other side of the car. "I just hate it."

And Rex wouldn't.

He'd never sell his daughter's location. Not for anything.

"Rex Sloane is surrounded by a lot of greedy bastards," the cameraman responds, reading my thoughts. "Maybe you should look at who's in his life—or who he's kicked to the curb—before cursing me out."

I don't give him any more ammo and open the passenger door, but the asshole paparazzi guy persists. "If it's not you giving me the info on his kid, then who is?"

The last thing I see before our driver pulls into traffic is the pap's sneer through my window.

"Thank you, Harper. For taking me to the show."

Stella's sleepy voice draws my attention to her. I'm surprisingly warmed by her acknowledgment. "You're welcome, hon—Stella."

Her head lolls in my direction. "That was awesome."

Stella's eyes are drifting closed as she submits to the comforting lull of a moving car. I should enjoy sitting in silence, the white noise of endless traffic. But I don't.

"Stella, when did you find out your mom was a dancer? Did your dad tell you?"

She gives a lazy shake of her head. "No. Patrice said so once. I don't think she was supposed to."

"Huh." I go back to staring out my window. "Have you told your dad?"

"No. I think he'd be mad. I don't like it when he's mad at me."

Understandable. I stop asking questions, and Stella drifts off, her neck cricked in doll-like fashion—unbearable for adults but comfortable for kids.

"I miss my mommy," she whispers.

I risk brushing one of her curls off her temple. "I miss my daddy, too."

Stella's eyelashes flutter open. "You don't have a daddy anymore?"

I take a deep breath, my fingers resting near her hair. "I actually had two daddies."

Stella considers this. "Charlotte in my class has two mommies."

I smile and stroke her forehead. She doesn't protest. "One of my daddies went to Heaven. The other…"

"Is like my mommy?"

My gaze narrows on this little girl. So many people don't give credit to children for seeing more than they let on. For *under-standing* the world better than a lot of adults, before societal rules and norms temper their instincts.

I won't ask where her mom is. I don't want to hurt Stella, or worse, traumatize or confuse her. It just means I have to become better than the companies hired to bury Google search results.

"I don't know where your mommy is, Stella, but I do know where my daddy is. He's just … too busy."

"Like my daddy?"

"No." I shake my head, my palm resting on the crown of her head. "Not like your daddy at all."

But my murmur isn't heard. Stella's fast asleep.

A nasty feeling coats my stomach. I feel subversive for asking as much from Stella as I did, but curiosity is a gnawing beast. So much secrecy surrounds Aesha. So much secrecy surrounds *Patrice.* It's as if any woman who touches Rex is gifted either a protective cloak or a blackout shawl. I haven't decided which one I fall into.

But what I do decide, as we get caught in the usual city start-and-stop traffic, is to do one last search on my phone. A nagging part of me has got to understand why a mother isn't in her child's life. Why the father is so tight-lipped about it. And why a cameraman keeps finding us.

You're imputing your past onto this child.

Shut up, brain.

Grimly, I ignore the subconscious warning and type into my phone's keyboard. This time, with more specifics.

Aesha "Rex Sloane girlfriend" NYC ballet injury.

When that still brings up little to no search results relevant to what I want, I resolve myself to the inevitable.

I will have to call my dad.

CHAPTER 21

Rex

"WHOA, DUDE. YOU SURE ABOUT THIS?"

Mason scrolls through my phone, taking a hard look at what I've written in the dead of last night, when I'd rather listen to my muse than the Sandman.

"Yup," I reply.

We're the first people in the dressing room. East and Wyn are taking their sweet time exiting the tour bus that transferred us from the plane to the stadium. The room is basic for our needs—dark walls, thin carpeting, chairs, couches, tables containing requests from our riders, consisting of Wyn's request for Skittles, Mason's demand for Hennessy and Coke, my inkling for deli sandwiches (especially when in Manhattan), and East's energy drinks, half at room temp and the other half frozen and thawing.

We remain teenaged idiots at heart.

Spinner will be here any second, along with the rest of our business posse, so I grab my phone from Mase and tuck it in my back pocket.

"I'm gonna do it," I say.

Mase eyes me warily.

"What?" I say.

After a moment of study, he looks away. I squint at him,

wondering what's made the guys walk eggshells around me this morning. I noticed it first when I meandered out of my seat on the plane, sniffing out coffee. The rest of the crew was awake, stuffing themselves around the small tables and couches in the aircraft and burying their faces in coffee mugs as soon as I appeared.

"What?" I remember growling, attempting to meet every one's eye. None would accommodate me.

East was the first to stand, possessing the thinnest and tallest body of all of us, therefore able to slither around crowded areas and get me the wake-up juice I so desperately needed. "Here, have some coffee."

I accepted it, but under great suspicion.

"Whatever gives you a boner," Mase says now, snapping out of the time-suck of that flashback. "But seriously, I like it. I'm interested to see the tunes you've put behind it."

"You'll see."

I don't intend to sound as cryptic as I do, but this is one of the most meaningful songs I've written in a long while. It took me ten minutes to write the first draft after I couldn't find my notebook in the scattering of luggage my bandmates and I stacked in our hotel rooms. I ended up falling victim to my phone, tapping through it under the electric blue glow in one of the bottom bunks as the plane roared through the dark sky.

The intensity with which these quick lyrics bled from my head could either be my death sentence or a top 100 Billboard maker. Such is the life of a creative.

This is the last stop on our tour. After hitting the major European cities: Brussels, Berlin, and Copenhagen, only naming a few, these two weeks on the road has sucked all the blood out of my body. Each night I give my everything, saving the tiniest amount for my FaceTime moments with Stella. I'm a husk of myself, but my baby doesn't see it. I don't allow her to.

Harper might. I sense her outside the lens. It's impossible to feel a person on the other side of an electronic device, but there you have it. I can smell her—roses and cherries—and touch her, the electrostatic waves coming off my phone becoming the hairs on her arm, rising against my caressing palm.

I can taste her, the subtle burst of berry against the tip of my tongue.

My hand twitches, aching to write more words.

It also reminds me of something. I say to Mason, "Hey, you know who I saw the other night?"

"Yeah, who?"

"Mack—"

But we're interrupted by the door bursting open with voices, movement, our keepers and our co-workers, everybody streaming in with purpose.

The rest of my band is here, and all the people paid or wanting to support us crowd in, surround the craft services table, slapping shoulders and guffawing, excited that this is the last stop on our tour and they can go home to their families.

Spinner's the last to step in. "All right, boys! We ready?"

The four of us hoot our acknowledgment and ready our instruments. Soundcheck earlier went well, and despite my ultimate pessimism, I'm eager for this last round. There's always something different in the final show. More passion. Increased energy.

I head out first, Spin patting me on the back as I pass. "This is gonna be epic, bud," he says.

My practiced smile leads the way. "Sure is."

Dude has no clue what I'm about to do. Freedom isn't exactly part of our contract with the major record labels.

"Oh and hey—your kid's here."

I stop in the hallway, Wyn plowing his practice keyboard into my back. I shove it out of my way and turn to Spin. "Yeah?"

"Yep, they made it. Put them in VIP seats up on the balcony. Stella'll have the perfect view of her dad."

This time, my smile's genuine. They're here.

"You're allowing Stella to see you in your element, huh?" Wyn asks my back as we start walking again.

"Yeah," I say, focusing on positioning my guitar as we move.

"Who is this new Rex? Gotta admit, I'm glad for it," Wyn continues. "I know it's been tough without Aesha."

The name freezes in my chest, but my movements don't show it. "Mm."

"I think it's nice, showing Stella her mom's roots. And now she's coming to our concert." Wyn keeps going. "You're doing a good thing, Rex. I don't know what's gotten into you, but introducing Stella to both her parents' careers, ballet and rock, can't be anything but a good thing. Hell, it could be a song—"

I halt. Wyn head-butts between my shoulders.

Cricking my neck ever so slightly, targeting Wyn out of the corner of my eye, I say with careful forcefulness, "What. The Fuck. Are you talking about?"

Wyn's dumbfounded, but accustomed to my moods. Hence why he isn't running in the other direction, clutching his asscheeks from the scald I'm about to give him.

"Uh, which part?" he asks.

"Can we keep it moving?" one of the production assistants asks from the back.

The hallway's clogged with bodies, more joining us the farther we walk and the additional doors we pass.

Fuck, it takes an army.

I'm feeling them closing in on all sides, not letting me breathe. But I don't move.

"Ballet," I grit out. "You said ballet."

"Uh ... yeah." Wyn's brows form confused, twisty wrinkles in his forehead. "Spin mentioned it this morning on the bus. The TMZ pic of Stella leaving the ballet theater. He was impressed with your nanny's ability to shield her. Weren't you listening?"

Vaguely. Not purposefully. My head was still wrapped in my

song. I hadn't even exited my seat to listen to Spin's usual mindless spiel of updates in the mornings.

But how the *fuck* did I miss something like that?

"Guys! Move it along!" someone else screams. "It's getting fucking hot in here!"

I stretch my legs and start striding, but they're stiff, blood and tendons thickening with adrenaline—and not the good kind.

"That's impossible," I say, but it's an unnecessary comment.

Harper did text me about taking Stella to the theater as some developmental day trip, and I don't recall any mention of ballet.

My mouth thins to a grim line. I'm now sensing it as a deliberate exclusion on her part.

My balls go hard, solid knots attached to my body at the thought of meting out punishment to that girl and what she's done.

What I allowed to happen because of my weakness for her.

I exhale through my teeth, a beast-like air taking over my lungs, feasting on anger and fueled by cruel imagination.

"Rex? You ... okay?"

Wyn asks this, though he can't see my face. Just the back of my head, the rigid line of my shoulders, and the grunt after every one of my footfalls. I'm morphing into a werewolf before their very eyes.

Mason sidles up next to me, squeezing my upper arm. Hard. It bulges under his grip.

"Keep it together, man," he murmurs under his breath.

I bare my teeth.

"It was bound to happen sometime," he continues. "You can't keep Stella in the dark forever."

I snap a look at him. He doesn't flinch. "She's a dead woman walking."

He knows I'm not talking about my daughter. Mason sighs. "At least give Harper a good severance check. She's been good for the little cherub."

"Dead," I repeat through my teeth. *"Dead."*

Shaking his head, Mase takes the lead and we shuffle through the maze of backstage, until we reach the curtain and I swallow back the wolf dying to be set free.

It's no longer about me. It's about them, those waiting, the fans chomping for a piece of my soul.

I put Harper in a special place at the back of my mind, reserved to pull out and slice and dice later, so I can become who they want.

Who they demand.

I'm Rex Sloane, lead singer and guitarist of Nocturne Court, and they get to have all of me, including my raging heart.

CHAPTER 22

Harper

I SENSE Rex's impending arrival on stage before I see him.

It's a pulse in the crowd that clues me in, humming, buzzing, sizzling higher until the air is so electric, the fine baby hairs on my head float from my scalp, as if invisible fingers trail through, coaxing them to become wild.

"Is Daddy coming?"

Stella's voice sounds muffled with the thousands of others mixing within the stadium, her pixie face standing out from the dimming spotlights like a full moon. Her ears are covered by special headphones meant for young children at concerts. Combined with the multicolor lights snaking across the darkened crowd, she appears more as a ethereal child from another planet than my human charge.

"I think so," I say.

My mind has yet to catch up to the static energy of my body in the massive stadium. I'm still thinking about the phone call with Nick Mei, and what it cost me.

"Mei Holdings, how may I direct your call?" a pert, young-sounding male voice asked, once I dialed the number when Stella and I reached home after the ballet recital.

"Um, can I speak to Mr. Mei?" I asked.

"I'm sorry, he doesn't take unsolicited calls. Appointment only."

"This—this is his daughter."

Pause. "I'm unaware of any daughter."

Of course you are. Yet, the disappointment slithers in, anyway. "I promise you, I am. Harper Mei. Just tell him it's me."

"One moment." The pert voice is no longer as eager.

After a few minutes, the line clicked over and I heard a deep baritone voice say to someone out of the speaker's range, "Babe, I'll explain everything later," before it became clearer and said, "Harper. This is unexpected."

"I-I know. This won't take long. I—"

"How much do you need?"

"I'm sorry?"

"I can't say I haven't been expecting a call like this from you. How much money do you want? I assume a large amount, since we haven't spoken in years."

"Enough to bury me under more paperwork?" I blurt out before I can help myself.

"Harper, please. You and I have both been happy with this arrangement, have we not? You enjoyed your time with my father."

"Don't you dare bring him up," I whisper. "You don't deserve to say ah gong's name."

Sigh. "If this is your way of asking for a check, Harper..."

"I'm not asking for any *money*." Despite my efforts, my voice clogs with the swell of incoming tears. "I wanted a favor. A small one, considering I've done you the favor of staying out of your life —and wallet—for the better part of eighteen years."

After a moment, he replied, "Fine. What is it."

It wasn't a question.

"The dance companies you donate to, there's one in particular I was wondering about. And a ballet dancer who worked for them. About three years ago."

"Go on."

I tell him all I can, which is the bare minimum but hopefully enough to understand what happened to Aesha.

"I'll have my assistant forward you any details," Nick said when I finished. "What's your email?"

It's amazing how my voice could still be affected, and hurt, by this man, yet there it was. I gave him the information, he promised he'd get it to me within the next few days, and then hung up.

And there we have my most recent communication with the last remaining member of my "family."

Swiping under my eyes, I didn't hope that Nick Mei would do anything for me, but to my surprise, my phone held an email the next morning with a simple sentence from Patrick Onus, Executive Assistant to Nick Mei, Founder of Nick Mei Holdings.

Aesha Anabella Shirapova, born May 13, 1990, was hired by the New York Dance Company in 2012 and made principal in 2013. Her career almost ended after a severe injury to her right knee during a 2013 Fall recital, in which she recovered and began dancing again. She also became pregnant with a daughter around this time, therefore had to take additional time off. However, she did come back and dance, though no longer as principal. She abruptly ended her career two years later with no letter of resignation, no forwarding address, and no known reasons. She never contacted the Company again.

Kind Regards.

PS - Mr. Mei has requested you not contact him again, unless in a dire emergency. Even then, call 9-1-1 first.

. . .

I ignored the assistant's—who I'm sure was who I spoke to—snarky last words, though it was difficult. That throat-thickness that happens every time I think about my father remains strong, even through an indirect email.

And, it turns out, I contacted my dad and opened up that wound for almost nothing.

Almost.

Aesha's injury wasn't what ended her career. It was something else. And it's this seed of doubt and curiosity that's growing weeds in my mind as I try to keep a handle on Stella in an overcrowded, thunderous stadium.

There's a sudden shift in the atmosphere, bringing me back to the present. I jostle Stella lightly and gesture toward the stage. "Look."

The men file out to roaring waves of approval. Stella flinches and tucks into my side, and I take that as permission to put a protective arm around her shoulders.

We're spaced out from other people pretty well, at the front of a balcony with an empty concrete walkway behind us and no one beside or in front of us. We're in a reserved row of four chairs only and have security guards on each side.

I should feel safe. I *do* feel protected. But I continue to wonder why Rex allowed this to happen, because I see now why he was averse to having her here, among thousands, exposed and vulnerable.

These are rabid fans. I've seen videos of them ripping the shirt off Rex's back, tearing at his guitar, climbing over shoulders to try to kiss him. No wonder he wants to keep Stella locked in a vault.

Yet, we're here at his request. I'm holding onto his daughter for dear life, lest she somehow slip away from me and get swallowed up in the crowd.

Rex takes up the mike, and Stella hops up and down upon seeing him. "Daddy! There he is! *Daddy!*"

I smile at the idea that Stella thinks he can hear her.

Rex glances up at us, and I hitch in a breath. Even from afar, his eyes are the iciest of blues, creating frozen craters through the crowd until his frost lands against my chest.

Oh shit. He's mad.

I don't know why that's my first thought. His face is a blur from this distance, save for his eyes, and he's looking for his daughter. But ... I can't shake the feeling that I'm in deep, irreparable trouble.

He knows.

The second thought isn't a surprise, considering what came first. He knows about the sneaky ballet recital, and I'm about to get my ass skinned down to the bone.

Worth it, I remind myself, and look down at Stella, who's wearing the same expression she did when she saw the dancers enter the stage for the first time. Enthralled and disbelieving that such a thing could exist outside of her sheltered, lonely world.

So freaking worth it.

"New York City, how're you feeling today?" Rex asks through the mike, his voice booming, surrounding, entering my veins.

It's a purr meant to draw in even the most resistant of fans, and I swallow against the instinct to peel off my shirt, throw my hands in the air and shout, "Take me! Take me now!" like every other female in here.

"Good, because I'm feeling *you*." Rex smiles, his lips touching the mike, reading my mind. His face pops up on the surrounding huge screens, at least five of them, his gorgeous, alluring expression a resonant gift even to those far off in the nosebleeds.

This time, my inhale isn't held in. Witnessing his face on so many screens at once, looking down the lens as if it's only me he sees, makes me feel like I'm back in his living room, under his scope.

In the bedroom with Stella while he sings.

Or in his kitchen, pivoting, meeting his lips for the barest of seconds to see if this was real. If *he* was real.

As if we could ever be real.

"Harper? You're holding onto me real tight."

"Sorry, Stella." I peel away the claw of my fingers from her shoulder, one by one.

The stadium screams as if it has become one creature, with one source of prey. Rex smiles as if he knew it all along, unafraid of the intense hunger coming at him in waves.

"You ready, Courtesans?" he asks, rolling his head to the side, the corner of his mouth all that touches the mike. As if that microphone could be me, and he's about to dip in for a forbidden kiss.

It's a different man up there.

All I can see is a sexy allure, an uncaring air, with complete focus on his fans' happiness as he opens up with a guitar riff that vibrates through the speakers and into our bodies. He knows exactly what to do to make every person in a crowd of thousands feel like he's singing just for them.

Stella jumps and claps her hands, screaming, "Go, Daddy! *Go!*" as he sings their current money-maker and panty-dropper, "Off-Road Nights."

They played their next hit, then their next, Stella and I never taking our seats but clinging to the railings, flailing like fangirls. Stella's enthusiasm was addictive, her lack of fear in such a crowded space even more so. She wasn't bothered by the screams, the demands for her dad. She loved the music and watching her father in real life and on-screen, playing the strings of his guitar, his long hair becoming slick with sweat, his shirt coming off, his muscular torso glistening under the harsh spotlight.

Okay, maybe those last bits were more from my perspective than Stella's.

Rex meanders back to the mike, hooks it with one hand, and says, "All right, the band's gonna take a quick break. You guys are wearing 'em out."

Boo's scatter across the stadium, shouts of disappointment soon following. Even Stella joins in.

Rex grins, the white of his teeth flashing across the screens. "Did I say *I* was taking a break?"

The stadium vibrates with approval.

"I have a song for you, a new one," Rex continues. "And because I haven't clued my band in—sorry, guys—I'll do it acoustic. Just me and the guitar. You guys okay with that?"

"*Yes! Yes!*"

The stadium creature writhes, winding its centipede tentacles around the stage, pulsing closer to Rex's feet. He's undeterred.

Once the cries die down, Rex says, "This one, I'm calling 'Forbidden Cherry.'"

Stella stands on her tip-toes to see over the top railing. My hand hovers near, ready to scoop her up and run if the crowd gets out of hand.

My fears are quietly, seductively squelched when Rex sings, when he takes over the stadium with his voice and his guitar, and I forget where I am, who I'm with, and what I'm doing here. I only want to listen to him. To follow where he goes wherever he wants to take me.

Then, the words hit home.

"You show up on a rain-filled stardust night,
Your body so ripe,
The readiness you have to protect what's mine,
Pales against my spotlight.

I'm not supposed to like you,
I can't need you,
Yet my everything wants you,
Even if scandal claims my stardom,
And we explode in a supernova doom.

You're forbidden to me,
You're next to me,

You hold my baby's hand,
And I'm doing the best I can,
To stop holding you by the hips,
And leave the marks of my lips."

Oh, boy.

My thighs clench together, and I wonder how fast denim can dampen. Can I even walk out of here without the mark of horniness between my legs?

Jesus Christ. He's talking about me.

He is, isn't he?

I glance around, as if I can ask someone—as if I can ask Stella, "oh hey, is your dad singing about seducing me?"

Stella bops along as if nothing's awry, clutching the blanket she could bring into her chest, her chin resting on the thick folds as she listens to her father, not understanding the meaning, but not needing to, because the song's beautiful.

Its beauty rips through my heart.

I press my lips together and cross my arms, unable to sit, unable to stand, afraid to touch Stella, like she could be a conduit to the explosion Rex has all but promised.

Supernova doom.

"*That* should've been your title," I mutter to no one.

For if he feels an ounce of the attraction I feel, we are doomed.

It doesn't seem so bad that he's mad at me now that I may have betrayed him by taking Stella to see something forbidden. He's *singing* about forbidden fruit, the seduction of doing bad things. Maybe he won't be so angry after all.

Ha. *Ha!*

He will probably eat my heart for dinner. After he dines on the breasts that cage it.

My core flutters, threatening more intense, erotic pulses down my center.

I can't have this. Not now.

I focus on Stella instead.

At last—or maybe, to my sorrow—Rex finishes. For mere seconds, the stadium is silent. Seduced. The band behind Rex remains a darkened, shadowy blur, the instruments resembling more menacing, mechanical beasts than music-makers.

Then, Hell comes alive, and the audience goes nuts, screaming, jumping, hailing to their king.

Rex, hoarser now, says, "Glad you enjoyed it."

The stadium booms. Stella claps, the most emotional I've ever seen her.

He turns his head back to the band. "Let's get back into this and give them the epic show we promised."

The lights of the stage blink on. The band comes alive, the instruments shine, and Rex is but one of many highlighted on stage, an essential cog to all the parts that make up Nocturne Court's machine.

Except, it doesn't matter how many other people are high-lighted, or the way the members of his band take over and play. The stadium could have spotlights on everyone but Rex. He could be at the center of a dark cone in the stage, the one person with the broken spotlight, and it wouldn't matter.

Because all I can see ...

Is my sexual fantasy coming to life.

CHAPTER 23

Rex

"THE HELL WAS THAT?"

Easton tosses his drumsticks onto the couch in the dressing room, then rounds on me.

I rest my guitar against the wall before I say anything. We're sweat-soaked, beaten down by the demands of our fans, yet we're breathing like bulls, the adrenaline taking its time leaking from our systems.

Wyn and Mason walk in, their expressions similar to East's. Flushed. Confused.

Well, Mase is more wary, since he knew what I was up to and stayed silent. We know a lot of each other's secrets, he and I.

"It was a song," I say, as nonchalantly as I can while my heart hammers against my ribs.

"Were you going to clue us in?" Easton asks. He makes a face, clutching at his right ear, then emits a frustrated growl.

I tip my chin. "That giving you problems?"

"Not as much as you at the moment," Easton snaps. "I thought we were a team here. I thought we share things."

I scoff.

"Fine, I thought the deal was, we share things *now*," East amends. "Remember when you kicked me out of the band for things you weren't clear on? I'm thinking about tossing your ass out for the same damned reasons."

"You can't toss me out. I'm the lead fucking singer." I rest my hands on my belt buckle, my shirt long discarded into the mob amassed at the front of the stage. The sea of their hands, reaching up like tentacles, mouths open in gaping, rabid maws.

Chest heaving, I face my band members in the quiet of our dressing room. So different from the raging storm of the stadium.

I peel out my protective ear pieces. "It hit me last night, that song. I wanted to test it out before taking it to a recording studio." I offer an arrogant smile I don't feel. "Admit it. You liked it."

Easton sneers. "I fucking liked it. We all did. It's stuff we haven't heard from you since—in a long while," he corrects.

"You can say it." I don't know what's happening, whether it's the mighty claw of our thousands of fans that makes me want to push the boundaries, or if I'm just pissed off. "Her name. Aesha."

Wyn licks his lips. Mason scratches at his cheek and says, "We don't have to get into this."

"Why not?" I throw my hands up. "She's what cock-blocked me. I was a powerhouse before her, penning lyrics in my sleep. Then, after it all, after she chewed me up and spat out ... whatever you call this." I slam my palms against my pecs. "Whatever I am now, I couldn't put a crayon to a coloring book. At least this is something. At least I've been"—*inspired by Harper*—"able to write a fucking song again."

"Aesha left you something good in your life," Mase says. "Stella."

"Yes," I agree, but it comes out as an argumentative roar. "One hundred fucking percent *yes*. And maybe, with 'Forbidden Cherry,' I'm getting the last of Aesha's venom out of my system."

"Damned straight," Easton says, but his expression remains twisted with anger. "Stop keeping your process from us, Rex. We're here to help you. You may have made this band, been in charge of it since we were kids and sucked up all the responsibility so we didn't have to, but you don't have to constantly brood alone."

"Maybe I like it," I snap back.

"Hang on," Wyn says. "Are we all in agreement? Rex's song is epic, we're always gonna be there for him, and we have a new track to lay beats on in the studio. Why are we still arguing?"

"The atmosphere, man," Mason says, referring to the shouts and calls we can no longer hear. "It's still with us."

He searches the room for a blunt.

"You're impossible," East says to me, but moves out of the way as Mason passes. "Fucking ridiculously impossible."

I smile with my teeth. "It's why you love me best."

"Whatever you got going for you now," Wyn says, offering a light when Mase at last finds his blunt. "It's working. I won't hate on it. But East is right. Include us in this shit, okay?"

"Yeah." I scrub my face with one hand. "Yeah, okay."

Somehow, Mase has made it to my side in the blink of an eye. He clasps my shoulder. "Now go home to that lovely daughter of yours and appreciate the life you lead."

I glare at him sideways.

"And bonus," he says, lit blunt dangling from between his teeth. "You got that hot nanny living with you these days. Maybe sleeping with her will get rid of some of that stick you got up your—"

I flick the blunt out of his mouth.

"Hey!"

When I push open the front door of my penthouse, everything is dark.

No lights are left on, not even the dimmer switch in the kitchen, but this shouldn't come as a surprise. Harper has been with Stella for over two weeks on their own, with no one coming home late at night, searching for a guiding light to bed.

It was one of our shorter tours, but I felt it harder. Longer. The older Stella gets, the more I think I'm leaving behind, and it's with increased difficulty that I shut and lock the front door when I leave, Stella's quiet, lonesome face hidden behind the wood.

But I'm here now. When Stella wakes up, I'll be there to greet her. That's what counts.

I drop my duffel near the door, my assistant promising to bring the rest of my things off the tour bus in the morning, and kick off my shoes, running my hands through my hair on a sigh.

Fuck, I'm tired.

Adrenaline no longer buzzes in my veins. Instead, extreme fatigue takes over my limbs, demanding my brain fall unconscious to begin healing—of entering back into real life and not continue the rush of the frenzied fame of fandom.

I'm rounding the stairs, a hand on the glass paneled banister, when I see her.

I pause with half a foot on the first step.

Harper's curled up on the couch, her head drooped to the side, hair swishing across her forehead in a blindfold of black. The wall of windows framing the lightbulb grid of the city outside highlights her cheekbones, the white line of her neck, and I find my eyes grazing over all her exposed points. Her collarbone between the deep V of her t-shirt. Her short, manicured hands. The tops of her ankles, the soles of her feet. Flawless, pale skin curled against black leather, her chest rising and falling with the slow meditation of slumber.

Witnessing her vulnerable beauty should make me soft. It should compel me to wander over and stroke my fingers down, starting at her cheek and cascading over her breasts. I should wake her gently, coax her to bed.

I wrote a song about her.

Yet, all I feel is anger.

It's a fuse I can't control, a reminder that I'm not a patient man and never will be.

I push off the stairs and stalk into the living room, taking a seat next to her, spreading my legs, propping my elbows on my knees, and resting my chin against my folded hands.

"Harper."

My voice is soft, but deadly. Harper snorts at the sound and shifts.

"Harper," I repeat. "Wake up."

My tone remains buttered and sweet for my prey, but it builds. It threatens.

Harper mumbles, cracks the dark crescents of her eyes open. Upon seeing me, she jerks to a sitting position.

"Rex—Mr. Sloane." She wipes her mouth with the back of her hand. "I—I didn't know you were—when did you get here?"

I angle my head. "Just now."

She rubs her hands against her thighs, a clear sign of nervousness. "I must've fallen asleep. I tried waiting up for you, figuring you might want an update on Stella, how she liked your concert."

I lean back against the sofa chair, crossing one leg at the ankle. "Do tell."

Her tongue flicks out against her bottom lip. She's unsure at the friendly tone of my voice, but she isn't uncomfortable. Yet.

"Well, she loved it," Harper says. "I'm so glad you let her see you live. I've never seen her *more* alive, watching her dad, trying to sing along with him. It was wonderful."

A small piece of my heart chips away. Melts into my center.

"I ... I took pictures," Harper continues. "If you'd like to see them, I—"

"Send them to my cell."

"Sure. No problem. Uh, do you want some coffee?" Harper blinks, still waking up.

"No."

She swallows. "Okay." Harper lets out an uncomfortable laugh. "Mr. Sloane, is there something wrong? You seem … off."

"It's been a long tour," I say with a grin in the shadows. "And I'm happy to be home. Glad my daughter had such a good time with you and that you kept her safe and happy."

"That's great," Harper says. "I think she's warming up to me."

"Wonderful to hear," I say, with extra enthusiasm. Harper flinches like I've flung a whip at her.

Time for the final blow.

"Now, tell me why the fuck my daughter was photographed leaving fucking Swan Lake."

CHAPTER 24

Harper

I WANT to chew my lower lip off.

Instead, I release said lip from the grip of my teeth and say, as affably as possible, "It was the theater show. I asked your permission before we went."

"Theater show."

Rex repeats the words with predatory precision as he sits in the gloom. Electric city lights outline the frame of his head in a bright blue-white halo.

But he isn't an angel. He isn't even good. Rex is hardened and bitter and knows exactly what I've done.

I choose a different tactic. "It was all planned with a few other trusted nannies. I have no idea how the photographer knew we were there."

"We'll get to that," Rex snaps. "But first, I want to know why you think I'm a fucking moron."

Rex peels off the chair, rising, standing over me. I resist the urge to cower.

"I don't think that," I say, with very little tremor.

"Oh, no? Then why did you so eloquently and sneakily plan a day trip that includes a ballet, which you *know* is forbidden, and couch it as theater?"

"It *is* theater—"

"*Do not* be obtuse with me, Harper."

He spits out my name like it was a meal containing bone shards. My insides shrink, but my shoulders remain set.

Screw sitting beneath him. *Fuck* being seen as a lower being by him. I stand.

"Stella loved it," I say through my teeth. "And because she's deprived of everything ballet at home, because she isn't allowed to even learn to dance, I thought taking to her a show where she sits outside the boundaries, where she doesn't *dare* step on stage, would be a gift to her. She was a witness, Rex, that's all. A simple audience member among some of her peers and she had a great goddamned time."

"You're fired."

"I expected as much," I spit, though it was the last thing I expected.

Spinning around, I search the confines of the couch for my purse, or wherever I've tossed it, but I'm fueled by too much energy. I'm flinging throw pillows and picturing them as his head.

It was worth it.

I spin around and say, "At least tell me why. Tell me why that little girl can't see a show that made her smile for the first time in the span I've known her. Explain to me why you hate that so much."

Even in the gloom, I see his eyes narrow. "You think I'm trying to prevent my daughter from being happy?"

I put my hands on my hips. "That's exactly what I'm coming to learn."

He bares his teeth. "You are so off the mark, so out of line—"

"*Why*, Rex? What is it about her mother and ballet that repulses you?"

Now I'm out of the solar system of decorum. But what's he going to do? Fire me? He's been banking on that since the moment I signed an NDA for him.

Rex hisses in a breath and I brace myself for whatever will come next. Whatever I've unleashed.

"How dare you." Rex whispers it, but it's the low tone of a demon pacing along a shadowy edge, waiting for its moment to strike. "You come here thinking you know what's best for my daughter when you have no fucking *clue* what we've been through. You have no right to assume that what I've chosen for Stella is worse for her. I went through years—" Another teeth bare, his elongated canines flashing through the dark. But he stops himself from confessing further. "It is what's best for her. No one knows that better than her father. You're nothing but a passing influence that she'll forget within the next week. Get out."

The barb hurts, as intended, but I stand my ground. "It was a *show*, Rex. A pretend reality with beautiful dancers and the heart of a story that Stella absorbed like wildfire. You can't contain that for much longer. Once she's older and deciding for herself, she will search out what's forbidden to her. We all do."

"I will address that when the time comes," he says, then points to the door. "You're done here, Harper."

A need to rebel seizes me with unexpected force. "Am I?"

His eyes, nothing but black and white discs, glint as he shifts. I've caught him off-guard. "My word is final."

I lick my lips, thankful he can't see the slightest hitch in nerves. "Why did you write a song about me, then?"

His slightest inhale, the quietest intake of breath, tells me I've hit the mark. "You ask way too many questions for someone in your position."

"I have no position left." I shrug, though it feels heavy and forced. "And I'll never see you again after this. Might as well get all my curiosity out."

After a pause where I don't know whether he'll explode with fury or go cold with rage, he says, "How do you know it's about you?"

I lift my chin. "Because of what happened the last time I saw you. Because you tasted it on my lips. That off-brand cherry chapstick I buy at my local drugstore has somehow impacted a world famous rockstar. I want to know why that is."

His laughter rumbles through the wide space, and I'm reminded of a storybook villain who's conquered the good guy. It vibrates through my veins, providing extra, erratic beats to my heart. "You're a bold girl, to ask a singer about his muse."

"Fine." I spot my purse on the floor, half hidden under the couch. "I don't need you to tell me what I've already concluded. Have a nice life, Rex—"

He hooks me by the elbow as I'm bending down, swinging me toward him. "That's Mr. Sloane to you."

I lift my head so we're almost nose-to-nose. Or as close as I can be, considering his height. "No. Calling you that is a sign of respect and professionalism, of which I have none left. You can take your morals and your high ground, your assumption that everything you decide is the correct and only way, and you can shove that *fucking* Dossier up your—"

Rex dips his head. This close, his smile is that of a lion facing its wounded prey. "Shove it where, Harper?"

I won't be felled by the smell of him, the sex of him, a magnetic frequency that buzzes louder the closer I'm pulled by his lure. *I won't.*

I say, through stiffened lips, "Up your ass. Down your throat. Stabbed through your urethra, for all I care. You're a mean bastard. You're a single-minded jerk." I breathe in a gasping exhale. "*God*, that felt good to say."

His eyes search mine. Rex doesn't step back with insult, like I hoped. Nor does he react with anger, like I expected.

Rex murmurs, "You're right, Harper, 'Forbidden Cherry' is about you."

That I've won should fuel my fire to get the hell out of here and never come back. But my feet have become anchors, lodged at the bottom of Rex's saltwater stare. In the dark of night, when there's no sunlight to guide me to the surface.

"But I've fired you," he continues.

All I can do is give a single, jerky nod. I don't trust my voice.

"Which means," he says, "now I can kiss you."

Breath escapes through the hard clench of my teeth. "You don't like me. Why would you ever want to kiss me?"

He angles his head. "I don't have to like a person to want to fuck them senseless."

I let out a sound of disgust. His hand is still on my arm and I fling it away. "See? You're an asshole with no concept of humility—"

He steps further into my comfort zone. "That song is nothing but desire for you," he says. "Since the second you stepped through these doors, you've been annoyingly on my mind, yet I couldn't touch you. You were my employee. The nanny to my daughter. So I wrote about you instead. What I wanted to do to you, given the chance. How I'd explore your body, given the opportunity. Say the word, and I will."

I'm shocked to find I still want him to. I crave his touch. He's saying everything I've wanted him to say since we met for the first time and I experienced the full force of him.

"I can't stand you," I lie.

"That makes two of us."

"You've fired me so you can fuck me. My best friend's a lawyer. Do you understand the consequences of that?"

"I terminated you because you broke our contractual agreement," he replies easily, then steps aside. "And you are free to leave."

I whisper instead, "You could be in so much trouble."

It's worth it.

"You *are* nothing but trouble," he retorts.

Neither of us move. We're in a forced stalemate, and it's up to me to decide on whether to leave or to stay. Yet I can't. He's my fantasy, and Rex is here, explaining in no uncertain terms that he'll give me what I want, no strings. I can have my night with him, get my last paycheck, and leave this sad, lonely home for good.

With a sad, lonely girl inside, and her bitter, isolated father.

Too familiar. It's all *too recognizable.*

Rex steps closer, lays two fingers under my chin, and tips my head up. His face blocks out my horizon until all I see is the moon-lighted curves of his cheekbones, the shadowy crevices, demonic intentions with human features, ethereal and promising.

Oh, boy. I'm in so much trouble.

"Just say the word," Rex murmurs.

Rex speaks, and stands, stoic. Unhurried. Like he has all the time in the world to wait for my reply. His fingers hover near the tender underside of my chin, electric currents riding between the small space he's left between us.

My lips part.

"Kiss me," I breathe.

And the devil takes me for his own.

CHAPTER 25

Rex

I DEVOUR HARPER the way I wish I could tear out my heart. And not feel. Not think. Just touch.

I'll channel my fury into her body, allowing us both the climax and release I'm falling desperately short of.

My hands skate under her shirt and span her waist as she moans into my mouth, as I press her up against the floor-to-ceiling window as the neon city looks on.

Harper's arms fling to the side at the impact of her body against the glass, but she lets out an appreciative, unexpected purr as I hike her legs up and lock them around my hips.

We don't talk, but grind. Denim to denim, hardness to softness, my scruff marking the pale purity of her cheeks, and her lips massaging mine, my tongue stroking over hers, and *damn* that mouth of hers knows what to do.

It's like she crawls inside me, the way she clings, the way Harper groans and writhes. She pulls at my shirt, up, off, and flings it to the side. She scrapes at my scalp and pulls out my hair tie. Now she's after my belt buckle, and I drop her legs to stop her.

We're both huffing, breathing unsteady, but our stares are grounded. She's flushed from my kisses—Hell, I should call it what it is, an outright ravishing—her eyes bright with want.

"You're sure," I grind out, "this is what you want."

"Yes, goddamnit, *yes*, Rex," Harper says. She clasps my neck and pulls me closer, my head down. "Don't stop and second-guess now."

The bright stars in her eyes are blinding. At this moment, she doesn't resemble Harper, Stella's nanny. She appears more like a fan, struck dumb because a half-naked, fully hard Rex Sloane stands in front of her, ready to fuck her against skyscrapers and city lights.

I blink, unsettled by the vision. Harper isn't anywhere close to a Courtesan. She isn't even my employee anymore. She's a person, yes. A woman wet for me. A girl who ran from her future and hides within the childhood of others, information which shouldn't matter to me.

Fucking isn't about personality, tragedy or truth. It's about sex, plain and simple.

And still, something holds me back.

On a frustrated mewl, Harper presses her lips against mine again, and the sweet cherry of her sends my mind back to an animalistic blankness where all I'm meant to do is come inside her.

I growl into her lips, teeth nipping, as I pull at her jeans' buttons and yank her pants down. She wears lace, delicate seams I rip into after a mere flick.

Harper's exposed, bare, her breathy notes hot against the side of my neck as my fingers explore, find, and stroke.

Damn, she's wet. And bare.

I hope the freeze of the window against her ass adds to the fire-and-ice effect that's consuming my chest, without the help of outside elements. She's slick, pliable, her legs buckling until I throw one up against my hip to balance her ... or, if I'm to be truthful, to give myself better access and spread her wide.

I use my free hand to grip her short hair and pull her head

back, still searching for that brightness in her eyes, to see if it's still there, though I can't claim it. I can't even name what it is.

And though she's half-lidded with desire, panting as I stroke and circle the folds of her, Harper meets my stare, swollen lips parted, asking—

"Don't stop," she pants. "God, don't stop."

My upper lip curls. I clamp one side of my lower lip with my teeth, biting hard, drawing blood, then release it only to paint my mouth on hers.

I swallow her gasp with ease, absorb her circular movements with fluid expertise. All it will take is one more rub, one more circle of her swollen nub, to experience the full sweetness of her, if only just the physical.

Thrusting her harder against the window, I do just that. Her cries are muffled by my lips, but I hear them all the same. She bucks once, twice, one hand gripping my wrist so tightly she'll leave marks, pushing my fingers in further until she all but folds into herself after the climax.

I tip my head up as hers falls against my chest and she catches her breath. I watch as the sky blinks with red and white lights through the clouds, planes entering and leaving the airspace. And I'm thinking ... that I just made a big fucking mistake.

Harper's fumbling hands at my belt draw my attention down.

"Here. I..."

I grip her wrist. "Stop. It's okay."

She glances up, brightness dimmed. "But don't you want...?"

I do, Forbidden Cherry. Do I ever.

Cock straining, I give us space. Her hands drop to her sides, frozen with confusion for mere seconds before she steps into and pulls up her pants. Her ripped panties are useless and tangled on the floor.

"I shouldn't've..." I clear my throat. Cough. "I shouldn't have taken advantage of you like that."

Her brows form confused arcs. "Taken advantage? I'm a willing participant here, Rex."

"Maybe so, but I'm tired of my temper clouding my judgment. Of making rash decisions. And this—what's just gone on between you and me—can't happen again."

After fastening the last button on her pants, Harper throws her hands on her hips. "Why not? I'm no longer in your employ. I'm just a girl in your apartment ready to screw your brains out, and you're saying no? After ... after doing everything to make me say yes?"

Her last sentence hits hard. I'm no tease. But I am an asshole. "That's just it. I made a rash decision."

"Rex, what are you *talking* about?"

I release pent up breath, angry that I can't say things the way I want or get them across the way I mean. "There's something more important than me or you. Than us."

Harper goes quiet, and I know the instant she comes to the same conclusion I have.

"Stella," she says.

I give a single, hard nod. "Even though it doesn't seem like it, we're screwing her over by doing this."

"But..." Harper licks her swollen lips, and my dick twitches at the sight. "I'm fired. It doesn't matter what happens now."

This. This is what I have so much trouble handling. So, I spit it out. "It's why I can't fire you, Harper."

"Excuse me?"

"You went against my wishes. You continue to defy my rules, yet one thing continues to hold true. My daughter likes you."

With deliberate emphasis, Harper shakes her head. "Rex," she whispers. "What the hell?"

"I know." I claw my hands through my hair and pace away. "This is fucked up. But I can't in good conscience terminate you, fuck you, and then believe my daughter will be okay with it the next day. Not that she needs to ever know the last part."

"Obviously," Harper drawls. "So, let me see if I get this straight. You went into a rage that I took Stella to a ballet, *then* you turned that anger into sex, then, after fingering me, you've somehow found a moral compass and have now decided to re-hire me, no hard feelings? Do I have that right?"

I bare my teeth, failing, as usual, at explanations. "Yes."

Harper throws her hands up, laughing. "What in God's name makes you think I—"

"I understand if you say no," I say. "I've crossed the line. All I can say is that I hope to see you tomorrow morning at breakfast as Stella's nanny. And if not, I'll understand."

"That's it?" Harper pauses in an attempt to control her voice. "That's all you can give me?"

I offer something else. "I'm sorry."

Turning, I don't wait for her response. I know I'm leaving her in the middle of the room, more empty and hollow than she was upon entering it, but there's not much left to say, other than the truth, and I can't give her that.

How do I tell her about recognizing the light in her eyes?

Harper has more love inside her than I ever will and depriving Stella of that would make me more beastly and callous than I already am.

Harper will come to understand this. I know she will.

And, as I glance over my shoulder when taking the stairs and see her, lit from behind, standing in the shadows, I'm certain it will be at my expense.

CHAPTER 26

Harper

THERE. I think I have everything packed.

Nope—never mind.

I throw on the crumpled navy plaid shirt I find stuffed under my bed's pillow over my jeans and tank that I haven't changed since Rex's concert.

Now everything's packed.

Glancing around the small but luxurious room I've stayed in for the past three weeks, I'll miss that bed. It gave me some good, sleep-filled nights with its memory foam. Now, instead of cushy foam clouding my head until I fall asleep, I'll be plagued with the very real memory of Rex slamming me against the window, his large hands searching for my naked skin, then finding, and bringing me to a kind of climax I've never experienced from a man's fingers before.

But I mean, he plays guitar with those dexterous hands, coaxing strings to play the same way my body played to him.

Ugh.

Scraping my hands against my face, I wish for more bed than memories.

He manipulated me. I fell right into his ego-driven hands.

My lips form thin, tight lines as I give one last scan of the room.

I'm not about to stay within his grip.

"Harper?"

Stella's voice jolts me out of my stone-cold decision. I turn to find her standing in my doorway in her nightgown, clutching her ratty pink blanket. Her curlicue hair is a bird's nest, and she uses one fist to rub her eye.

"What was all the noise for?" she asks.

"Noise?" I repeat, then look around as if searching for the source. *Please don't say you heard us a few hours ago.* "Uh ... what noise?"

"Lots of banging."

The statement lights a fire in my cheeks, but she can't mean that. "Banging?" I ask.

"Yeah." Stella points to my unmade bed, where my duffel lies open and stuffed full of the haphazard items of my life. "It sounds like you were throwing things. That's not allowed, you know. You're not supposed to have a tantrum."

A balloon of relief deflates in my chest. "You know what? You're right. I shouldn't have made so much noise and woken you up. I'm sorry."

"Why were you being so loud?" she asks.

Because your father played me like a fool, and I foolishly let him, and would have continued to let him.

"I was ... looking for stuff," I reply lamely. I might've been a bit too aggressive when finding my things and stuffing them into my bag, muttering curses and hexes against Rex ... and mostly against myself. Especially when I packed up my bathroom in one fell swoop of the counter, glass and plastic clanging against ceramic.

"Are you leaving?"

The tone of Stella's question catches me off-guard. It's tremulous and filled with dread. Stella's eyes widen and her lower lip trembles as she clutches her baby blanket tighter. I open my mouth to tell her *yes*, but I'm stopped by the sweet devastation written across her face.

I didn't think Stella liked me, yet she's upset I might leave for good?

Then again, this job is never about becoming best friends with the children. It shouldn't matter if she likes me or not. Being her nanny is all about protecting her and doing what's best for her.

I cringe. *I'm even starting to sound like him.*

"Don't go," she blurts before I can respond. "I don't want you to."

The idea that Stella cares for me, even a tiny iota, and doesn't want me to leave, warms my heart. And the realization that Stella knows when women are about to leave her breaks it.

"I..." I'm at a loss for words.

It should be easy to be blunt with Stella, tell her this didn't work out, especially if I put her father at the forefront of my mind. But I can't, because Rex *isn't* the priority on my mind. Stella is.

Just like Rex made a point of saying in the early morning hours, before the sun rose.

"Stella, I..." I tuck my hands in the front pockets of my pants. "I'm not sure if this is..."

"Is it because I haven't been good?" she asks.

A specific, roiling lurch uncoils in my belly. I step closer and bend down to her level.

"Stella, I would never want you to think that. You've done nothing wrong."

"Then why?"

She keeps asking, and I can't answer. *Because I'm a coward,* I think.

Then, under the watchful, too-wise stare of a girl who's been left without explanation too many times, I break.

"I'm only packing up my dirty laundry," I say, shoulders sloped. "And also, your dad's here. He came in last night."

"You are? He is?" Stella releases the blanket from under her chin. Her head tips up, but her eyes remain wise to my excuse.

I smile and say, "Yeah," while tucking a lock of hair behind her ear. She doesn't flinch from the contact. "Should we go see him? I think he's waiting in the breakfast nook in the kitchen."

She must forgive my hesitation, because Stella does a quick two-step dance in place before spinning around and running through the hallway, calling, "Daddy!"

I hope he's there. I do a quick swipe under my eyes with my fingers to catch any dried, old clumps of mascara since I haven't been to bed yet, and, if Stella's awake, it must be close to six in the morning. I wonder if Rex got any sleep, or if he's snoring now, unaware that I'm about to do exactly what he wants.

No, I correct myself. *I'm doing it for Stella.*

Our torrid night aside, my instant climax at his fingers forgotten, I'll continue to do my job, because I'm a professional, because I'm strong, and because I can't seem to walk away from this family or their secrets.

Or the man behind them.

"Stella!" I call, moving fast through the hallway. "Slow down! Don't trip!"

"I won't!" her echoing voice calls back. Then: "*Daddy!*"

"Hey, sweets."

I don't have to witness the hug to know it's happening, Rex wrapping his strong arms around Stella and lifting her from the ground, spinning her in place. I step into the kitchen just as he lays a kiss on her cheek, his iced-over eyes soft, his lips curved, as he sets his daughter down.

"I had June make us pancakes," he says as Stella clutches his hand and he leads them to the breakfast table.

"Chocolate chip special?" Stella asks.

"You bet. Come, sit by me." As Rex slides onto a cushioned bench, he pats the spot next to him.

As he moves, his stare flicks up over Stella's head and connects to mine for an instant. It's in the time of a split second that magnets fuse, cars crash, stars implode, lips touch, farewells occur. Accidents happen and fate intervenes.

I'm not sure where on the spectrum Rex and my's shared glance falls, but it feels like two stars crashing together before the implosion.

It throws me off balance. The right decision isn't to stay here with these two. The prudent thing would be to leave and start over somewhere else. Continue living my life within the confines of my control. To tell the universe to back the fuck off.

Except, I can't. I remain rooted to the spot as Rex dishes out stacks of pancakes and emits a low laugh at something Stella says. I remember the way those very hands explored me.

Here is Rex in his element, warmed by his daughter before facing the coolness of his day. The aloof lead singer whose private life is more protected than a billionaire's underground vault. Cold, unattainable, and still my boss.

And there is Stella, opening up like a rose in bloom, enjoying this time and her father, smiling more than she's frowning. With the concert last night coupled with pancakes with her dad the next morning, she's blossoming. The both of them are healing, even if they don't know it.

"Harper? Pancakes?"

I blink and notice Rex is staring at me. But it's bland and with none of the blue fire I experienced last night. He holds up a plate.

"Yeah, sure," I say, tucking a strand of hair behind my ear as I sit opposite the two of them and assist Stella in digging in.

"Thank you," he says.

At first, I'm not sure I heard it. I glance at him, but Rex remains composed and attentive toward his daughter, busying himself hiding blueberries on Stella's plate when she's not looking.

But those words came from him. They were soft and gentle.

I don't let on that his gratitude affects me. Instead, I focus on dousing maple syrup over all my pancakes, but the bottom tip of my heart flutters with warmth, like a firefly before sputtering out.

CHAPTER 27

Rex

"You're pissier than usual today."

I cut a look to Wyn. "According to you fuckers, I'm pissy all day, every day. This shouldn't be any different."

"*Ooh*, he's extra sassy today, too," Mason pipes in.

I resist storming out, knowing my mood has nothing to do with the guys and everything to do with my home situation and the fact I didn't want Harper to leave, despite it being the best option for both of us.

I settle for a growl. "Everyone shut up and get back to cutting 'Forbidden Cherry.'"

The studio is small for four tall men, plus production assistants, producers and composers, but we're making it work. As soon as we got off the tour, we were back in the studio putting the finishing touches on our next album.

"First off," Mase says, squinting at his iPad and tap, tap, tapping away. "There's no real verse melody, B section and hook, which we need to fix if we want the fans singing it back to us. And replaying it repeatedly on their streaming apps."

I nod. "I wrote it with all feeling and no thought, so I'm fine with any changes to make it marketable."

Wyn cocks a brow. "Seriously?" He glances at the rest of the band. "This isn't the Rex I know. I'm getting scared."

"Doesn't matter, 'cause this is exactly the Rex I want." Mase smacks a palm on his iPad. "Let's get to work."

We do. Mason grabs my guitar and plays a few chords to help bring the song to sellable standards. Easton helps by scribbling on the iPad with a stylus pen. I don't consider their chopping up and choosing my words to be selling out—not anymore. Not since the paychecks started coming in did I realize that aiming for the title of special snowflake doesn't always make a career.

The theme will remain the same. The lyrics I'll sing out will ring true. The girl I shouldn't have. Not *can't*, as last night proved, but should stand back from.

If my head wins over my cock, which is always debatable.

"Uh, Rex? Mr. Sloane?"

Bobby, my PA, pokes his head in. I stare him down at the interruption.

"There's someone here to see you," he says.

"Who?" I bite out the word.

"She says she used to work for you?" Bobby glances down at his phone. "Patrice?"

What could she want? I set aside my notebook and rise from the small leather couch.

"Take five," I say to the guys as I exit the studio. I ignore their curious stares.

I follow Bobby into the reception out front, where Patrice stands, staring out the large windows onto the busy street. She's not in her usual sundress, since the weather is changing and dipping into the cool autumn winds and pumpkin spice lattes of New York City's fall season. Her jeans are tight on her hips and taper down her long legs, topped with an oversized plaid shirt unbuttoned to a wide V.

Patrice has always been pretty and well put-together. Paparazzi and managers alike (read: Spinner) have often wondered why I've never given her a chance, especially after she left the nanny position, and I've always had trouble explaining that perfection is not something I'm able to pursue in a partner. It's in every other facet of my life, but I've never wanted it in a woman.

"Patrice."

She turns at the sound of my voice and smiles, holding two to-go cups of coffee. "Hey, Rex."

I step up to her, accepting the second cup, the scent of her vanilla-caramel latte wafting into my nostrils. Smells delicious. Tastes worse. "You brought me coffee?"

"Just how you like it," she says. "Black and bitter."

I search for the double meaning, but don't find it within her careful, placid mask.

"To what do I owe the spontaneous visit?" I ask. "I'd think your new teaching job would keep you busy."

Patrice shifts her balance. She never does this—shuffles her feet or appears at all uncomfortable.

"Well—I wanted to ask you something," she says, eyes averted.

"What's up, Pats?" I make a show of checking my watch, but do take a sip of coffee. She knows I can't resist street cart caffeine.

"I want my job back."

Patrice blurts out the sentence like it was too hot for her tongue to hold on to much longer.

I blink.

"You what?" I ask.

"My job." She sips at her drink, glancing away, then back. "I made a mistake. I'd like to come back, Rex."

"That's..." I run my tongue along my top teeth. Her timing is impeccable. Or impeccably wrong. What happened between Harper and me is on a constant highlight reel in my head and I expected her to disappear this morning, never to come back. At that point, I would've needed Patrice and accepted her offer with no hesitation. Yet, Harper showed up in the kitchen. She sat down and ate breakfast like she would stay.

You want Harper. It's not good for Harper's job, for Stella, for me, *to keep her around.*

Harper rebels against your rules...

And you want to expose her ass and spank her for it.

"I'm sorry, Pats," I say. "But Harper's settled in and Stella's starting to get attached."

"But—" Patrice screws up her expression. "Everything I've read, all the blogs—Harper's doing everything you *hate.* Like taking Stella to the ballet. I thought that was forbidden—"

"You're right." I can't fault Patrice for her reasoning, but I also can't stand being made out to be a fool. "And I was prepared to fire her over it. But my daughter..." I expose my teeth in a flash of frustration. "She's opening up more. Smiling. Talking about things other than death and the black plague. It pains me to admit ... maybe exposing Stella to dance wasn't a bad thing."

Patrice's eyes bug out of her head. "Are you saying I wasn't able to do that? Are you *seriously* saying Harper knows what's best for that child? Do you even know her past? What she hides? Because I do, and I can tell you, she has no idea what a family's supposed to be, never mind how to handle Stella's psychological development. Harper's bad for her, Rex—"

"Then why'd you fight for her?" I ask it softly, since I'm curious. "Why did you go to bat for Harper as your replacement if you believe she's such a failure?"

Patrice throws her hands to the side, the lid almost popping off the lid of her coffee. "Isn't it obvious, Rex? Stop being so goddamned *dense!*"

I don't move from my position. Don't twitch. Don't blink. "Excuse me?"

"Because no one can replace me." Patrice seethes. "And while I know it was my idea to leave, to move on to other things, I just don't—I can't—I can't lose you. Or Stella."

I shake my head. "Pats…"

"No," she blurts. "You want the truth? I didn't want to be a nanny to you because I wanted to be *more*. I thought if I quit, if someone less qualified than me took over, you'd want me back. You'd need me. Or … with my absence, you'd … *miss* me. And maybe take me on as more than a nanny."

I angle my head while I parse through her words.

"At what point," I ask, "did you think hiring someone who you thought could be unsafe for my daughter would make me want you back?"

"Don't." She uses the sleeve of her shirt to wipe at her eyes. "Don't twist my meaning. Harper's not unsafe. I'm not that much of an idiot."

I let out a breath. "Patrice … there was never anything between us."

"Yes, there was." Patrice lifts her chin, her expression determined. "Don't you remember? That one time late at night, when I stepped out of the shower, and you…"

"No." I hold up my hand. "That was a mistake."

"You looked at me," she whispers fiercely. "You *really* looked at me."

"That's—" I curse the male response to the naked female body. "You know you're beautiful. Flawless, even. But *I* know you set that moment up. I'd come home late that night from rehearsal and you were showering in my room, Pats. I cracked the door open to see what the hell was letting out so much steam and *who* the hell had the gall to shower in my quarters—"

"The water heater was out downstairs. I had to be up there."

I level her with a look. "I've never considered you to be an idiot. Don't consider me to be one."

"You let me touch you," she says.

I shake off the image, but it sticks. The moment a few months ago when I was so dog-tired, I stripped off my clothes as I headed upstairs, clad in a bare ass by the time I made it to my bedroom and noticed the heat. Steam, rising under my bathroom door and the humming voice coming out of it.

I knew who it was. Who it could only be. Yet, I still padded over, pushed the door open further, and discovered the silhouette of Patrice, arms raised as she slicked her hair back in the shower, breasts pert, pussy shaved…

Fuck. How could I not notice?

But I snapped out of it the moment her eyes met mine and I read the intention behind them. When she stepped out, wet and dewy, and laid a hand against my chest, dragging it down my torso.

I caught her by the wrist before she could squeeze my—yes, hard—dick.

She was my kid's nanny, and it'd be easy to glide her to my bed, screw her senseless, then keep up pretenses the next day. But I didn't, because of principles. And, because I knew the instant I slept with Patrice, she would want more.

And Harper? What about her?

Now, I let out a quiet growl. "Nothing happened, Pats. And nothing ever will."

Patrice shakes her head. "You are the most frustrating man alive."

"And you want to teach. Make more of yourself. I know that to be true," I say. "Don't come here asking for a job you don't want simply because—"

"*Simply*? This isn't simple, Rex. This is the most complicated decision I've ever made. I'm unhappy. I'm happy with you and Stella. I want to come back."

"You can't."

"You're a bastard."

"I know."

"You—" Patrice lets out a frustrated breath and turns away. "I can't believe I've reduced myself to this. This isn't me. Do you see what you've done? You've made me *do* things I normally wouldn't.

Cause problems I usually mend. You're messing with my head, Rex! My mind, my heart … I know you feel the same way about me. I know you do."

I seize on a certain sentence. "What things have you done, Patrice?"

She waves me off. I'm almost intrigued at witnessing the real Patrice, the one hidden under all the groundwork and guise of the woman she thought I'd want. But I'm more concerned.

"I'm sure you and Harper will figure it out," she mumbles.

I resist the urge to grab her arm and shake sense back into her. "Patrice, tell me what you've done or so help me—"

"Rex!" Mason barks behind me.

On instinct, I turn, and Patrice takes that moment to sprint out of the studio, bell dangling above her as she opens the door to outside and disappears.

"You're eating up valuable studio time and we have a shitload more to do," Mason says. "Unless you want the time to put more of your lady problems into a song, we need you in here with us."

I rub at the line that's becoming permanent between my brows. "I'll be right there."

Mason nods and turns back into the hallway.

Staring out the windows, I see no further sign of Patrice. The memory of her flushed, angry expression, her trembling fingers, remains triggered in my mind, and what's worse, the things she said won't tumble from my ears and follow her out.

She's done things, she says.

Harper has a secret past, she insists.

And it's my job to protect my daughter.

After a quick glance the way Mason went, I pull out my phone and send my band a group text. Family emergency, be back in a few hours, will personally pay for any overage costs.

The gut-wrench of feeling after I send the text is expected. How our band has now become more business than pleasure, catering to record companies and production costs rather than fans and music. I wonder if any of the guys see it as I do.

Then, I send a second text to Harper.

Meet me at the apartment in an hour.

Mason's right about one thing. I have too many lady problems.

It's time to find some fucking solutions.

CHAPTER 28

Harper

STELLA SQUEALS as she takes the slide in the park, arms up like she's on a roller coaster.

I'm happy to see it. Even happier to be a part of the blossoming flower that is this child coming back into herself. I'm not sure how much I have to do with it, other than the certainty that this morning, when Stella saw me packing, she did not want me to leave. It felt good—warm—to be wanted, but there was also a sickly lurch behind it.

I do not want to be responsible for Stella's disappointment, but I fear the road I'm on will only take me there.

I'm attracted to her father. I don't know how much longer I can work for him, even to keep Stella happy.

Stella's the most important, my brain insists.

But what about you? my heart retorts.

I can keep up pretenses a little longer, but what about the day Rex brings a woman home? He's a bachelor for now, one the press insists will never get married after the heartbreak of his baby's mother, but I'm no fool. There will come a time, come a *woman*, who will take his breath away, and I'm not so senseless to think that it could be me. But it could be someone, and will I be able to handle it? As the nanny? As a professional within his employ?

No.

Rex leaves a broken trail of hearts behind his every footstep and doesn't even realize it. I don't want to be part of the collection.

"Harper! Look!"

Stella jumps for the monkey bars, her fingers grazing the metal before she flops back down, butt first on the ground.

I cup my hands around my mouth and call, "Try again, Stella! Second time's the charm!"

Stella side-eyes me in the way only she can, suspicion forever remaining at the forefront of that kid's mind. Stella hates motivational speeches, but I smile and hoot extra hard at her. She frowns.

"Gorgeous child."

I jolt at the woman who has sidled up beside me undetected. It irks, since I've been on high alert for paparazzi and should've sensed this woman's presence. Rex is way too much of a distraction, even when he's miles away.

"She sure is," I say.

"You must be a proud mom, cheering for her like that."

I guffaw. "Oh, I'm not her mom, I'm her nanny. And I do it because she hates it."

The woman laughs, and I glance over at the sound. She has long, wavy chestnut hair, light brown eyes, and a smattering of freckles across her nose. She's tall and slim, but not a mammoth, wearing a simple beige coat and a light gray wool hat because of the increasing chill in the air.

"Which one's yours?" I ask.

"That one."

She points at a little boy who's grabbing unsuspecting children's ankles under the bridge of the playground.

"Ah. He seems nice," I say.

"You're too kind," the woman says wryly. "We just moved here. He's … adjusting."

I nod. "I know something about change. This park is a great

start. Tons of supportive nannies and parents, and the kids are great."

"Good to know." The woman turns to me. "Would you like to grab a coffee sometime? Being new and all, I'd love to make a friend and chat..."

"Sure," I say. "Though I have Stella most of the time. Maybe we can make it a playdate."

Did I imagine it, or did her eyes flicker at the use of Stella's name? I'm wary of Rex's superfans infiltrating private areas, especially places involving Stella, and I hesitate when she offers a gloved hand.

But she's here with a child. Or, if she isn't, that will become obvious soon. And I don't have to meet her anywhere.

She withdraws her hand when I don't take it.

"Should I get your number?" she asks.

"Um, how about I get yours?" I pull out my phone from my jacket pocket, ready to tap it in. "What's your name?"

"I'm—"

My phone chimes with a message from Rex. **Meet me at the apartment in an hour.**

I sigh and black out my screen before tucking my phone back in my pocket. "Sorry, that's my boss. We have to go. Stella!"

Stella looks over and then takes her sweet time exiting the playground. I watch her with my hands on my hips during her whole, meandering journey.

"Maybe another time," the woman says, and steps back as Stella appears. "Hi, Stella."

Stella glances up at the woman as she grabs her backpack from my feet. She doesn't say hello. Usually I urge Stella to be polite, but something holds me back.

"You're beautiful," the woman continues. Stella scrunches her nose at this.

I steer Stella in the other direction, put-off by the woman's weighted gaze. "It was nice to meet you."

"Likewise. We'll connect next time. *Andrew!* Stop biting those kids' ankles or I swear to crickets I will take your gaming system away!"

The troll-boy under the bridge jolts at the woman's voice, then, head bowed, exits from under. It's somewhat of a relief to note the woman actually has a child here, and I feel bad at dismissing her compliment to Stella. Lots of parents and nannies alike comment on Stella's beauty. I don't know why this one was any different.

"Come on," I say to Stella. "Your dad's getting home early."

"That's cool," Stella says, but she's distracted, glancing between the kid named Andrew and the woman.

"Everything okay?" I ask.

"Yeah." Stella turns to look straight ahead, keeping step with me. "I just haven't seen Andy's mom before. He's always with his nanny. He's a jerk."

I nod, glancing back once myself.

"We'll avoid the playground bridge from now on," I say, then usher her into our car.

Stella glides through the apartment door in front of me, taking off her backpack and placing it on the floor by her shoes.

The child barely makes noise, always so quiet, like she's afraid what will happen if she's noticed. I wait for her to call out to her dad or barrel down the hallway, but she doesn't.

I call out, "Mr. Sloane?"

"In here," comes the answering reply, in the direction of the main room.

"There he is," I say brightly to Stella. "Let's go say hello."

She nods and leads the way out of the foyer, her socked feet shushing against the floorboards.

Rex rises from the sofa upon seeing us, his expression warming. "Hey, baby sweets."

"I'm not a baby," Stella says, but wanders up to her father to receive his open arms.

"You sure aren't." He kisses the top of her head. "Would you want some big girl alone time? How about you go to your room, crack open one of your books, and I'll be there in a little while to read with you."

Stella tilts her head up. "You're going to help me read in the afternoon?"

"Sure." He palms one of her cheeks, and I wonder if I'm one of the few to witness the thawing of his ice-blue eyes. "I haven't been too great lately, but I'm going to carve out more time for us, Stella. Because you make my day better, and it's a wonder I don't give myself better days more often."

I smile at this, remaining standing, clasping my hands in front of me. "How about you start on your *Peppa Pig* book? You can show your dad how good you're getting at reading it."

"Okay." Stella pushes off her father's knees, winds around me, and heads down the hallway to her bedroom without looking back.

"I appreciate you coming home early," Rex says.

At the sound of his voice, I stop watching Stella and turn my attention back to him. "No problem. The park was getting a little chilly as it is. We're going to have to pull out Stella's winter gear sooner than expected, I think."

I'm blabbering, but I can't seem to stop myself. I'm also refusing to sit down.

"Can I offer you a drink?" Rex asks. "June made some coffee earlier."

"I'm fine." My answering smile is tight. I'm not sure how I'm supposed to act when Rex treats me as a guest.

He nods. Swallows. Sweeps out his hand. "Take a seat."

Standing off to the side isn't exactly working for me, so I do as he asks and sit on the sofa across from him. It occurs to me that

Rex never chooses the long sofa to sit in. Always one of the adjacent chairs.

Rex clears his throat. "I'll get straight to it. I saw Patrice today. She wants her job back."

"Oh." My stomach *plonks* with disappointment. "I guess I should've expected this."

Rex's brows come together.

"Because of last night," I continue through my racing heart. "And what happened between us. It can't keep working, can it? Not how it used to."

He clasps his hands, leaning his elbows on his thighs. "That's not what I'm getting at."

"It's not?"

Those same hands glided up my shirt. Those same fingers curled into my body, coaxing ecstasy to the surface of my skin.

"Patrice confessed to a few things," Rex says. "She has feelings for me, and going forward, it just wouldn't work between us."

I chew on my lower lip, sensing the parallel between me and Patrice. The *Rex* between me and Patrice.

"Is it not the same thing with me?" I blurt out.

Rex gaze is centered on mine, and he says in a low voice, "I don't know, Harper. Is it?"

"I—" I don't like where this conversation is going. Not when we've only mended fences hours ago. When I've *just* convinced myself I can put any feelings for him last, and Stella first. This sizzle between him and I, it's nothing but hormones and chemistry. My brain can fight against it. My heart will.

"No," I say at last. "It's not the same. We can remain professional."

Rex straightens, his palms clasping his knees. "Good."

I stare at him a little longer. If I didn't consider him to be the grumpiest, most arrogant man alive, I'd swear he was as nervous as me right now.

"Patrice mentioned something else," he says.

"Was there anything going on between you and Patrice?"

He startles at my sudden question. I startled myself. But there's an odd sense of intimacy between us at the moment, one that will dissipate the instant one of us lets out a heavy breath. And I don't want to lose the chance.

"What makes you say that?" he asks.

I fight back an eye roll at his deliberate obtuseness. "When she was here, training me, I sensed a weird tenseness between you two. I thought..." I offer an uncomfortable laugh. "I thought something had gone on between you guys, and maybe that's why she was leaving."

And can you blame me? I want to add. *When something's happening between* us?

"Nothing," Rex says. "Patrice wanted more and perhaps set up a few situations where it could've, but I never took it any further with her than was professional."

I lean back, not quite convinced, but not sure he's lying, either.

"She's a wonderful woman," Rex continues, "Just not the one I see myself with. With Stella being the most important female in my life, I have to be sure. And that kind of surety is not something I'm looking for right now. It's just Stella and me, and I'm good with that."

I stiffen, but don't make it obvious. He's using more words than usual, and if that means he's trying to tell me something ... my stomach does another *plonk*.

"Yes, of course, obviously." I say. My fingers are interlaced too tightly together. I loosen them and, in an attempt to loosen the tension of my thoughts, add, "Is that what you wanted to talk to me about? To tell me my job is safe?"

"For as long as you want it—or are comfortable with it," he adds, but with the clipped tone that tells me he may not be as comfortable as he seems, either. "But I also need to ask ... something else Patrice mentioned. It's about your past."

I cock my head. "Oh yeah?"

Rex rubs at his scruff, glancing away. "I'm not very good at this kind of thing. So I'm just going to come out with it. Is there something in your life that could prevent you from taking proper care of Stella?"

"Of ... what?" My spine goes straight, and I stare at this man, unblinking. "What could Patrice have said to make you ask me that?"

And what does she know?

CHAPTER 29

Rex

HARPER'S QUESTION IS INNOCENT, her pallor the pale color of truth, yet I have to pry.

I dislike making a woman uncomfortable, and my lips twist at the irony that this is hardly the first time I've made Harper shift in her seat.

"If there's anything at all that would make Patrice bring her concerns to me, you must say so," I continue.

"There's—" Harper bites her lip. A ripe, reactive trait that gets me hard every time she does it, but I show no outward sign. I remain cold, calculating. The boss I must be with her from here on out.

"I don't know why," Harper says, "But I've always felt Patrice has had it in for me, even when she was cheering for me."

I nod. "I've felt the same."

"Yeah?" Harper brightens. "Even about the paparazzi photos?"

Now I raise a brow. "What about the photos?"

"I don't know—I have no proof." Harper holds out her hands, empty palms facing up. "But it's like this cameraman knows our schedule or asks someone with enough knowledge to figure out where Stella and I are going. Especially on the night of the ballet recital. The nannies I spoke to are trusted, long-term individuals who are well aware of Stella's situation and would never compromise their job—or a child—that way."

"And you think Patrice would?"

Harper's shoulders jerk like she wants to backtrack. "I don't—I'm not trying to accuse her. Not without proof."

"Oh no?" I cross a leg at the ankle, settling in. "Because she's all too ready to accuse you."

Harper's cheeks bloom with reddened rage. "I would never, *never*, sell secrets to the paparazzi. You want proof? Ask Taryn and Easton. I've worked with Jamie for years, some of those while Nocturne Court became famous, and there was never a *breath* on where we were."

Harper's eyes remain emboldened, her cheeks a flash-fire of indignant defense. If her hair were tousled, if she were pressed up against the window again, I'd say we were back to when I used my hands and lips instead of my words to entice her. I have the sudden urge to clear the coffee table, cup her neck and drag my lips over hers. Swell and color them cherry red from my scorching lust, rather than her store-bought lipstick brand.

But I remain composed.

"Harper," I reprimand. "I believe you. But I want to trust you. If you've left out something on your resume, or if you have a childhood that might—"

Harper scoffs, shocking me silent. "My *childhood*? You think Patrice has found something out about my pre-teen years that could affect my nannying career?"

"I don't know," I ask, though the sheen of her stare has me questioning how deep I should go. "Has she? Why did you quit your Computer Science degree?"

Harper's jaw locks and she glances out the window, to the city and sky beyond. It's a clear blue day, the sky settling thin, crisp fall clouds over the gray and silver buildings. I let her study the view, waiting.

"If you must know," she says, still focused on the outside, "No, my childhood wasn't very terrific. Not until my grandpa."

"You don't have to tell me why," I say, then, sensing my weakness, amend, "unless you think Stella will be affected by it."

Harper shakes her head, her eyes downcast, until she flicks them up and stares at me. "I'm the result of an embryo donor."

Every day, I carry the face of a mask. My emotions are rarely seen by others save for close, trusted friends, unless it's anger. But this has my brows jumping.

"I never had a mother," Harper continues. "But I had two dads."

I say, "I see."

"That's not what made things difficult. Not at all, in fact. My early years, I remember being loved. Cuddled. Spoiled rotten." She laughs, but it's with hollow remembrance. "Then, when I was around Stella's age, my Daddy died."

I frown. "Harper, I'm sorry."

Her tongue clicks as she looks to the ceiling. Trying not to cry. "It was a private plane crash. My parents were very wealthy, both being in worldwide finance. They traveled a lot, and I remember being in many hotels, since they never wanted to leave me behind. I'd either go with them together, or when they traveled separately, they'd trade off on time with me. I never felt unwanted until ... until there was only one dad left."

I don't speak, instead allowing her to work through her words on her own, but I listen.

"Maybe it was because I wasn't biologically his that Dad distanced after Daddy died. Maybe it was because I reminded him too much of Daddy, or too little, or maybe I was the direct reflection of the family he was supposed to have but that broke in the five minutes it took for the plane to hit the ground. Either way, Nick Mei washed his hands and threw me at my grandpa, my ah gong, who lived in a single apartment in Chinatown and elected to stay there despite his son's wealth, wanting nothing to do with what Dad—Nick Mei—had become."

There is so much information in her words, yet not enough. I want to sit next to her, to coax details out of her, but I don't dare do it. Instead, I remain still and watch her through lidded eyes, fingers resting on my chin.

Harper fills the thickened silence. "I'm half-Taiwanese. Nick is half-Taiwanese, too, so obviously there was thought put into my resemblance when they chose the embryo, but I guess it wasn't enough. And with my ah gong, who's Taiwanese, who's to say he would've accepted me? Not only am I made from science, but his son is gay, and ... well, it ended up not mattering. He took me in. Loved me like his own. Said that the only shame brought into this household was a father who refused to raise his daughter." She adds, "his *bought* daughter."

A lick of flame hits me in the gut. "Your grandfather said that to you?"

"No, he would never," Harper rushes to say. "That's just how I see myself in Nick's eyes. Yes, science is advancing, there are plenty of children born with surrogates and donor eggs and sperm, and it's all wonderful. Wonderful for the curious and the progressive ... but not so wonderful for some of the products. The kids."

"Don't call yourself that," I say. "A product."

"Why? That's what Nick reduced me to. He's a powerful man in New York, written up in all kinds of articles and donating to a bunch of charities and the arts and dance companies. On paper, he's a doting philanthropist. You think there's any mention of the child he made? That he has no genetic connection to? That he has no responsibility for other than to legally keep me fed and in school and under the care of a guardian?"

I take some time to digest her words, rubbing my eyes with my forefinger and thumb. "Do you think this truth of yours is what Patrice was trying to bring to light? To make me question you?"

Harper shrugs, but it's a sad movement. "It's the only thing I have that's considered controversial. My grandfather died when I was almost eighteen. I could find affordable living and use my small inheritance to attend a few months of college, get into computers..."

A lightning bolt of realization pings between my eyes. "Until the money ran out."

Harper nods. "Right about the time I met Taryn, who desperately needed a nanny. I was temping in many administrative jobs, hated every second, and turned to babysitting, instead."

"And your father didn't help you? Not at all?"

Her expression closes off. "I never asked him to."

I lean forward again, despising that I possess such a lack of words. Of comfort to this girl. "I'm sorry for everything that's happened to you."

"I'm not," Harper says. "It's made me who I am, and my ah gong loved me fiercely. I fought the bullies in school and focused on my studies and made a future for myself. It's a little hand-stitched, I admit, but I'm happy with it. Happy I've found Stella. She and I..." For the first time in this conversation, Harper's gaze flits away from mine. "She and I have something in common, and I think that makes me more than able to care for her, not the other way around. I'm not an unloved orphan."

"Never, during everything you've said to me, have I thought that," I say. "I'm furious at Patrice for conning me into forcing you to come forward about this. A past that's none of my business. I have no doubt you're capable of supervising my daughter. We don't have to speak of this again."

"It's okay. Really."

"No. It's not. In fact, I'm now able to see that yes, Patrice could be vindictive enough, hurt enough, to leak information about my daughter to the press. An unforgivable move, and one I will make sure she answers for.

"What was your father's name?" I ask. "The one who died?"

Harper's brows furrow, her only sign of surprise. "Dylan. Dylan Chadwick."

I nod, clasping my knees as I rise. "It may have been under duress, but I'm glad you told me. I won't air this out to anyone else. Not if you don't want me to."

"Can I tell Stella?"

I pause.

"Not everything," Harper amends. "I know it's complicated and confusing. But I want her to know she's not alone. That missing a parent doesn't always have to mean..."

"She's missing a piece of herself," I add under my breath.

"Exactly," Harper whispers.

I run my teeth along my lower lip, then say, "I can't see the harm in it."

"Only if it comes up," Harper assures, and rises from her seat. "Or if she's curious. I promise not to push the issue."

I shake my head, smiling. "I'm not so dumb as to think she doesn't ask questions. Or wonder where her mother is. It's good Stella has someone like you."

"Where is she? Stella's mom?"

I'm jarred and wary when I glance back at Harper.

"I'm sorry. I didn't mean—well, maybe I did. I've just unloaded my deep, dark, shady past on you and I'm feeling pretty vulnerable. Forget I said anything."

"Dinner."

Harper raises her eyes to mine. "What?"

"Stella will be looking for us by now. After you put her to bed, let's have dinner."

"Um..."

"We can talk more then."

I don't wait for Harper's response and stride into the hallway to Stella's room.

Harper opened up, and I listened, ears cocked, but my chest stayed closed off. Her words can't strike me where I'm vulnerable

—no woman can. Not anymore. But there's a crack in my cage of bones, a shocking fracture upon hearing Harper's story.

I rub at the area, pressing my palm hard between my pecs, and pretend it's a phantom ache from a woman long ago and not from the one standing in front of me.

There's time to read one book with Stella, then get back to the band. If the strain of balancing my career, my child, and my nanny is getting to me, I won't show it. I'll give Harper enough to satisfy her curiosity, then get back to what's important.

And I sure as hell won't make the mistake of increasing Harper's importance in my life.

CHAPTER 30

Harper

STELLA GOES DOWN with frustrating ease after a single read-through of *Peppa Pig*. I'm left to twiddle my thumbs in front of the bathroom mirror, wondering if I should comb my hair. Change my outfit. Spritz some perfume.

No, none of that. He's your boss. It's just a casual dinner at home.

Huffing out a breath, I reach for my translucent powder. I can justify getting rid of T-zone shine for a simple dinner.

He fingered you. You know his touch. What his mouth tastes like.

I grapple for my eyeliner and flat iron next, then check for stray hairs … anywhere.

Satisfied, and wearing the same shirt and pants I've been wearing all day, I figure I'm the perfect combination of trying but not trying too hard, since Rex and I have laid out our boundaries and nothing further will ever happen between us.

His naked chest flashes in my mind's eye. The way it pressed against mine, his muscled ridges made stark and sharp in the darkness, his lips scoring down my neck as we almost fuck against a window.

A whisper of "oh, boy," flutters from my throat as I smooth down my shirt that doesn't need smoothing.

When I exit Stella's wing and enter the main area of the penthouse, then the kitchen, I become confused. The lights are on, the counters pristine from June's cleaning and her addition of a small bouquet of greenery on the table, but no one's here.

Not June, not dinner, not Rex.

"Hello?" I ask.

Nothing but a lone faucet drip answers back.

I get it. Rex must be running late at the studio and I'm not exactly a priority. But a text would've been nice. A head's up of any sort. Except, that would mean he owes me something beyond a paycheck, and since I'm here, caring for his daughter full-time, he doesn't need to provide me with his schedule—only Stella's.

Only Stella matters. Not your stupid, crushy feelings.

I cover my face with my hands. "Jesus, I am such an idiot."

To even *think*, after Rex and I spoke, that there's still some spark, some *something*, between us, is such a naïve idea. I'm smarter than that.

Turning to the fridge, I search for something to scrounge up and eat within the confines of my room, with an angsty, teenage drama Netflix series and a glass of wine.

"Hey."

I glance over the top of the fridge's door at the voice. *Rex's voice.*

He muscles himself through the kitchen entrance, carrying a small box with an open top.

"Hi." I shut the fridge and head over to help.

"I got it," he says as I try to reach for the box, and he sets it on the kitchen counter. "Costco."

I nod like this makes sense, then gesture behind me. "I was just about to make something, if you want to eat."

"No, that's what I'm saying. I got us Costco for dinner."

"You ... huh?"

"Not me," he says, shoving his thumbs in his denim pockets. The movement stretches his tight white tee farther, his nipples erect, his pecs defined. I clear my throat and pretend deep interest in what he brought home.

"I sent Bobby to Brooklyn to get it," Rex continues. "One of their roast chickens and some fresh rolls. June keeps the pantry stocked with avocados and tomatoes and stuff, so I figure we can make some roast chicken sandwiches for dinner."

"Right." Realizing I'm standing frozen in the middle of the kitchen, I jerk into motion. "I'll get us some plates and stuff."

"Is this not okay?" Rex asks behind me.

I root around the silverware drawer, grab some dinner knives, then maybe slam it shut with my hip too hard. "No, it's fine. Totally fine. I love Costco chicken."

One side of his mouth quirks. "Doesn't everyone?"

Damn it, does he have to look so boyish and cute while so obviously making this the most casual dinner ever? It's clear what he's doing. And no surprise. I just wish my heart would agree with me.

We set up the kitchen table, the only sounds the light clanging of dishes and silverware. At one point, my elbow brushes his and I jump away.

"Sorry," I say, and continue slicing an avocado.

Rex halts me with a hand on my shoulder. He waits for me to look up at him, then says, "This is awkward."

"It's not," I say while gesturing with the knife. I put it down. "You said we should have dinner together. We're having dinner."

"Harper." His hand remains on my shoulder, like a heat-seeking missile searching to blow up my heart. "Sit."

I don't argue. I sit.

Rex pulls out the chair beside me, and he's too close. I can smell him, the clean, soapy scent of him, despite his working all day. What's most disconcerting is I can *feel* him. Rex's proximity, his nuclear power, just inches away from my lips.

"I'm not trying to make light of this," he says in a low voice. I watch him through my lashes, too afraid of what my cheeks will do if I look at him. "I promised you some information on Aesha, and that's what I'll give. I thought a laid-back dinner would put less pressure on the whole thing."

I nod behind the small curtain of my hair. "Sure. I understand."

Rex lifts his hand as if to put it over mine, which is clenched on the table, but he second-guesses and draws back.

"Is there something else you want to talk about?" he asks.

Us. I want to talk about us. I want there to be an us.

"No." I sit back in my chair, folding my arms lightly. "Tell me about Stella's mom. Why she's so forbidden in this household."

There's a flash in Rex's eyes at my use of the word *forbidden*, but he stifles it. Maybe because it's on point.

"We met young," Rex starts. He reaches for a bread roll, cuts it, then concentrates on stacking the sandwich. As if to keep himself busy. Or from looking at me. "We were twenty-two. The band was kind of in static mode, since East went to college. For me, school wasn't my thing. I bartended, fixed bikes, to make ends meet, and in my spare time, I focused on music. There was a ballet studio near the bike shop, and I could always hear the music. I also started predicting the lulls in their rehearsals. It was in those times I'd sneak in to the concert hall and spend some time with the piano. Composing. Singing."

To also give myself something to do, I mirrored Rex in making a sandwich, reaching around him for tomatoes or mayo or lettuce, but keeping my eyes on him. "And you ran into Aesha there?"

A sad smile flits across his mouth. "She also took advantage of the lulls. I was using the piano one night, and she took the stage. Alone. Hearing my music, I guess, she started dancing—having no idea it was some punk who snuck in, of course."

I smile. "Of course."

"She moved like a ... like a swan. I was fascinated. Mesmerized. Stunned to where my fingers stopped moving. And when they did, she froze in the silence. Looked down. Saw me. I thought she'd scream."

No one would scream upon seeing you.

I could imagine spotting Rex within the shadows, the halo of his long blonde hair, the bright blue eyes and tanned, lean jaw. His broad shoulders and the heartbreaking mold of him, etched into Aesha's vision.

"Instead, Aesha asked, *Who the hell are you*? And I answered honestly." Rex shrugs. "I'm Rex. I work next door. I need an instrument to write music."

And that straight truth probably drew her even closer.

"Let me guess," I say. "The two of you naturally began meeting up most nights, her practicing her dance, you practicing your music."

"Mm." Rex takes a bite of his sandwich, the muscles in his jaw working as he chews. I'm fascinated by the carving of him, the sharp angles and straight lines of his profile.

He swallows. "Of a sort. We had instant attraction. She and I ended up together almost instantly. Insta-love, I think the cool kids call it now." He licks mayo off his thumb and puts his sandwich down. "Ended up dating for a few years, then moving in together. While I hustled, so did she. She ended up becoming a dancer for a major company."

"That's huge," I say. Here's the part where I have to pretend there was never a time I stuck my nose in Aesha's business.

"Very," Rex says. "Aesha was at the top of her game. I was getting close, too. East was out of college, the band was back together..."

And then she—

"And then we got pregnant."

I nod, unsurprised. "And everything changed."

"Actually, no." Rex wipes his mouth with a napkin. "She took it in stride. We both did. We could do this. And we did. She worked with her pregnancy, went to all her appointments. Aesha took it seriously. It was only after the baby was born, Stella was maybe six months, that everything went to shit."

"Aesha was injured."

Blue eyes clash with mine. I'm thrown by the sudden stare. "I tried to do some research," I say as a lame explanation. "When you wouldn't really talk about it, and Stella had all these strange quirks. I *had* to figure it out. Please don't be mad."

After a moment, he sighs. "I can't be surprised you attempted to find answers."

I offer a wry smile.

"What did you find?" he asks.

"Honestly? Not much. The internet doesn't say a lot about her."

Rex nods. "My team scrubbed a lot, or buried it low in search results, once the public became more interested in me. Not only to protect me from criticism, but her, too."

"To where she almost doesn't exist," I say without thinking. With a jolt, I reach for my sandwich, perturbed over what I blurted out. "I didn't mean…"

"She was injured. Badly." Rex takes another bite, and I wait with suspense for him to finish chewing to find out what has been so thoroughly scrubbed online. "Her knee. She took a terrible fall with her dance partner in the middle of a major recital."

I could predict the answer but want to ask. "Was she able to recover?"

"That depends." Rex licks his lips. "How do you define recovery? Was her knee going to return to normal? No, but she could still dance. She'd have to do a lot more physical therapy and stretching beforehand, but the prognosis wasn't as bad as it could've been."

I draw my brows down. "Then why…?"

"The pain meds." Rex clears his throat, rubs his eyes. "She was over-prescribed. Given something like eighty Oxy pills per refill. She was hooked."

"Oh…"

"Yeah, you hear about it, right? In the news, the whole national painkiller crisis. But you never think it'll affect your family. You never think your girlfriend, with a serious knee injury, will be prescribed too much after a standard, run-of-the-mill surgery. You think you have an eye on it. That you'd see if the woman you love was changing, seeming how you've dabbled in off-market drugs yourself. Right?"

The question doesn't need an answer, but I reach out. Touch his forearm.

Rex laughs. "By the time I figured out what was going on, she was hooked. Sneaking it in her drinks, snorting it as powder. Aesha had ways of taking that stuff I didn't think was possible. And she hid it so damn well. Until—"

Oh, God, I think. *Something happened with Stella.*

"We were in a small apartment." Rex's voice cracks, snapping my attention back to him. "On the second floor. I was getting ready for a gig at this local Brooklyn bar with my band, and I wasn't there. Aesha overdosed, and Stella, almost two years old, was left on her own in that apartment. Roaming free. With an open window because our air conditioning never worked. We only cracked the window, never opened it all the way. But not on that day. That day, Aesha was overheating and needed the extra air before she passed out."

I cover my mouth, swirls of dread adding heavy layers to my stomach.

"There was scaffolding directly below us. Stella ended up falling onto that, maybe three feet below our window. A pedestrian saw her, climbed up, and got her down. And called the police. Christ, that phone call." Rex covers his face, his shoulders shaking. But he's not crying. He's trembling with emotion.

"If that scaffolding weren't there ... Harper, I can't think on it. I can't, because if I do—"

"Shh." I rub his back, leaning close. "It didn't happen. She's okay."

"Aesha was taken to the hospital. This was before the availability of Zorcan. You know, the nose spray that instantly revives some ODs. Her stomach was pumped, child services was called. It was a fucking nightmare."

I lower my head, hand still on his back.

"We worked on ourselves, Aesha and I. I was determined to get my family back." Rex straightens, sniffs hard, then takes a long swig of his beer. "Aesha was in the hospital for two weeks, then tried rehab but dropped out. All her time with Stella was supervised until Aesha stopped showing up to her NA meetings. I stayed up all night, watching Aesha sleep—*hoping* she'd sleep, but any time she stopped the pain meds, the withdrawal became too much. She screamed, I held her. She hit, I held her. She spewed hatred at me ... I left her. Took Stella and told Aesha that if she didn't get clean, she'd never see her daughter again. Aesha responded that she didn't want to see either of us ever again. She loved the high too much. She stopped trying, Harper."

I rub my lips together, searching for the right thing to say. "With addicts, it's difficult to discern their true motives. The drug takes over."

"I said to her, any time you show up on my doorstep, clean, you can see Stella. That I wanted to help her, but I had to put our daughter first. I'd help with rehab and be there for Aesha to call. I tried to figure out all the best ways to be there for her yet keep our daughter safe. Because I didn't love Aesha anymore. I couldn't—I *couldn't*, not after Stella almost...*argh.*"

Rex takes another drink, his shaking subsiding somewhat.

I whisper, "Did she ever come back?"

"No. Not in the physical sense. I got famous, so that made a difference to her."

My brows rise. "She tried for some monetary support?"

"Yep. It was some years back. I haven't heard from her since. I agreed to help her, though, because I promised I would. I couldn't leave her to the drug, though a big part of me wishes I was that cold. I'm not that man."

I know.

"My lawyers and I figured out a kind of payment plan. Where any money I provide goes to assist with rent or utilities. It never lands in Aesha's hands."

"Does that mean you know where she is?"

He nods. "I started out that way. So I could watch out for Stella. I kept tabs on Aesha to see if she was doing anything to improve her life, but mostly, she's lived as she wanted, without the burden of a kid. Then I gave up hoping."

"Is she clean?"

"That, I don't know." Rex tips his head back and finishes his beer. "She seems to be, but Aesha's very good at disguising her highs."

"And as a result, you keep Stella from asking too much about her," I say. "To prevent any heartbreak."

He nods. "To have her mom back would mean the world to Stella. But to only have Aesha leave again, another spontaneous disappearance, would be so unfair to Stella. Because Stella can remember now."

"I know the absence of a parent," I say. "But I know the pain of unreliable love even better. I understand what you've done. Why you protect her the way you do."

I hesitate but do it, anyway. Lay a hand over his, still damp from the condensation of his beer bottle.

His lashes flicker as his stare meets my own. As his palm flips so both of ours touch. His fingers entwine with mine.

"Thank you, Harper," he says. "Because hell, I was not meaning to tell you this much."

I grin. "It's my face. So open and trusting and baby-like. Many people can't resist it."

My attempt to lighten the mood falls flat once the softness around his lips falls away. His stare turns hard. Penetrating.

"Your face," he says, so close I can open my mouth and curl my tongue against his breath. "Is anything but baby-like."

My lower lip trembles, like I'm trying to say something, but I can't. It's impossible to do anything but fall into his gaze.

The roughness of his palm touches my cheek as he cups my jaw, his thumb drawing patterns against my chin. At every movement, my skin tingles. My heart slams.

"Rex…"

"Shh." His finger brushes against my lips.

I squeak out, "Your emotions are running hard right now. This isn't a good idea. Don't do anything you'll regret—"

"*Shh* might've been too polite," he murmurs, his gaze on my lips. "How about I shut you up with my mouth?"

My jaw drops open in shock.

Rex smiles, the predatory one that preempts him getting his way.

Then, he pounces.

CHAPTER 31

Rex

MISTAKE.

Harper is nothing but a tempting regret, a moment of weakness, a taming of such severe emotion, I can't staunch it on my own.

I shouldn't touch her. Shouldn't drag my fingers through her hair, along her chin. Shouldn't explore her mouth with my tongue. But it can't be helped. Aesha brings with her memories with such frustrating emotion—

But it's not about Aesha anymore.

It's only Harper and her guileless eyes. Her soft smile. Her understanding touch. I haven't had anything like that since ... ever.

"Rex..." she murmurs, her lips moving over mine as she speaks. "I thought we worked through this."

I drag my other hand across her thigh until I hit a hole in the denim.

"Still wearing ripped jeans in the fall," I say, lowering my gaze to the apex of her legs. "It's so tempting to tear them wide. Spread you open."

"R-Rex," Harper stutters. But doesn't move away. "You're not yourself. We've talked about something emotional and now you're looking for an outlet. I don't think it should be me."

I play with the stray denim strings. She shudders at the contact.

"No?" I ask. "That's unfortunate, since I disagree."

"We—we'll compromise too much if we—"

I cut her off with a brush of my thumb against her zipper. So close to what I want.

"I need to get you out of my system." I'm mesmerized by the circle of my thumb against the metal threading, how easy it would be to pull the zipper down, dip my fingers in... "It's the only way."

"I..." Harper's head tips back as I do just that. "Oh, God. Rex. I'm trying to be strong, and you're..."

"Doing what we both want. I'm tired of fighting this, Harper. I thought I could, but—*sweet Jesus.*" My index finger slips inside her. She's not wearing underwear and she's wet, so wet, and hot. "If we do this, it could be over. We'd get what we want, what we've been fantasizing over ... tell me you've been fantasizing about me."

"I ... have," she breathes out, her eyes on the ceiling. Her back arches, allowing me better entry.

"And I, you," I say. My breaths are hard. I'm not sure how much longer I can hold out.

I risk a glance at the security monitor on the counter. Stella is curled up in bed and out like a light.

Harper uses that moment to catch my wrist and bring me to a standstill.

Don't resist, I think, but don't say.

"My turn," she says as she pulls my hand away and slides off her chair.

Perplexed, I wait to see what she's up to, and if I'll have blue balls for the rest of the night.

On her knees, she fits between my thighs, her smile impish as she unbuttons my pants and pulls down the zipper.

"We can't have sex," she says, focused on her actions. "It means too much to me and will cause way too many problems. But I can give you your outlet, what you so need." At this, she looks up. I'm close to burning her with the quiet fire of desire in my stare. "I'll give you my mouth on your cock."

The sudden, dirty statement coming out of what I consider such an innocent mouth nearly has me popping off. And when she tucks her hair behind both ears, licking her top lip, readying to swallow me, I can't contain the groan of approval.

Harper pulls my dick out with surprising deftness. At her gasp, my lips quirk, but I'm not about to ruin the moment with a quip about my girth. I want her mouth on me. Now.

Harper must've heard my low, commanding growl. Her gaze flicks up to mine, then back to my cock. She strokes it in her small, tight grip, and my hips pick up the rhythm, wanting more, demanding.

Harper's lips part, her head dips down. Her hot, silky mouth hits the tip of my dick and I throw my head back, teeth clenched and bared, as she takes me in.

She goes deep and gags when my tip hits the back of her throat. The sound lights a match near my groin and I want to grip the back of her head and drive deeper, but I'm a controlled man. I wait for her to realign my dick, to stroke and stir with her tongue, and to use every horny skill she has to get me to come, rather than swallowing me whole.

"That's it, darling," I say through my teeth. The controlled thrust of my hips is brutal on the ecstasy. Fuck, I want to press her against the wall and shove my dick all the way inside her. "That's it…"

She moans something, the vibration of her vocal cords hitting my sensitive skin, and I grip the side of the table, plates clanging and glasses clattering at the sudden contact of wood to palm.

Her hand reaches around my pants and into my briefs, cupping my balls, massaging and squeezing as she sucks, and my eyes about roll into the back of my head.

Anyone walking into the kitchen right now would see nothing but myself, staring at the ceiling, Harper hidden from view.

But she's there. Holy fuck, she's there, sliding and gripping and sucking and…

"Harper, I'm gonna come."

She doesn't stop. Harper's head bobs, her sucking turning urgent.

"Harp…" I grit out. "You'd better … I'm gonna …"

Harper doesn't fall back or switch to jerking me off. Her mouth stays latched, her suction loud, smacking, and determined. My focus remains on her as my lips peel back and I let out an ecstatic snarl and I fill her mouth with my hot seed. She tastes all of it.

I catch my breath and she sits back on her haunches, dabbing at the corners of her mouth. The sight has me wanting to pounce and take her right there on the floor, damn all the furniture.

Harper stands. She glances at me, but the words following hit their mark. "Am I out of your system?"

No. Not even close.

I tuck myself in and button my pants, standing with her. Reaching between us, I scrape my thumb across the corner of her lips. She freezes at the contact, but her mouth is supple and hot against my touch.

I angle my head and ask, "Am I out of yours?"

I feel her lips tilt before I see them. "Good night, Mr. Sloane," she says.

"Night, Harper." I drop my hand.

She takes her sandwich and a beer with her. I wish I could join Harper in bed, share our meal and drinks together, maybe laugh at whatever show she'll be putting on her computer after fucking her blind a few times, but that's not us.

It'll never be, even with the blurred lines we've drawn in front of ourselves.

I take my seat again, constructing another sandwich and uncapping another beer in the midnight silence of the kitchen. I'm ravenous, but no roast chicken sandwich will fill the hungry crater that's opened up inside my groin.

I eat with the closed-mouth chew of a man on a mission, yet I have no destination in mind.

Harper.

I don't think I will ever be sated.

CHAPTER 32

Harper

"GET A MOVE ON, Stella. We'll be late for school," I say while stacking her last-minute homework on the kitchen table among sliced bananas, spilled milk and scattered Cheerios.

It's June's day off, so I made us breakfast on the fly, only to be told by Stella that four pages of math homework was due, which she "forgotted" last night.

We worked through it while munching on our cereal, one of my ears pricked for Rex's arrival. At any noise, my chin would jerk up. The hum of the fridge, the cycle of the dishwasher, what sounded like a door opening ... Rex was behind none of them.

"Are you still looking for my daddy?" Stella asks as she hoists on her backpack.

"Me? No." I grab my denim jacket from the back of the kitchen chair and pull it on.

"'Cause it looks like you're looking for him." Stella levels me with one of her too-wise stares.

"If I was, it's only so we can say goodbye," I say, and swipe my purse off the table.

"He left early." Stella shrugs. "You're not going to see him."

"Too bad for us," I say airily, and gently swing her to the door with a wave of my hand.

"I think you like him."

My fingers clench on the doorknob. "Huh?"

"I do." Stella waits for me to open the door and strides through with all the confidence in the world. "It's easy to notice."

"Well, sure I like him." The heavy door slams shut behind us, and not only do I jolt, I squeak. Stella crosses her arms.

I'm being interrogated by a five-year-old.

"Nobody likes my dad, and you *like* him," Stella says. "You get all weird when he's around. And when he's not around."

"He's just—he's my boss." I can't believe I'm being forced to reason with a small child. "I respect him. That's different from liking him. We're getting along, so maybe that's what you see. Us being friendly."

Stella rolls her eyes as we take the elevator. "Just so you know, I'm fine with it. Because you're not trying to be my mommy. Ladies that dad brings around, they always try."

"Really?" I hit the button for the lobby. "You've met some of your dad's ... ladies?"

"Kinda, but not really. I'm not supposed to be around, or Daddy forgets I'm home. Or Patrice doesn't tell Daddy we're home. Then I see them. And sometimes they see me when I'm hiding in the hallway."

"Hang on." I'm close to hitting the emergency stop button so I can glean more information. "You're saying you've been in the house when there are ladies present?"

"It hasn't happened in a while." Stella looks down at her feet and I'm afraid she thinks I'm scolding her. "It used to happen a lot."

I parse through the facts. "And Patrice, she's been there, too? Did your dad know you guys were there?"

Stella shakes her head. "I ran away before he could see me. But sometimes the ladies see, and they try to talk to me and be all super-nice and gross. One lady told Daddy she saw me, and that's when they stopped coming around. Daddy had a stern talk with Patrice, too."

I'm confused, appalled and worried, all at the same time. Did Patrice set it up so she and Stella would be in the home? But why? Because Patrice is in love with Rex and wants to sabotage him? It reminds me of what else Patrice has done, like force Rex into suspicion about my past, all while appearing innocent and concerned.

"Oh, she's good," I mutter. "*Too* good."

I'm hoping, with an appeal to Rex, that Patrice can be out of Stella's life for good. I don't think any of this happened through coincidence. Manipulation is more like it. I'm tempted to confront her myself and ask just what it took for her to nose into my private life and think it was okay.

Then again, you nosed into Aesha's private life, no problem.

"Harper, you look mad. Did I do something wrong?"

"Not at all," I say as the elevator doors slide open into the lobby. "Thank you for telling me."

"And anyway." Stella continues, nonplussed, "You and Daddy can like each other. I don't know if I like you yet, but I don't *not* like you."

Her reasoning fosters a smile against my lips, which I stifle.

"Your daddy and I are just friends," I say, proud I sound believable. We head outside to the waiting car.

"Uh-huh." Stella slips into the back seat and I buckle her into her booster. "That's what the ladies say, too."

"Stella." I meet her, nose-to-nose, and cross my eyes and stick out my tongue. "I don't know where you get your information from, but I'm no lady."

To my utter astonishment and pleasure, Stella wheezes out what sounds close to a laugh in response.

I swear I could taste Rex with my coffee this morning.

The feel of him in my mouth—the ridges and softness—is a phantom memory that has my tongue constantly stroking against the back of my teeth. It's like, even if my brain is convinced it had to be a nighttime fantasy that never happened, my heart reminds me that *oh yes*, it happened.

And I swallowed.

I *never* swallow. It was the heat of the moment that did it. The smell of sex on him. The pleasure I gave and the notion of *my* control brought him to the edge, along with the want to take him all the way.

And it wasn't bad, really. Sort of creamy frosting, and then ... gone. Done.

Crashing back into reality shouldn't be allowed to taste so good.

I massage my temple, breaking out of my revere as I wait for Stella to exit her school. I'm standing near the crosswalk with the rest of the parents, as I always do, taking part in small talk with those around me but not really paying attention to how much I say "uh-huh," and "that's nice."

"Oh my Gosh, Harper, I'm so glad to see you here!"

I turn at the sound of the voice. "Oh, hey, uh—Andy's mom."

It's the woman from the playground, the one whose son was latching onto kids' ankles under the bridge. She's in the same beige coat but chose a wide-brimmed hat this time and oversized sunglasses. If I'm to be honest, she looks like she chooses her wardrobe from the pages of *Vogue*.

"That's right." Her smile stretches wide. "Stella hasn't come out yet?"

"Stella's the last to amble out," I say. "She likes to pack up her stuff just right."

"Type A personality." The woman sidles up to me, crossing her arms and nodding. "Who do you think she takes after? Her mom or dad?"

The woman studies me like I'm about to fail or pass a test. I massage the back of my neck as a cover for searching around, hoping another nanny's nearby to strike up a conversation with. All nannies and parents seem to have dissipated into the line of trees on the crosswalk. As soon as the kids are picked up, they disperse.

Enough time has passed that if I don't say something, I'll look weird for not answering what seems to be a simple question. "Uh, I'd say her dad."

"Oh, yeah?" The woman glances over at the open doors. Stella has yet to come through them, but I'm not worried. She straggles behind.

"It's funny," she says. "Most daughters take after their mothers."

"Do you have a daughter besides a son?" I snap. Her statement hits me in all the wrong places, both for my and Stella's sake. I have to work to gentle my tone. "I mean, that's the first time I've heard that."

The woman turns back to me. "Well, I—"

"Stella!" I wave as soon as I see her hovering in the doorframe, her teacher not far behind. "Hey, slowpoke."

Stella frowns, but it freezes halfway when she notices who's beside me.

"Go on, Stella," the teacher, Miss Sammy, urges. "Harper's right there."

But Stella doesn't move from the top of the small staircase. "Andy's not here."

I purse my lips. "Stella, c'mon. It's starting to get cold. I've got some hot chocolate in the car."

That wasn't the way I wanted to introduce the treat, but the lady beside me is making things awkward, Stella is doing her best interpretation of a stone statue for unknown reasons, and my head is still reeling from pleasuring Rex. So yes, the chocolate idea could be just as much for me as it is for Stella.

"Are you sure that's good for her?" the woman asks me.

"No, but that's the point of a surprise treat," I say, then move to take up the space between Stella and me. I hold out my hand, knowing Stella won't take it but offering it nonetheless. "Come on, before it gets cold and the whipped cream goes all gross."

"Stella's right," Miss Sammy says, a perplexed cock to her brow as she regards the other woman. "Andy left a while ago with his nanny." She stares harder at the woman. "I assumed you were with Harper and Stella."

"Oh, I am." The woman nods.

"You are?" I ask, at the same time Stella adds, "No, you're not."

The woman's lips pry apart. Another clownish smile forms across her face. She takes off her sunglasses and hat, then bends down, hands on her knees, and says to Stella, "Honey, don't you recognize me?"

A *whoosh* of denial drowns my airways at the same time my feet hit pavement and I hook Stella by the elbow. "We're leaving. Now."

"Harper—ow. That hurts," Stella says.

Stella struggles, but only somewhat, as I half stumble, half drag her to our waiting car.

"Stella," the woman tries again. "I'm your mo—"

I whirl, pushing Stella behind me and say to the woman through a clenched jaw, "Don't. You. Dare."

The woman's—Aesha, she *has* to be Aesha—smile falls, and is replaced by cool disdain as she straightens. "Stella has a right to know who I am."

I say, through adrenaline-chattering teeth, "Take it up with Rex," then usher Stella into the backseat.

Stella goes quiet and doesn't argue when I buckle her in and shut the passenger door a little too hard. I stumble around to my side, glancing at Aesha, who isn't moving. Just standing there watching, her hat and glasses clutched between her hands.

"Should I call the police?" Miss Sammy calls from her perch.

I wave her off, finding no words as I slide into the backseat. What do I say? I have to protect Stella, that's all I know. And I must get her as far away from Aesha as possible. At least until there's more understanding of what's going on.

Aesha remains where she is as we pull away from the curb. I hand Stella her hot chocolate while staring out the rear window, wondering what the hell this woman is trying to prove.

And how badly she wants her family back.

CHAPTER 33

Rex

YOU NEED TO COME HOME. Stella's fine, but I need to talk to you about something.

I swipe Harper's message off the screen and shove my phone into my pocket. Break's over, and I'm expected to finish "Forbidden Cherry" in time for it to be put on our next album.

"Ready for the verse?" Easton asks behind me, seated behind his drum kit.

I take the guitar pick out of my mouth and test my strings. "Let's do it."

Focusing on the song is important. Being present with my band is even more of a priority. Harper wants to talk because she gave me head last night. That's the long and short of it. My plan is to avoid her until I can figure out why I let it happen, and why the *fuck* I want it to happen again. Actually, I just want more. More of her mouth, more of her skin, more of me on top of her...

I sneer into the studio mike before I open my mouth to sing, more annoyed by my thoughts than prepared to solve them. Therefore, I sing it out.

The producers and sound techs are on the other side of the

glass, pushing buttons and flicking switches on their mixing boards, eyes on their computers more than on us as my voice and our music turns into digital audio bars for their dissection.

We finish, Mason coughing and searching for his tea and Wyn pressing out aimless notes on his keyboard.

When did we become so silent after a song?

I look to Easton. He spins his drumsticks, but my attention catches his. East is the most comfortable in the silence, but through his stare I can tell he isn't impressed with the way the band is communicating, either.

Maybe we need a refresher. A getaway. Renting a mansion upstate or something, so we can rediscover to our brotherhood and what came before our fame—

"You know what?" I say to the room. All eyes turn to me, but my phone buzzes hard in my pocket. And insistent. I ignore it.

"I think we need some time." I continue. "All four of us"—my phone goes off again—"Damn it. One sec."

"Some time?" Mase echoes as he set his guitar aside.

"Yeah, what do you mean by that, Rex?" Wyn asks. "You want us to peace out from each other?"

"Like take a break?" Easton asks, rising predatorily from his seat.

These questions all happen in the span it takes to pull out my phone and answer it. I hold up a finger to them. "No, that's not— Harper? What's good, I'm kinda in the middle of something, and—"

"Did you get my text?" Harper cuts in. "You need to come home."

"It's my next stop." I lower my voice and turn away from the guys. "But I have to finish what's going on here first."

"No, you don't."

I frown. "Harper, I get that what happened last night needs to be addressed, but there's—"

"It's not about that. Well—yes, we should talk about it, but Aesha came to Stella's school today."

"Good, so when I get home—" I pause. Then roar, "*What?*"

"Aesha. At Stella's school."

"That's not possible." I spit the words out.

"Then some other woman is posing as Aesha and trying to get Stella's attention." Harper sounds exasperated. "Either way, come home, Rex. I don't know if she will show up here next."

"She better fucking not," I grind out. "I'll be right there."

"Okay, drop a bomb on us," Mason says as I click off from Harper. "And then bounce."

"There's no bomb," I say. "Scratch that—there is. Aesha's back."

All three boys of mine—guys who've been there through it all—stiffen.

"The fuck?" Mason says.

"How?" Wyn asks. "I thought you had that chick on lock. Payments to California or some shit."

"So did I," I mumble. "I have to go. She's already gone after Stella."

"Go." Easton motions for me to leave. "We'll talk later."

"Yeah, 'cause what you said isn't something we can ignore," Mason says. "But we can sure as shit put it aside while you deal with your baby mama."

Even that term, as innocuous and distanced as it is from the word *family*, bothers me in places I wish I could scratch.

"I don't want the band to break up," I say as I shove my guitar in its case. Wyn stops me with a hand.

"We got your instrument, bro. Go on ahead," he says.

"And maybe," Easton adds, "You have a point. We could use a break."

"What?" I reel on him, but my brain is soaked, swelling with stress and yes, fear, over Aesha, the fate of Nocturne Court, Harper—I'm afraid I'm gonna blow. "You're not thinking straight, East."

He levels me with a flat look. "Neither are you. Nor have you been. We need some serious discussion, but not before you protect your daughter first."

My daughter. Stella.

The thought of my kid going anywhere, with anyone, and my not being there forces my face numb. I swipe my jacket from a chair and, ignoring Spinner's babbling on the mike through the two-way glass, I exit the recording room.

Storming through the hallway, my expression contorts at the idea that my band wants to separate. It's a realization I banish to dark recesses of my mind, where Aesha once lay.

Before she somehow escaped.

"Where is she?" I shout as I shove the door to my penthouse open. "Is she here?"

Harper rushes into the foyer, shushing me. "No, and Stella's in the other room watching *Peppa Pig*, but if she hears you roaring, she'll be out here in a second wondering why her daddy sounds so angry."

I breathe out hard, despite my chest wanting to explode. "I'm fine. I'm calm."

Harper's hands have landed on my biceps, and there they stay, until she glances down and jerks them back. "I made us some coffee. Let's go sit."

I follow her into the kitchen, peering into Stella's wing on the way and catching a glimpse of her sitting on one of her over-stuffed pink chairs and watching something on her tablet. Her hand reaches down for some popcorn as I finish passing by.

"She's okay?" I ask Harper's back. "Stella?"

Harper nods, heading to the carafe and pouring us two mugs as I head to the kitchen table but don't sit down. I can't sit.

"Stella was weirded out by the woman, but I think I stopped

any sort of confession from getting out," Harper says as she spins to the fridge for some cream. Almost on instinct, she leaves my coffee the way I like it and hands the mug over before she pours a gallon of cream in hers.

Harper takes a seat, and since I don't want to lord over her with my size *and* anger, I follow suit.

"I don't know if I can stop it the next time," she murmurs before taking a sip, but her eyes are on me over the rim.

Normally her stare is unsteady when it meets mine. Nervous and twitchy. In this moment, she's level, calm and searching. She's on my side. Harper will do whatever I need. It forces me to look away, a reaction I don't enjoy gaining.

I set my mug on the table. "There won't be a next time. I called my lawyers on the way here. I've never asked for it, because I've never needed to, but an agreement is being created for her to give up her maternal rights. And if that doesn't work, we're taking it to the courts."

"An agreement? Involving what?"

"Money."

"Like … you're going to pay her off?"

I respond with a single nod. "Aesha'll take a lump sum payment."

"Are you sure about that?"

"It's what she's wanted all these years. Instead of doing that, I gave her restricted income. Paying her bills, her rent, utilities. I wanted to keep her safe from her addiction. But she's come here, into my territory, breaking into *my* daughter's safe space to detonate my child's life as she knows it, for what? A threat? A power move?"

"Could she want to be a part of Stella's life?" Harper ventures. "Rex, Aesha didn't look—I mean, she seemed sober."

"I don't care how she seemed," I snap, then temper as soon as I register Harper's surprised jump. "In three years, Aesha has never tried to know Stella. Even before that, Aesha treated our baby like she was a chore, something to get through until she could have more pills. And need I remind you, she almost killed Stella—"

"I know." Harper raises her hand in surrender. "I would never try to defend the actions of a woman I have no history with. I'm only coming from the experience of an abandoned child." She takes a breath, her attention skittering to the side. "Rex, if my father ever did an about-face ... if he ever showed an inkling of interest, especially when I was young, I would've jumped at the chance to be in his life. I would've felt whole."

"Harper." Unable to resist, I lay my hand on hers on the table. "It's for that precise reason I will never do that to Stella."

Harper lifts her eyes to mine.

"It's too uncertain," I say, and lower my head closer to hers. "I can't take that chance with my daughter's heart. Aesha may want to connect, for now. But odds are, she wants to threaten me for more cash. She wants to bring our daughter into the middle to make that threat irredeemable. If Stella ever found out her mother was here, not to see her but to gain more currency, it would break her." After a beat, I say, "Just as it would break you."

Nodding, Harper's fingers clench under my hands. "I wish love weren't so blind."

Angling my chin, I caress the side of her face with my fingers. Amazing, how in a time of such turmoil and hatred, Harper softens me. She drifts into my touch.

"If there were even an inkling Aesha wanted to make it work," I say, "I'd hear her out. I want a mother for Stella more than anything. I just don't think it's the woman who birthed her."

"As long as you're sure," Harper responds.

Frowning, I draw away, the pads of my fingers feeling cool where they once touched Harper's skin. "I must talk to her. For myself. To be sure."

A sliver of light in Harper's eyes seems to flicker out, but her words betray her expression. "I think that's wise. Stella never has to know."

I glance behind me, my mind blueprinting my home despite the walls between my daughter and me, and I picture her in her room, snacking, watching a show, innocent and ignorant.

How long can I keep her that way?

Harper's hand finds my forearm. "It'll be okay."

I turn back to her with newfound resolve. "It will. Once I get that woman to sign her rights away, it will be just peachy."

I don't glance down at Harper's expression when I stand and what might be written across it. She doesn't empathize. Or maybe she does, but it's with the wrong side now.

"I can't walk in my daughter's shoes," I say to her. "Because I must remain a parent. Always. And my role is to protect her heart for as long as I can. Empathizing with Stella's situation and seeing her mother through her eyes will not help me do that. I hope you can understand." I swallow, then grit out, "Your opinion matters, Harper. And I'd hate for you to be disappointed in me."

I don't wait for her response. She doesn't need to. Instead, I leave her behind, with my cooling coffee for company.

CHAPTER 34

Harper

I DO one last check-in on Stella, curled up under her covers, the deep magenta of her nightlight haloing her curls in a neon pink glow.

It took three reads of her *Don't Bring Your Dragon to Dinner* book before she went to sleep, two by me and the last by Rex, his husky, baritone voice lulling her to slumber better than any of my high-pitched character voices ever could.

Around Stella, Rex and I assume our respective positions, our bodies and minds attuned to one thing—keeping a child safe and happy. There's no further mention of Aesha's looming presence or our unavoidable libidos. Rex nodded his good night to me as he unfurled his large body from Stella's bed. I nodded back as he left, then tucked Stella in.

And that's that.

The mere remembrance of how stiff and awkward we've become has me rolling my shoulders back as I shut the door to my room, craving a hot shower to massage some stress-filled shivers out of my skin.

And prevent Rex from sinking into my bones.

Whatever we were, whatever we're becoming, can't happen now. Aesha's in town. Rex is determined to cut her out, but maybe she's changed. Maybe Aesha's different and willing to be a mother. In which case … she belongs in this life a lot more than I do. She has more skin in the game than I ever will.

Despair tugs at my soul, and I scrunch my eyes shut, hoping a forced blackout will make the feeling go away.

The idea of a shower invigorates me and I step into the attached bathroom and twist the shower faucet. Patrice left a few toiletries behind, notably some creamy, sparkly, extra fancy orange vanilla body wash which I plan to use.

But the thought of her name brings on a sourness in complete contrast to the citrusy-sweet scent. Patrice wants me out of here so she can get back in. I'm confident she won't, now that Rex knows the truth. It's what I *don't* know that gives me pause on what my position is with Rex—both personally and professionally.

Did Rex ever sleep with Patrice?

It's a question I'm not sure I want to ask. I don't want to hear the answer.

I strip off my shirt and step out of my pants, then pull out my hair tie and give my short hair a tussle. Steam rises from behind the shower curtain, and I push it aside to pick up the body wash and toss it into the small trash bin by the toilet. I'll stick to my usual Dove soap.

One foot is in the bath when I hear my bedroom door creak open. I've left the bathroom door ajar and peer around the frame.

"Stella, you okay?"

My mouth goes dry at the shadow in my bedroom doorway. It's much too big to be Stella. To broad, too sharp, too strong … too overwhelming.

I press my lips shut long enough to accumulate the saliva needed to whisper, "Rex?"

Rex steps into the sliver of light caused by the single lamp on my nightstand. He's shirtless. His jeans ride low on his hips, flashing the elastic band of his briefs. More importantly—flashing the V of his hips.

In such low light, I shouldn't register the flare of his pupils or the depth of his stare as he focuses below my face ... below my collarbone.

I let out a squeak and cover my bare breasts. In a panic, I realize my privates are exposed too and rush out of view, back into the bathroom.

"Don't," he says.

Hands still on my chest, I say, through dry lips, "Don't what?"

"Run away." Rex's voice is husky, unusual in its unhurried, arcing tone.

I lean against the wall separating us, near the bathroom door, head resting against the plaster. "W-what are you doing here, Rex?"

"I can't sleep."

His voice sounds closer, like he's rounded my bed and stands near the open bathroom door. Inches away.

"It's been a hard day," I say. "For both of us. Let me get dressed and we can sit on the couch and talk—"

"No."

Rex's body shadows mine as he steps in, the glaring, halogen lights of the bathroom adding to the wild sheen of his stare.

I feel encompassed by him. Fearful yet ... turned on.

"Rex," I breathe out, and yank a towel from the rod. I cover myself.

The rush of the shower's spray acts like a noisy balm against the furious silence between us, but I keep my chin up.

"Aesha's return has nothing to do with this," Rex says, though his lips barely move. He's hardly focused on what he's saying. Only on what he's seeing.

"It has everything to do with it," I say. "You're here because your emotions are high. You're trapped in anxiety, and the only way you know how to release it is to—"

"Fuck you blind?" Rex cocks his head.

"I—" *Oh, dear.* A tingling sensation rises from my core. "It's not right. Please don't take your frustration out on me."

"Even if I can turn it into ecstasy? For both of us? Even if I can hold you against this wall and do things to you a thousand times more pleasurable than the last time I had you pressed against something hard?"

I swallow. It does nothing to relieve the swell. But I forge on. This is my heart he's playing with, despite his determination to own my body.

"I see the look in your eyes when you talk about her. Aesha. She broke you, Rex." I push off the wall, my grip tight against the towel. "But she also mended you by giving you a daughter. I-I can't compete with that kind of connection. I can't be the outlet you use to *break* that kind of connection."

Rex shakes his head in one, slow arc. "You have it wrong, Harper. I'm not using you to get over Aesha, because I am over her, I can assure you of that. And I have no fear she will take away my child. She'd have better luck wrestling a tiger. I'm here because I want you. Plain and simple. I want your body. I want to be inside you. I don't want you to leave."

"I'm not planning to go anywhere," I say. Though, after this, I'm not sure it's appropriate I stay. The thought lights up an alert in my head. "If we do this, Rex, it changes everything. You're right— maybe I can't stay. If we have sex, if we cross that line, I won't be your nanny anymore. I'll be—"

"You'll still be mine."

His statement hardens my jaw, despite the flutter it brings to my heart. "I'm not property. Not yours or anyone's."

Rex's brow furrows. For the first time, he looks away. But just as fast, he's back, a calloused thumb hooked under my chin. "I do not—will never—consider you to be property. Especially after what you've been through, how your father made you feel. I want you. I know it will change us—I know it could ruin us, but fuck, Harper, I can't keep seeing you every day and not know how you taste. How you feel. We're beyond professional. You've licked, sucked and tasted me."

My resulting blush is fire on my cheeks, but I don't cover it. I don't stop falling into his eyes.

"It's only fair I taste you, too," he murmurs.

"But Stella—"

"Don't." He lays a finger against my lips. "Tonight needs to be just the two of us. No consequences, no one else. Just us. Tell me you feel it too, Harper."

God. Yes, I do. Without hesitation, my grip loosens on my towel.

"Tell me you want me as much as I want you," he continues.

Since the first day I crossed over your threshold, wet in all the wrong places.

"Tell me..." he leans closer. "You want my mouth on you."

The sound of the shower rises in my ears. The heat of the small bathroom prickles against my skin, but its temperature is nothing compared to what rages inside.

I want him.

I want to feel him inside me.

"I want to forget everything but you," I whisper before his mouth covers mine, and he presses me flat against the wall.

Rex's tongue is liquid fire, his hands hard and calloused as he pulls mine away from my body and holds them above my head, his fingers tangling.

I rise on my toes to meet his mouth better. Harder. I'm hungry, un-sated, and he's the entrée I've been craving for perhaps my entire life.

Rex releases my hands and pulls at his belt, then his jeans. He steps out of his briefs, naked and untamed, and I hurry to have him pressed against me again, to feel the ridges of muscle against the suppleness of my stomach and breasts.

Instead, he takes my hand, leading me into the shower, a half-smile on his face. My stomach shimmies at the idea that my first time with this man will involve shower sex, but I give nothing away as I follow him in.

The shower's spray hits his back. He can barely fit in the small bath, and I don't have time to consider if we both can because once I join him, Rex lifts me by the thighs and presses me against the tile wall, nothing but his rigid shaft between us, almost spanning the entire length of my stomach.

Rex devours my lips, now that we're at eye level. I meet him all the way, arms wrapped around his neck. He begins a rhythm, shifting himself to tease against my clit, using an unhurried up-and-down motion that is more punishingly cruel than the instant gratification I want.

"Rex," I moan. "Get inside me. Now."

I feel his smile before he draws back enough to say, "Not before I get my taste."

Rex untangles my legs from his hips, lowering me gently but directing one of my legs to stay on the lip of the tub. He bends down. My eyes widen at the sight of him in his knees.

The spray dampens his hair and creates dots of dew on his shoulders. The muscles and tendons underneath his tanned skin undulate as he shifts and coaxes my legs farther apart.

I say nothing. I'm speechless. I'm terrified, yet the most intimate part of me is swelling larger than my heart at the thought of receiving the pleasure of his lips and tongue.

At the ... oh *yes*, at the *feeling* of it all.

Rex's tongue strokes up, around, circles, and my head falls back, my eyes close, and the only thing I focus on is the sense of him, his exploration.

My fingers dig into his wet hair, urging him closer, deeper. I can't for the life of me remember *why* I hesitated about this or why I thought this was a bad idea.

This is paradise.

He groans, nips lightly, and goosebumps trail down my inner thighs despite the steam. My hips circle where he guides. Rex palms my ass and pushes me closer so he can tongue deeper. I ride his mouth like it's a sex toy made just for me, and I'm making sounds I've never made but will be sure to be embarrassed about later but *who the fuck cares because—*

"Rex—" I groan through my tightened jaw.

His encouraging moan vibrates inside me, bringing me closer.

"Rex, I'm—"

I don't finish my sentence. The pleasure rushes through my body, beginning where Rex plays, an instrumental song that crests from my center all the way through to my dancing fingers and toes. He's singing to me, a song written only for us, a private lullaby that rings through my veins.

I melt like the candle wax that I am, pliable and hot to his touch. It's only his strength that keeps me upright. Only him as he rises, his mouth reddened by the erotic massage, but the tilt of his lips says we're nowhere near done.

"You're mine for tonight," he says, then lifts and wraps me around him like I weigh as much as his guitar. "Now I want to see if you feel as sweet and addictive as you taste."

When he thrusts inside me, I don't register my own gasp.

All I consider is that I never knew a single feeling could be met with such blinding sparkle.

CHAPTER 35

Rex

We move to the bed, the feather down of her comforter doing nothing to soften my dick.

"I need to fuck you again." I groan, pulling Harper on top of me, my palms scraping from her bare thighs to her hips.

Her pussy cups my shaft, and she grinds against it as it's pressed against my stomach, but she won't allow entry.

"Harper…"

I hate how my voice sounds, the way my Adam's apple bobs, as Harper grapples for her version of control. But she's an addiction. One that's blinding and deletes all my other priorities. Worries. Stresses.

"What are you trying to forget?" Harper asks above me.

I crack an eye open. "Nothing. All I want to think about is you."

She lifts enough to wrap a hand around my cock, damp from her juices, and positions it near her entrance. I raise my hips, but still, she denies access.

Her eyes are heavy-lidded. "I'm using you to forget, too."

I grit my teeth. *Fine.* If Harper wants to play this game, I'll take part, so long as I get to sink into her at the finish line. "What is it you're trying to forget as you fuck me?"

"You have it the wrong way around," she pants. The wait is

getting to her, too. "Fucking you *allows* me to forget. I feel nothing but you. Want nothing but the fullness of your dick."

I growl and thrust against her palm, trying to sneak in.

"It helps me remember that life isn't a list of disappointments and losses," she says. "There's pleasure in it, too. Fleeting, but there."

Her words hit too close. They mean enough that my jaw locks. I grip her wrist and get her hand out of the way so I can drive into her, pumping, pounding, and give her the memory loss she's asking for.

I'm asking for it.

Harper yelps with surprise and ecstasy the moment I take her, gripping my hands on her hips as she rides me wildly.

I don't allow myself to come until she does, watching her, those gorgeous coastal eyes of hers flashing bright, then fading, as she slows down from the wave of orgasm, my cock still inside her.

"Not yet," I say, and flip us around until I'm on top, driving into her tightness, the slick sheath of her causing temporary blindness.

I groan into her neck, dragging my teeth down her sensitive skin, once I finish. She clutches my shoulders like they're some kind of counterpoint to our lust, and I think, *I need to fuck you again.*

"Rex," she says, her voice mostly dragged out air. "What's wrong?"

Lifting my head from the sweet scent of her neck, I don't meet her gaze as I roll off. "Unless you think wanting to screw you again, and again, and again, is wrong, then there's nothing to worry about."

"You're driving into me like I'm the last female on Earth before the final Armageddon," she says beside me.

I close my eyes. "There's a lot on my mind. You're helping me—"

"Forget." A sad smile follows the word.

She then props herself up on her elbow. "What are you afraid of?"

This time, my groan has no sexual component. "Harper, have I ever told you I hate pillow talk?"

"No, because we haven't had sex until now."

"Right." I rub at my eyes. "I'm not afraid of anything."

"Hm." She falls back against her pillow.

I squint at her through my fingers. "What?"

Harper shrugs. "Everybody's afraid of something. Me? I'm afraid of family."

A chuckle escapes. I repeat, with different meaning, "What?"

"I've never had one. Not a complete one, anyway. I wasn't even *made* through one. Who's to say I won't screw up any chance I have at making one of my own?"

"You seriously think that?"

"I do. It's why I nanny. I get to see what true families look like."

I frown up at the ceiling and at the complete innocence of her statement. *She's so goddamned young sometimes.* "Is there even such a thing?"

"To me there is."

"Well, then you might've chosen the wrong case study. Stella and I—me, mostly—we're pretty fucked up in our own right. I'm barely a father to her."

I try to see it from Harper's perspective. To be created in a lab by scientists and doctors through anonymous donors, then inserted into a surrogate stranger, all people Harper will never meet, has to do something to the child's psyche.

No wonder Harper's picture of a perfect family is so imaginary.

"The medical advances and scientific breakthroughs of our time are mind-blowing," I say. "To come into this world the way you have … I won't insult you by trying to sympathize. However, to have that kind of cold and sterile start perpetrated by your living father, that is unforgivable." Rage builds at the thought. "It's one thing to be created because for some reason or another, your fathers couldn't do it naturally and wanted a baby. But to transfer that kind of loveless environment over to a child instead of nurture her..." My upper lip curls. "Despicable."

To my surprise, Harper isn't repelled by my frankness. Her mouth curves in the dark. "You're more of a father than you give yourself credit for."

I laugh, but it's hollow. "Oh, yeah?"

"You don't see what I see. Yes, you're gruff. Rude. Brutally strict—"

"Great start."

"But the love you have for that little girl is *fierce*," Harper continues. "If I had even a sliver of—never mind. What I want to say is, give yourself some credit. Day by day, Stella gains something from you. Whether it's going to your concert for the first time or eating pancakes with you, it's those small things that matter. Not the grand meaning of the word *father*. You should remember that."

"Mm." Her words have hit home, but I don't let it show. It feels good to be validated, even if it might be because of the flush of multiple fucks and orgasms instead of the truth. "Maybe take your own advice, Miss Mei, and avoid the grand meaning of *family*. Love, in all its forms, is never perfect."

Harper rolls to face me, cupping my cheek. "Maybe we both need to grow out of our fears."

The unexpected, affectionate contact is jarring—unstoppable— yet I sever it by pulling her hand away. We can't be this. I'm no family man.

She pulls her hand back to her chest, under the covers she's thrown over herself.

I dip my hand under those same covers, finding her soft thigh and playfully drifting toward her center.

"Rex..." she says to the ceiling, but writhes against my touch. "We're in the middle of a meaningful conversation..."

I move to suck her nape as my fingers find their target and sink in.

Her sigh flutters against my ear. She says, before she bends to my will, "Don't stop."

We don't sleep together.

Not in the same bed.

I ravish Harper in all the ways I craved, thinking if she doesn't always like it dirty then I'll also give her slow and sexy. Turns out, she desires both.

The intention behind showing up at her bedroom door was to get her out of me. The want and the need. Too much flies around my head, and to get rid of one issue would realistically open up space for the others to resolve.

That's not what happened.

As soon as I hear Harper's light snores, her body reddened and malleable from my ravenous use, I slip out from under the covers, careful not to disturb her as I hook my clothes from the bathroom floor and sneak out.

Sneak out might not be the right term, since it's my home, but I don't want to wake her. I can't handle the inevitable talk that will break down our actions and see where we go from here. My promise to her was a night without consequence, a crucial meet-up of our bodies to satisfy the endless salivating we seem to do over each other. It was supposed to end here.

I shut her door with a quiet click and pad out into the hallway, then the kitchen where I crack open a beer and drink the entire bottle while standing in front of the fridge.

With a groan, and a covered belch, I shut the fridge door and lean my forehead against it.

Instead of getting Harper out of my system, her taste, her scent, her moans and her mind, have all creeped in with the satisfaction of claiming their territory within my chest.

CHAPTER 36

Rex

"SO, I'M NOT A FAMILY LAWYER."

Taryn's voice comes through on my phone as I lean back against the kitchen counter the following morning. Harper got Stella off to school before I'd even roused awake.

Stella left a cute note on the table saying **BYE DADDY HAV A GOD DAY**, written in black crayon only. Just as I'm worrying the kid doesn't want enough color in her life, I flip the page over to see a multi-colored heart with an arrow pointing to the words underneath spelling out, **HARPR MADE ME DRAW THIS**.

"But," Taryn continues, "I can hook you up with a very good one."

"That'd be great," I say.

After I gave Taryn all the facts of Aesha's return—and Easton's fiancé demands *details*—Taryn stated her plans to get a full breakdown from Harper and what she witnessed and then take it to the Family Law department of her top-level firm. I have lawyers, but none who specialize in family matters.

"To be frank, Aesha Shirapova doesn't have a leg to stand on," Taryn says. I wince at her unintended reference to what led to Aesha's downfall in the first place. "She's been gone for three years with no contact with her daughter. She's a drug addict. She's unre-liable. On paper, she's unfit to be a mother."

"My thoughts exactly." I scrub at my face. "I sense a *but* here, Taryn."

She sighs. "New York favors the mother in custody cases. And I have to say, if she's turned herself around and can prove stable living conditions as well as sobriety, she could get her custody restored."

"Despite fucking off for three years?"

"Yes. Rex…"

I swallow a groan. "Just say what you want to say, Taryn."

"I … look, as someone who's been in a very similar situation, I feel I can offer unsolicited advice. Are you sure this is the way you want to go? If Aesha proves she's fit, if she wants to be a part of Stella's life—"

"She doesn't. She wants money. She's always wanted money."

"I don't know, But it's your decision. You know her best."

"You're damned right I do."

"What if she's turned her life around?" Taryn persists. "Think about this. It could change everything."

I ignore the pit forming in my gut. "Would it have changed it for you? Knowing what your ex has done? Especially to your own kid?"

Taryn hesitates and I feel a second of guilt for throwing her terrible past in her face.

"I apologize for that," I say. "This is a sensitive topic, and if there's any inkling that Stella could be taken away—"

"My firm will make sure that doesn't happen," Taryn says. "This is not about giving Stella's mother full custody. It's about allowing her—a reformed, repentant her—back into Stella's life. And maybe avoiding the court system if you can."

I frown and stare out my windows at the vast expanse of Manhattan. It feels about as wide open and uncertain as my daughter's future right about now.

"There's a saying," Taryn continues. "Lawyers should be hired for three reasons only—money, property, and bad decisions. Dragging children and families through the courts, with its outdated laws and slow processing times ... well, there's a reason I don't do family law cases, Rex."

I grunt because she's right. Stella will never be reduced to property. I resolve to never make her feel that way, especially after hearing Harper's experience.

"The last thing I want to do is traumatize Stella," I say. "It's what I'm trying to avoid at all costs by protecting her from whatever Aesha has up her sleeve."

"I understand all that you're saying," Taryn says. "But sometimes you only see things as black or white—"

"Hey, now."

"I'm sorry, Rex, but you do. I'm only recommending that you have all the facts first. Maybe listen to what Aesha has to say before any lawyers get involved."

"Are you telling me that as my lawyer or my friend?"

"As your friend," Taryn says. "Because any good lawyer will shred this woman to bits, and I need to make sure you want that."

Damn it. My jaw goes tight. I should have images of the Aesha that left me bursting through my head at Taryn's warning. The underweight, stringy haired, red-faced, angry woman who cared about nothing but her next fix. Who screamed for it and trashed our apartment. Who stole what little money I was making and put it towards street Oxy instead of baby food.

Instead, I see the Aesha I met, the one glowing in the spotlight, her body bending and arcing with a graceful sixth sense. Her smile. Her long brown hair that would get caught between us in the wind when we kissed or in bed when we fucked.

I press my forefinger and thumb to the bridge of my nose, fighting off an incoming headache. "Despite what she's done," I say to Taryn, "I don't want to make things worse for her. I'll ... fuck. I guess I'll talk to her."

I sense Taryn's sad smile on the other end. "It's not easy being a parent, is it?"

"Not in any way that makes any fucking sense," I say. "Thanks, T. I appreciate your input."

"Any time. And hey, one more thing."

I stifle a groan, since it's rare for Taryn and me to engage in small talk.

"You should talk to East," she says.

My head falls back to stare at the ceiling. "Yeah. We have some issues to clear up."

"That black and white vision I said you have? I think it's applying to more than you know. Like the band. It's clear to me that you don't want to break up Nocturne Court, but that's coming from the perspective of a person who's been knee deep in shit and knows what real issues are. I'm not sure if the guys comprehend it as well as I do, especially if you don't open up to them."

"Thank you, therapist T. I'll keep that in mind."

"You know I'm right."

"Yeah." I exhale. "I'll talk to them, too."

"And Harper."

"And—" I pause. "Come again?"

"Harper," Taryn repeats. "Pretty sure you two need to have a talk as well."

"Seems like I'm gonna be on a talking tour," I say.

"It's your own damned fault," Taryn says. "Start seeing in the gray, Sloane."

"How'd you—"

But I'm talking to dead air.

Taryn, in all her cleverness, has left me to my own decisions.

And I'm not nearly as wise.

I TOOK Stella out of the house extra early and to a local diner for breakfast.

Technically, it's against the rules of her Dossier, but after a night like last night, I doubt Rex will go after me for bending them.

Plus, I made Stella get milk in addition to her chocolate chip pancakes while I mainlined caffeine, so she isn't without nutrients.

It would've been too awkward to greet Rex this morning, especially while I still ached in forbidden places. As a gesture of peace, however, I had Stella leave him a note from us in hopes he didn't think I was avoiding him.

Which I am.

But it's for the opposite reason than what he probably thinks.

Once Stella and I finish our stack, I pay the check and drop her off at her school, casting a wide visual net for any sign of Aesha. I don't see her and I want to ask Rex what his plans are. I remind myself it's none of my business what he decides, despite having him retain the type of knowledge about me very few men have acquired mere hours ago.

Once Stella is safely inside with her teacher, I wave off Duncan the driver, choosing to walk for a while on this crisp fall day before getting back to the penthouse.

The TriBeCa streets are crowded this morning with strollers, dogs on leashes (or also in strollers), and early morning commuters getting their caffeine on before heading to the modern business lofts in one of the most expensive areas in the city.

Being the pro pedestrian that I am, I dodge oncoming people traffic with my head down, thumbing through my phone until I reach who I want, then bluetooth the call to the wireless buds in my ears.

"Hey," Taryn says.

"I should've stayed this morning," I blurt out.

"You did what instinct told you to do. And that was to get the fuck out of there until you got your head on straight."

I'd low-key texted Taryn on the ride to Stella's school, confessing everything and hopelessly whining about my lack of judgment when faced with the hottest man alive. Naked.

"I should've sat down with him this morning and had a mature discussion like a responsible human being." I sigh, eyes on the concrete horizon as I hold the phone near my mouth and stop at a light. "What have I done? It was bad enough we were groping each other, but now ... now there's no going back."

"You did what you were meant to. It was only a matter of time between the two of you, nanny or no nanny. You've been attracted to him from the very beginning. Now, are you sated?"

"Not nearly enough."

I've merely had a taste of that man, and my hunger for more surprises even me. Stroking his pecs in the shadows, clutching his arms, dragging my nails down his back as he entered me, then slid out, then entered, excruciatingly slowly, then rapidly climbing and reaching and pounding and ... *Whew.*

Taryn chuckles. She must read my thoughts.

"If it's any consolation," she says, "I talked to him this morning, too."

"You *what*?"

Cars have cleared the intersection and a man behind me

mumbles, "Take your sweet-ass time," as he walks around me. I get a move on, but my attention's glued to my phone. "What do you mean you talked to him?"

"Not entirely about you, stop fretting and scaring the yummy mummies around you. It was about Stella's mother."

I pull my lower lip out from the clench of my teeth. "Do you know what he's going to do?"

"I know enough that you should talk to him," Taryn responds. "Now that you've gotten coffee, pancakes, fresh air and a clear perspective into your system."

"Stop talking like you know me."

"I think it's time you had a real conversation with him. You've earned that much."

I exhale. "Yeah. I'm just not sure where I stand."

"You stand next to two people you care very much about. Stella and Rex. Start there."

I halt in the middle of the sidewalk, pissing off the man who's fallen behind me again. "Wait. You said *entirely*."

"Huh? Harp, I really gotta go. I'm at the office and Yang's already up my ass—"

"You said entirely," I repeat. "And that your conversation with Rex wasn't *entirely* about me. Does that mean there *was* something said about me?"

"Girl, I am not the net between your and Rex's tennis match. Go to the source. Get your answers. They may not be as dire as you think."

"So you do know something."

"Only that the two of you have more in common than you're willing to admit," she retorts. "And that *maybe*, if either of you would get your stupid ostrich heads out of the sand, you'd see the support being offered right in front of your faces."

My brows pinch together. "You honestly think Rex needs or wants my support during complicated custody issues with his daughter?"

"*Yes*, you dolt. And vice versa."

I scoff. "I'm fine. There's nothing in my life that requires support beams. I don't need—"

"Bye, Harper. Godspeed. Love you."

"But I'm not—"

Click. Dead air.

Taryn's doled out her advice and has left me to my own devices.

"Thank God you can fucking walk again without your phone," the man says as he darts by.

I flip him the bird, but he doesn't bother to glance back.

Stuffing my phone and my hands in my denim jacket pockets, I head back the way I came.

To Rex.

If I'm to be honest, I'm not sure if I've ever left him.

CHAPTER 38

Rex

A CORNER, hole in the wall, hipster coffee shop is my safe space.

There are about four tables and one long bench towards the back, low lighting, and the calm, never-ending sound of a milk steamer as patrons come in and order their caffeine hit, but don't stay.

Birdwatch is often a cafe I hold private meetings in, with managers and press alike, and the young, millennial owner knows of my moves and has never blown up my spot for money, exposure, or simple entertainment. I'm not sure why, but I tip him well after every private visit.

It's the perfect place to meet Aesha.

The woman that broke my heart, but also the person who gifted me a newly born one. It's a dichotomy I don't think I'll ever come to terms with.

She's not in the café yet when I arrive, meandering past the line of people and snagging my favorite corner table. It barely has the capacity to fit my legs, but it's the spot with the lowest lighting and is partially hidden by a wooden column separating the barista bar from the rest of the space. It's also an excellent blind spot for those in line.

I keep my beanie on anyway and pull out my phone, scrolling aimlessly.

Raheem, the owner, sets down a mug of black coffee and we share nods of acknowledgment. He goes back to his station as silently as he arrived.

Aesha's late, but I'm not surprised. I attempt to keep my frown as tame as possible as I wait, in case I'm photographed by a crafty, bored individual whose social media scrolling isn't providing enough entertainment while waiting in line.

The bell above the entrance tinkles, and I glance up, tilting my chair back to see around the column.

Long, wavy brown hair greets me first, the top half bundled in a wool cap. She's chosen a gray hoodie and denim jacket to wear over her lean, dancer's body, and black leggings with wool stockings and black military boots.

Aesha's fashion is on point, as is her body, but she's always been that way. And my response remains the same—stiff, waiting for the anchor to fall and sink me into the depths.

Her honey brown eyes scan the place, so much like Stella's, and when she lands on me, her whole body goes rigid, including the thin lines of her lips. But when she makes her way over, that ballerina life shoots through her limbs, so graceful and at ease, even as she takes the seat across from me and folds her legs under the table. Our knees glance together, but I spread my legs wider, further away from her.

She swallows. Her cheeks are flushed with an autumn hue.

"Hi," she says.

I set my phone down and focus on my coffee. I don't want her to see my heartbeat in my fingers.

She looks around. "Um. Should I order?"

I lift my gaze and find Raheem's. He pads over and Aesha orders a Pumpkin Spice Latte. It's an interesting piece of information. When she worked for the ballet company, she was on a strict, no sugar diet. Of course, that still allowed for copious amounts of codeine.

When Raheem departs with her order, I find the will to speak. "So. I'm here. You can say what you have to say before I involve the lawyers."

She sighs and pulls off her wool cap. "How's Stella?"

The question catches me off guard but doesn't take the sting out of my words. "Why do you care?"

"I'm clean, Rex." She folds her hands on the table. They're white, as pale as they've always been, whether in the chill of winter or the heat of summer. "I've been sober for about a year and a half now."

I tilt my head. Take another sip. "Why should I believe you?"

"You want me to take a drug test? Or grab a hair sample?" She tugs on a hunk of hair. "Do it all, Rex. It's taken a lot for me to come here and face you, to finally be ready. But I am. I want to be in Stella's life. I want to be her mom."

"And it's taken a lot for me to raise a baby on my own," I say, then draw back. I never enjoyed hurting her, and the crack in her gaze tells me I have. "Why did you start by approaching my nanny? Realize how suspicious that was. How frightening for Harper. And me."

Her brows furrow. "What, did you think I'd try to kidnap Stella or something?" At my silence, her eyes lose any remaining light they had. "Okay. I deserve that assumption."

We're interrupted by Raheem placing Aesha's drink in front of her. She takes what seems to be a fortifying sip, closing her eyes, inhaling the steam. When we first started dating, she did that every time she had a hot drink.

The sudden *yank*—the ache—at the memory, swells my vocal cords for a mere moment. That's a remembrance of her mother Stella doesn't have. Stella doesn't know Aesha's habits. Her moods. She knows nothing about her.

"My daughter has no memories of you," I begin. Aesha's thick lashes flutter open. "Not any good ones and zero bad. How confident are you that by coming into her life, you'll give her more good than bad? Because she doesn't know she almost died because of you. Stella doesn't know she fell out of a window because you OD'd on the couch—" I stop myself as soon as my voice becomes too strangled and emotional.

"I-I know that." Aesha's lower lip trembles, but she maintains eye contact. "I'm aware of all the awful things I did to that child. The lack of attention, the ignoring of her needs ..." A tear crests down her cheek, but I have no idea if it's real. *I don't know her anymore.* "But I've been going to therapy after rehab, I've created a good, stable life. I'm a dance instructor, you know. I teach young kids, about Stella's age—"

That fact infuriates me. "How wonderful for you, Aesha. How comfortable your life is, teaching other parents' children, all the while living off my dime in Cali-fucking-fornia, about as far away from Stella as you can get in the United States."

Aesha's lips peel back. "*I haven't spent a single penny of your money for an entire year.*"

I'm startled, but don't show it. Suspicion overrides any surprise. "Then where has it been going? Because you cash it every damned month."

She falls back in her chair, cupping her drink. "I've been putting it into a savings account. For Stella. For when she's older."

My lips part, my tongue ready to tell her off, but the vulnerability on her face—the same age as mine, yet so much older in some ways and childish in others—fuses them shut. I work my jaw, thinking how best to approach this.

"Aesha, what in God's name makes you think I haven't been setting money aside for her since I started getting a steady paycheck? Since I became successful? Stella is well taken care of and will be for the rest of her life. That money I've been giving you..."

She brushes another tear away. "Means nothing to Stella or you. Understood."

I shake my head, my breath catching on a sigh. It goes to show just how far Aesha still needs to go to become any sort of mother to Stella, financially and otherwise.

But you're thinking about it.

"Look, I appreciate the gesture," I say. "If that's what you've done. If you've been living independently the past year, that's excellent. And I'm happy for you. But you can't come to New York expecting to play mom because you've been handling your own finances and sobriety for a year. Parenting takes..." I pause. "Everything out of you. It squeezes you dry, then fills you up such copious amounts, you think your heart will burst. Then it crushes you again. Raising Stella is the most difficult and rewarding thing I've ever done, but I've earned it. I've been there for her. When she's sick, when she's terrified. When she's happy or sad. When—" I stop.

Have I been there for her as much as I should? Stella opened up when Harper came into her life. A kindred spirit with a parallel life. Providing a need and a damage I couldn't fathom, not until it was thrown right in my face.

I study Aesha, who also mirrors need. Damage.

And Harper. Who only wanted two parents who loved her.

"Rex, if my father ever did an about-face ... if he ever showed an inkling of interest, especially when I was young, I would've jumped at the chance to be in his life. I would've felt whole."

On a snarl, I fall back into my chair and gulp the dregs of my coffee.

"I've missed so much," Aesha says in a quiet, shaken tone. "And I don't expect to be forgiven. Not at all. What I hope is to be given a chance, because I *do* love her, Rex. I think about her all the time. I miss her—" She grabs my hand across the table, cold and thin to my hot and rigid one. "Please. I don't want to elbow into her life or scare her. Or, God, hurt her. I just want some time.

Then, when you see fit, maybe some days. I don't plan on moving here. I'll still live in California. I'm not here to blow up your life—"

"I don't give a shit about what you do with my life," I cut in. "You've demolished it plenty. But I refuse to let you crater our daughter's."

"A few minutes," she whispers. "That's all I ask. Light conversation with her, nothing dubious or confusing. I just want to be face-to-face with Stella, after all this time."

My lips pull inward, clamped by my teeth. My jaw aches so hard, it's about to lock up.

Struggling, I find myself saying, "Ten minutes. That's all I'll give you. And you do not mention to her who you are. You do not scare her or intimidate her. Understand?"

Aesha's eyes flare open. "Yes. Yes, I understand. Thank you, Rex."

Something about her gratitude makes me feel unclean, like I'm depriving Stella from a relationship with her mother, when all Aesha wants to do is start one.

I lean forward over the table. "I will continue to remember our past and what you almost did to Stella," I say in a low tone. "In fact, I will never forget it. Do not for one moment think I will weaken for you or any of the truths or half-truths you give me. I am my daughter's protector and always will be. I will even protect her from her own mother if need be."

I stand, and Aesha's gaze follows me upward. "I'm not fighting you, Rex. And it'll take a lot of time and effort for you to see I'm genuine, and that's okay. I have the time. The patience. Just tell me when and where, and we can start in that moment."

I throw a few bills on the table. "Now."

Aesha jolts. "Wh—now?"

"Yes. Stella does half days. I'll pick her up early. Meet us at my apartment. I assume you know where that is."

Aesha scrambles to a stand. "Y-yes, I do. I'll go there right now. I'll wait."

The eagerness with which she accepts my proposal sets my teeth on edge, but not in an off-putting manner.

It's a fearful one.

My daughter, always home when I come home, with her rare smiles and displays of affection lighting up all the darkness in my heart, could be counted on to be *there*. By my side.

And despite my continued control over the situation, I feel the tethers to her slipping from my fingers.

CHAPTER 39

Harper

I TAKE a deep breath before fitting my keys into Rex's front door.

He's home this afternoon, working in his private studio, and I'm hoping to get some time before I pick Stella up from school to say all I need to say.

The only problem is, every time I blink, I see him on top of me, our skin scraping, igniting, his hard body transforming my supple one into elegant, arching orgasms.

When my eyes are open, it's also tough—really tough—to be right in front of him, conversing normally, knowing my fingernails still mark the ridges and muscles of his back.

"You can do this," I mumble to the carpet beneath my feet. "It's Mr. Sloane. Rex. He'll be ready for you."

Will he?

Ugh. God.

I shake myself out of the tenuous self-doubt and shove my keys in, clicking the door open.

"Hello—?" my greeting is cut off when I hear the rumbles of Rex's voice, matched with the high-tones of Stella's.

"Stella?" I ask instead. After kicking off my shoes, I step out of the foyer.

And there they are. The three of them.

They sit in the main room, Stella beside her dad on the sofa, and Aesha perched on a chair across from them. Aesha's hands are on her knees as she leans forward, and she's beaming.

Stella regards Aesha with careful consideration, but her shoulders aren't tense. She remains close to Rex, but she's listening to what Aesha has to say.

All three glance up at my presence, and with a sudden, vicious urge, I wish to melt into the floorboards and never be seen again.

"Harper, hey." Rex says, so, so casually. "Did you get my texts?"

"I—no." *I was too determined to bolt my way over here and express my love to you.*

The crash that follows my thought, that heart-rendering sinking of a thousand ships in my gut, causes my lower lip to tremble, but I catch it in time to prevent the swaying sea-sickness from sounding out of my throat.

"I'm interrupting," I say. Rex opens his mouth, but I add, "I apologize for not receiving your texts, Mr. Sloane. I'll be more aware next time. I'll—I'll leave now. This is a private event and I shouldn't be—"

"Harper, stay," Stella says. "Meet Miss Shirapova. We thought she was Andy's mom, but she's one of Daddy's new ladies."

Rex chokes on his own spit. "Stella, no, she's not—she's a friend." He rises from his seat. "Harper, sit down with us, we can—"

"Perhaps it's best if you do leave," Aesha cuts in. I see no malice in her stare, but I do note her casual, raking gaze up and down my body. It seems my fiery cheeks have betrayed me yet again. "We'll only be a few more minutes."

"Sure," I whisper. "Uh—Mr. Sloane, let me know when you need my assistance again."

Rex throws up a hand. "Harper—"

I spin to the exit too fast to catch anything else that's said.

That's Rex's family. He's trying to make them whole again. I should be happy.

But I don't belong.

I risk one last glance over my shoulder, hoping my heartbreak isn't written all over my face, and I see Rex's expression wrenched wide open.

It doesn't matter, because I should know my position. What I was hired for.

I'm his nanny.

I'll never be his lover.

CHAPTER 40

Rex

"YOU HAVE A RELATIONSHIP WITH HER," Aesha says to me.

It's mentioned casually and innocuously enough that Stella doesn't catch any undertones, but I nip it in the bud.

"Stella, go read in your room," I say, squeezing my kid's shoulder.

Stella mumbles, "You're always telling me to open books in my bedroom."

"Because it helps your brain. Now go."

Reluctantly, Stella slides off the couch. She waves off-handedly to Aesha, who flutters her fingers back. Anyone who's not a child can see the utter eagerness on Aesha's face, a whitewash of wishes, as she watches her daughter leave the room. And the darkness of fear that replaces it as soon as Stella disappears.

"What's going on in my life is none of your business," I say to Aesha once Stella's out of earshot.

"Is that smart? Taking up with our daughter's nanny?"

"Has one fifteen-minute visit with Stella given you the courage to face me down?" I bark.

Aesha blinks and reaches for her purse at her side. "I'm merely expressing concern. But you're right, it's none of my business."

I stand and wait for Aesha to rise from her seat. She takes her time, applying lip gloss first.

Yet, I'm no fool. I sense the cunningness in her expression, the filing away of my failings, to maybe take to court.

Damned if I'll let her.

"I'll bury you," I growl.

Her index finger pauses in its application. "Whatever do you mean?"

"In lawyers. In the courts. I will use all my money and it is copious amounts to make it so you will never exist in Stella's life."

Aesha flies to a stand. She whisper-yells, "Don't you threaten me. *You're* the one sleeping with your nannies and acting surprised when it comes back to bite you in the ass. All I'm wanting is to make up time with Stella, to right my wrongs. I don't need to be thrown in with your dirty laundry and tied up in your shit! I have enough of mine to deal with. And yes, I agree it's not my place to give advice to you, but I swear to God, Rex, tread carefully with these girls. Not all of them are as innocent, young and sweet as that one looks to be."

I glance behind me, at the space where Harper once stood, so vulnerable and alone. An intended outcast that crushed me to look at. "That girl—Harper—has done more for Stella in a few months than you have in three years. Harper is bright, funny, loyal, and dedicated to Stella. I do not make my moves rashly when it comes to her."

I'm furious. Angry. Rigid at being questioned and ultra pissed at the fact that Aesha, former girlfriend, mother to my child, and disappearing act for years, may be fucking right.

But under Aesha's steady, silent gaze, it clicks. I say, "These girls? What do you mean, *these girls*? There are no other nannies, Aesha."

Aesha lifts a brow, shifts her purse strap on her shoulder, and walks around me.

"Aesha," I demand. She slows. I ask her denim-clad back, "Are you referring to Patrice?"

Aesha tilts her chin over her shoulder. "You know, you're right, Rex. At any moment, you can pull the rug out from under me. I don't dare overstep, because despite your suspicions, I am here for Stella, and Stella only. Just look at your own life, okay? I'm not the only one hiding skeletons."

"What the hell is that supposed to mean? Aesha, talk to me. If we're ever to move forward, we can't keep slinging veiled threats at each other."

Aesha's shoulders slump. She turns to face me. "It was Patrice who contacted me. About a month ago."

The ribs in my chest calcify, closing off any access to the tender organs underneath. I spit out in a harsh whisper, "What?"

"She said..." Aesha licks her lips. "She said Stella needed a mother. That she heard from you that I was doing well, and that it was time for me to come back into Stella's life, if I wanted to."

"She ... *what*?"

"How could I not believe her, Rex? She was Stella's nanny for three years. The entire three years I was gone! And she was so kind. She listened so whole-heartedly and was so encouraging over the phone. That's why, when I came to see Stella at school, I was so surprised it wasn't Patrice. It was someone else. And I was even more shocked at how viciously you rejected my attempts to see Stella. I thought ... I thought you approved all this."

"I..." I'm choking on saliva. Spit. Emotions. I have no fucking words to fill the circular rage of fire that's expanding and blowing my bones to dust. "I did no such thing. I *authorized* no such thing. Patrice had no right to contact you, to say those things, to do anything to make you believe I would accept you into Stella's life with no preparation. How could you believe that? How could you believe I'd allow *Patrice* to introduce you to Stella without my presence?"

I'm misdirecting my fury, but Aesha is the closest collateral damage I have.

"Rex, you're scaring me. You're going so red. Please calm down."

"I *will not* calm the fuck down," I respond. Though it's in a low whisper. I do not want to terrify my child, as much as I want to burn this place down in explosive hellfire. "I will address this with Patrice."

And Harper. Dear God, Harper, who could be halfway to Philadelphia, escaping at the right time, except she doesn't know I need her for all the wrong moments. All the mistakes and fears, the pain-fueled misfires like losing my grip over my band, losing my head, losing ... my daughter.

Harper, come the fuck back.

"I will never approve your presence in Stella's life until we rake through your past and do enough home visits and psychological studies to prove you're fit for visitation, mark my words." I have to restrain myself from roaring. "You will never approach Stella and her nanny on school grounds, at this home, in any park or restaurant or *loading dock* without my prior authorization. Do you understand?"

"Yes," Aesha says in a small voice. "I keep telling you, I'm not here to fight—"

"Do not be meek," I say. "You want your daughter so bad, you better be prepared to face the worst parts of me, because I do not allow access to her lightly. Now go, Aesha. I'll be in touch."

"Does this ruin my chances?" she asks. "Has Patrice prevented any reconciliation between us?"

"I may be tough as balls for Stella, but I do not play with her heart so cruelly. If I let you into her life, it will be permanent, Aesha. I'm not about to rip her away every time you piss me off."

Aesha lets out a trembling breath. "Thank you."

"Don't thank me yet," I say, gritting the words out. "Please leave."

"I'll be here a few more days," she says, but moves towards the door. "You have my number."

I remain standing, listening to the door open and shut behind her, fists clenched at my side. The sun shines bright through my windows, and I know its warm rays are hitting my body.

I just can't feel them.

The realization that I want Harper to help me figure this out is far too numbing.

CHAPTER 41

Harper

I'M NOT sure where I should go. Or what I just did.

Did I just quit?

Did Rex just fire me?

Have I been made redundant?

Perhaps these are all the things I should've asked in the moment, but I was too shell-shocked to wonder about my future when the woman who is the source of all Rex's heartbreak and dark moods is sitting and sipping coffee with him and Stella on the couch.

Is Aesha back in their lives?

The idea that a mother wants to be back in a child's life shouldn't cause such stones in my stomach, yet there they form: hard and round and *heavy*.

My phone vibrates as I'm crossing an intersection, looking for a coffee shop or maybe a bar—hopefully both—and I pull it out without pausing in my strides.

Come back.

· · ·

Those two words send me toppling against a building. A lady and a stroller have to bypass my sagging form, but she does it with the ease of a settled New Yorker.

My thumbs hover over my phone's keyboard. Should I go back to Rex? So many questions, so little to answer for…

I sigh and stare up at the clouds.

My phone drops to my side.

Of course I'm going back.

There's a familiar figure leaning against Rex's building when I approach.

The sun, shining bright and blinding on this day of clear clouds and chilly air, makes it tough to recognize the form until I'm a few feet away. And when I do, I gasp.

"Patrice," I say.

She looks up from her phone, one booted leg dropping to the ground after she had it propped against the stone wall. "Harper. I was looking for you."

The crisp outside air, when inhaled, chills my voice to a satisfying degree. "How convenient. I've been waiting for a perfect time to ask you, why the hell were you digging into my past and going behind my back, when all you had to do was ask?"

Patrice arches a brow as she comes to a stop in front of me. "For Stella's sake."

"Bullshit. You had no right."

"And you probably should've brought your poor daddies' story up in your first interview with *Mr. Sloane.*"

She says Rex's last name snidely, like I have yet to earn the privilege of calling him Rex. Even though I've moaned it on top of his naked body while he was buried balls deep inside of me.

How I *wish* I could throw that in this girl's face, but I refrain.

"My family history has nothing to do with my qualifications for a nannying position," I say.

"Is that why you kept it quiet?" Patrice asks. "Because you're proud of being made in a petri dish?"

I want to spit in her face. "Stella and I have formed a special bond because of my past. She's a quiet, lonely child, just like I was, and has been for years. And, I'm coming to realize, perhaps it's because of the nanny she gained. One who was more interested in banging her father than introducing her to the world."

It's below the belt but considering how Patrice keeps bringing up my dead father and my neglectful one like they're pawns to be played in her one-player game, it's irresistible to hurt her.

Patrice's gaze narrows. She says, through stiff lips, "Well, it looks like we're both out of a job. Aesha's still up there, you know. She's been up there a long while. I'm pretty sure they're discussing getting back together."

The jab hits where it's meant to, but I school my expression. "Is that why you're down here? Waiting for your moment to plead with *Mr. Sloane*? Again? I thought he already rejected you."

Patrice hitches a breath, but I don't feel any satisfaction. I feel immature, hurt, and stupid at fighting with Patrice over a man neither of us can have. *Should* have.

"I'm sorry," I say before she reacts. "But you and I aren't friends. We're not even co-workers. I don't have to justify anything, and I don't have to keep talking to you."

I brush past her shoulder towards the entrance, but Patrice's manicured hand latches onto my arm.

"You were supposed to be the *worst* of the bunch," she stage-whispers, her teeth all but fangs as she seethes. "Rex was meant to realize *I* was the perfect one for him, for Stella. You were meant to make him run to me, begging for me to come back!"

"Then why did you quit?" I ask, despite her nails digging in. "You had him. I knew him as nothing but the lead singer to my friend's fiancé's band."

"Please," Patrice scoffs. "You knew he was hot. A broken bachelor. A famous millionaire. You knew you could snag him the instant you showed up in a see-through shirt with your tits out."

I don't deign to rise to her bait.

"Careful, Patrice, your perfect veneer is slipping," I say.

Patrice lets go of my arm, but she doesn't walk away. "I resigned because I had to give him some kind of ultimatum. Rex had me there with him, always, like I would never leave and he was perfectly content with our arrangement. But I wasn't. I needed more. I *needed* him. And to prove to Rex how important I was to the family, how much he needed me but didn't know it, I had to leave. To show him what it would be like without me. I was convinced it would be awful." Patrice gives me a sidelong look. "Turns out, I didn't consider my variables. It forced me to take other measures."

"What kind?" I ask. "Patrice, what else could you possibly say or do to me—"

The large glass doors of Rex's building open, a woman exiting onto the carpeted sidewalk and stepping to the curb. She turns to hail a cab, her brunette waves blowing back, her long legs, clad in black leggings, exposed as her jacket lapels fling to the side with the wind, and it's Aesha.

I realize it at the same time she sees me, our eyes locking, then hers bouncing over to Patrice.

Aesha's arm falls to her side. She stalks over.

"You two? Together?" she says, glancing between us. Her honey eyes blaze. "So that's what I was, huh? A set-up? An injured bird with fucked up feathers for you two bitches to bat between yourselves?"

I raise my hand to plead, "Aesha, no—"

"So what if it was?" Patrice cuts in. "Did you have any success up there?"

I jerk back in surprise, but my mouth isn't as shocked. "Patrice, stop this right now. She's lying, Aesha. I had nothing to do with this."

"With what?" Aesha asks. "Oh, you mean meddling with a traumatized family so you could move in on rich guy? Play with his drug-addicted ex-girlfriend for a while? Because what does she care, right? She just wants to score. She doesn't think back every night, when she's lying in bed, on the baby she left behind. The baby she almost *killed* because she couldn't get the right fix. The life she ruined"—Aesha's voice breaks—"the perfect fucking *life* in a one-bedroom apartment in Bed-Stuy, living with a struggling musician, both of us with no college degrees. Both of us chasing insurmountable dreams. *Both* of us raising a gorgeous child."

Aesha stops for a breath, tears tracking down her face.

I step forward, my hand out again, whispering, "Aesha..."

"Don't you fucking step up to me," she says. "You think being young and cute and available to Rex is enough to dangle me back in his face, to show him how much he's progressed and moved on. You are playing with emotions you are too immature to understand, Harper. Involving people's traumas when you really shouldn't. How dare you? How dare you think you are *anything* close to what Rex needs? You are a mistake." She points at me. "And he's going to figure it out."

My mouth works, but nothing comes out. My throat is swollen and frozen all at once, Aesha's accuracy clear and true.

Patrice smiles. "Couldn't have said it better myself."

Aesha rounds on her. "And *you*. You lying, deceiving, manipulative cunt. Don't think I'm unaware of who the mastermind is, here. You're going to lose, too. You both will, because that man up there, in his ivory tower, with his daughter protected on all sides, will not give you what you want. All the money in the world won't fill the emptiness he'll put in you. All he cares about is Stella and his music. There's no room for anyone else. Believe me, I—"

"Well, well, well. This seems like a reunion I just *have* to document."

All three of us turn to the voice. Once I register the flash, I'm done. Overcooked. Ready for a knock-down.

"You sonofabitch," I scream, storming over to him and grabbing his camera, uncaring that it's strapped to his neck.

When I yank it out of his hands, he flails and almost loses his balance, forced to follow my trajectory, but I throw the machinery back at him just as hard. He catches it before falling on his ass, almost off the curb. "That's assault! I'm calling the police!"

"You've been harassing me since the day I was employed, you jackass. Call the police!" I say. I'm at my wit's end. I'm losing it, deciding to unleash anger and frustration in the only places I can at the moment, and I don't care. "I'll be happy to inform them of your loitering in playgrounds, trespassing on private property, and generally being a dick too small to do anything remotely useful in this life, including peeling your unwanted carcass off this sidewalk and *staying the fuck away from us!*"

I round on him again, my throat raw, but Aesha pulls at my arm. "Not worth it, Harper. Not worth it at all."

She tries to get my attention but I'm too busy enjoying the slimy photographer flinching on the ground, afraid of a five-foot-three girl.

In my periphery, I catch Patrice smoothing back her hair. Her candid smile as she waves. And I notice the amount of press and photographers coming out of the nooks and crevices of the city. Coming toward us.

"Fuck," I say. "Patrice, what did you do?"

Aesha steps away, hiding her face with a hand and using the other to lower her cap. "I'm getting a cab. I'm not doing this. I can't. I can't risk—"

"Go," I say, ushering her forward.

"What're you gonna do now, little lady?" The photographer on the ground sneers.

I glare at him and he cowers. But doesn't miss an opportunity to click his lens.

"Goodbye, Patrice," I say, shocked I'm even saying that much. But I don't look at her as I say it.

"You're leaving me to talk to the press alone?" she asks, the warning clear in her voice.

I say over my shoulder, "Do what you want. Say what you want. I'm tired."

And much too full of insecurity and doubt, all the flaws Aesha listed circling my head and refusing to be swallowed down any mental drain. Because she's right.

"Didn't think you'd give up so easily, Harper," Patrice says.

"Funny, because I *did* think you'd resort to leaking personal information to the press about a man you claim to care about and a vulnerable child you were responsible for. Selling them out must feel pretty good for you to keep doing it."

A ring of press surrounds Patrice, flashes highlighting the white of her face, voices and questions taking over any response she may have made, but I don't take the time to appreciate any guilt that may cross her features.

I was telling the truth. I am tired, and I know Rex must feel the same.

Maybe it's finally time to exit this fairy-tale I always knew would have an unhappy ending.

CHAPTER 42

Harper

THIS TIME, when I open the front door to Rex's apartment, I know what to expect.

A family attempting to be made whole and my services no longer being needed.

I rationalize that Stella will be full-time in school soon and is growing more mature by the hour. Hell, she's more mature than me at this point and can probably start paying her own bills.

It's fine. It's totally fine. I can get over Rex and miss Stella like a limb and spend months crying into my pillow, wishing things were different, but then I can be back on my feet. I can maybe even start dating again, do the whole single lady in NYC once more. I—

Rex stands in the middle of the main room, head dipped down, arms clenched and rigid at his sides.

"Rex?" I whisper, then look around. "Where's Stella?"

I almost don't expect him to answer since he seems so cast in bronze, but he replies, "In her room. I had June make her a snack and put on her shows."

"Okay." I wring my hands together, even as I tell myself not to be weak. "And Aesha? I saw she was here with you guys. That's great, right? She wants to be part of Stella's life again. It's a step—"

"Don't."

I swallow. He's still not looking at me, but I can't stand the silence and say, "I only meant for Stella's sake. I know you wouldn't let Aesha back in without—"

He barrels forward with the shadow of a brute and the speed of a snake, biting onto my lips, fusing us so surprisingly and forcefully that I have no time to take in air.

"Rex—" I say against his lips, but he won't heed. He digs and dips and searches, burying his hands in my hair and tilting my head so he can dive further. Take more.

I clasp his biceps, nails biting through his shirt, but I have to clutch at him, to pull and move with him, because his grit and his scruff, his scrapes and raw points, the rough tension and tugs and yanks, are everything that's anchoring me to the ground right now.

He is my flaw. My one mistake in life. And I don't want to say goodbye to the only fairytale I've ever known.

"Harper," he groans, trailing kisses across my cheek, down my neck, sucking and nipping. His hands slide down and cup my ass, gripping it and fusing me closer so I can feel the hardness of him through his jeans. "Fuck, I need you."

"Not—not now." It takes all my effort to say it, but I picture Stella, not far away. "You're not thinking clearly. You're upset, and I'm here to talk—"

"No. I want to fuck."

"We can't."

"We can." He grinds against me, moves so his hand goes down my pants. He cups my heat and I moan.

But, as much as I want it, too, I say the one thing that will send him crashing back to earth. "Stella."

The name has the expected effect. He drops his hold on me and I stumble back, catching my breath at the same time he rubs at his jaw, stalking the room.

"Rex, talk to me."

"I…" He digs his fingers into his hair. "I've taken advantage of you, Harper. I'm an asshole. A cutthroat dick, and you don't deserve how I've treated you."

I speak, despite the curveball apology he's thrown. "Rex, everything that's happened between us, I've chosen to do. I know I'm your nanny. I'm aware of the open trust your daughter has in me, and that I've probably burned that to the ground by sleeping with you. I'm just as culpable."

He turns, and his eyes scald. "I'm not as irresistible as you are. I could've stopped myself."

"I—" I don't know what to say to that. How to respond to such scathing want in his gaze. "We both succumbed to our cravings. And now it looks like we have to answer for them. So … if this is your way of dismissing me, if it's gone too far and your life has gotten too complicated, I can leave." Oh, it hurts in ways it shouldn't to say that. "I can go."

Rex eats up the space between us and squeezes my shoulders. This close, his eyes will leave nitrogen burns on my face. "That's the problem, Harper. I don't want you to go anywhere. Despite my life blowing up—despite the wrongs of us and the right of walking away—I need you." Rex bares his teeth, and repeats, "I. Need. You."

"Do you?" I ask, hating that my vision's blurring. "Or am I just a safe space for you right now? A secret hideout for you to escape to before you have to deal with reality again?"

He lets go. Spins so his back faces me. "I—I don't know. I'm so angry, so filled with hate, all the time. The only thing that used to loosen that grip on my soul was my kid. Just looking at her was enough. But now … now that Aesha's back, and Patrice has done what she's done … the first person I want to look at, is you."

I lay a hand between my breasts. "You know about Patrice?"

His responding laugh is hollowed out. "Everything. All that she's done. I also know she's downstairs with her court of reporters, making up some kind of redemptive story about herself. But wouldn't you know it, my security will soon arrive and escort her publicly and loudly away. And my lawyers will then hit her with a restraining order. And, I'm debating suing her ass. She's done, Harper. She'll never get near Stella or you again."

The information should soothe me, but it has the opposite effect. "You can really crush a person if you want to, can't you?"

"Yes," he says with no hesitation. When he meets my eyes, his narrow. "Don't think I do that lightly, or for just anyone. I'm not a king with a lethal trident."

I remain silent, giving him time for his brows smooth with realization. He says, "You're thinking about Aesha, aren't you? And what I could do to her."

"Do you want her gone?" I ask.

He searches my face, as if he's wondering what the right answer is.

"It's none of my business," I say at last. "I'm ... I'm gonna go."

"Harper, no."

"Please. I can't be here anymore."

"Why not?" He steps closer.

"Because ... because we've gone too far. Because Stella's mom's back. You have a lot on your plate. And I'm not—"

"Equipped to handle it?"

I pause. "What's that supposed to mean?"

"You want a true definition of family? This is it." Rex spreads his arms out wide. "Imperfect, fucked up, totally unpredictable insanity. Your idea of a wonderful mom and dad? Doting parents in an impeccable home? They don't exist, Harper. So how about instead of running away from reality, you face it?"

I shake my head. "You're going through a lot. But you don't have to be cruel."

Rex smiles, but it's toothy and unlike any expression I've seen on him before. "Am I crushing your dreams, Harper? I don't think so. You're well aware there's no such thing as *family*. Watching mine fall apart shouldn't surprise you."

"You're not falling—"

"Do I deprive Stella of her mother forever, or do I let Aesha in enough to take as much as she wants before leaving again? This time, Stella will have memories. I can't protect her like I've been able to these past three years. What's the move here, Harper?"

"I-I don't have an answer to that." Yet my stomach trembles with dread.

Rex paces away. "Maybe that's the conclusion, then. I'm here to prove you right. You don't deserve a family, and neither do I."

"Stop."

"What kind of father am I to keep a mother from her child? Or do I allow a mother to take advantage of her child? What choice should I make, Harper? Tell me!"

I flinch at the snarl, but not from fear. It's from what he's turning into.

"You're not considering a third option," I whisper.

"Oh yeah?" Rex's voice is thunderous compared to mine. "What's that?"

"That Aesha wants to stay. She wants clear, good memories with her daughter. That she wants to try again, this time for real."

Rex barks out a laugh. "And there it is. The naïve, hopeful side of you that keeps thinking there's a perfect family out there some-where, if only you could just wish hard enough."

I say with defiance, "Stella deserves that."

"You deserved it, too, and look what you got."

I pinch my lips together to halt the trembling. "I don't have to stay here and listen to this. You have *choices*, Rex. That's what being a father is. And they're not supposed to be easy. Raising a kid isn't black and white, it's instinctual. And you're going to make mistakes—of course you are! Stop beating yourself up every time you're forced to make a hard decision about Stella's well-being. I can only *wish* I had a father who dwelled as much as you've been."

I turn to the door, but can't resist adding, "And quit calling me hopeful like it's an insult."

"Wait."

I don't, but Rex uses his stealth and catches me by the shoulder.

He thumbs my chin, forcing it up. I'm ashamed he can see the tears.

Rex swipes under my eye.

"I'm not here to ruin your life," he says. Then adds, "Or maybe I am."

I reply with a whisper. "I'm not your outlet, Rex. I can't be your catalyst to forget. I'm a *person*. One with feelings." *For you.* "And we're in dangerous territory now. Stella deserves a family. One you're mending, as much as you hate to admit it. I don't belong here, anymore."

"That's the problem. I think maybe you do."

I extricate myself from his hold.

"Your family is being stitched back together," I say. "Even if you don't see it yet. It's the right thing for Stella, the right thing for *you*, if Aesha comes with true intentions."

"Harper—"

"And only you can and should decide if that's the case. I'd just impede that. Where are we going here, Rex?"

"I..." On a frustrated growl, he throws up his hands. "I don't know."

"We're having sex," I say. "Good sex."

"Great sex." He rakes down my body, eyes hot. I back away.

"But that's it, right?" My voice cracks. "To continue it would cloud your judgment—*my* judgment. And it doesn't leave much room for Stella."

"Harper, don't leave."

"If I stay," I say, my vision clouding with more tears. "It would only be for selfish reasons."

He doesn't chase after me as I sniff, turn, and walk as fast as I can through the foyer and out the door.

Rex can't find any other words to make me stay. I don't blame him.

This is just another chapter where I'm an intruder in someone else's story.

CHAPTER 43

Rex

As the door clicks shut behind Harper, I think, *Maybe she's right.*

I'm being selfish, putting my dick before Aesha. Maybe Stella's mother is here for the right reasons, despite her past. And the only way for me to discover if that's true is to see this through.

On a venomous growl, I kick at the nearest surface—my glass coffee table—and it shatters on impact. I don't flinch.

I'd have to give up every preconception, every *instinct*, to shield my daughter, if I'm to let Aesha in. And I'm not ready for it.

I'm not prepared for Harper to leave.

I prowl to the front door and throw it open, but I'm met with an empty hallway. The elevator has taken Harper, and she's forty floors below, too far for me to call out to her.

I do it anyway.

"You're wrong!" I yell into the deserted hallway. "About everything! Even if Aesha comes back, it'll only be as a mother, not a family. *She is not my family*! She does not complete me. She doesn't make me a better father. She doesn't…"

I trail off, deciding that punching my doorframe is better than any finishing punctuation.

"Sir?" The elevator doors open. It's my head of security. "Everything all right?"

"No." I seethe, clenching my bloody knuckles close to my chest. "Everything couldn't be farther from a-fucking-ok."

"I, uh, I figured I'd give you an update on the situation downstairs."

"Is Patrice gone?"

"Yessir."

"Is Harper?"

"Uh—sorry, sir?"

"Harper. The nanny. Is she gone?"

"I didn't see her, sir. Should I go back down and look?"

I mumble something incoherent, my brows casting shadows on the floor as I turn back into my home. I feel like I'm losing it, but that's only because it's true: I've lost something.

And I fucking want it back.

CHAPTER 44

Harper

I'M HIDING in plain sight and I'm not ashamed of it.

Taryn sits across from me at her dining room table while I hunch over another cranberry-vodka, mostly vodka, and take another long gulp.

"Tell me again what happened," Taryn says.

I shake my head. "There's nothing more to explain. I made a mistake getting close to Rex. I made a *colossal* fail when I slept with him. And now I must face the consequences." I hold my drink up in the air. "Cheers to bad decisions."

"Harper, you're drunk."

"Yep."

So drunk, in fact, that while ignoring Rex's texts and calls, I found an international website of families overseas looking for ex-pat nannies. Australia looked pretty good and far away, so I shot off my resume to a few of those searching parents.

"Though I'm pretty sure Rex is famous down under, too," I mumble now while flipping my phone over so the screen faces up. I've been ignoring it the past few hours, unwilling to see the notifications flashing against the table, since they're all from Rex.

"What was that?" Taryn asks.

"Nothing." I hide my mouth with another sip.

Taryn leans back in her chair and crosses her arms. "I've never known you to give up so easily."

I scrunch my brows. "I'm being smart. Walking away while I can before I get really hurt."

Taryn softens. "You seem pretty heartbroken to me."

"That's an illusion," I snap. "There was nothing between Rex and I except mind-blowing, explosive sexual chemistry."

"You think that's all it was?"

"*Yes.* And I'm not about to get between what could be amazing for Stella. She could have a complete set of parents, Taryn! I was never going to be that for her. I'd only be a barrier, and it's inevitable she'd figure that out and resent me for it. I'm not about to ruin it for her, T. She deserves..."

Taryn hand comes over mine. To my surprise, I'm still clutching my phone on the table. "Harper, don't you think that maybe ... I mean, that you could be ... imputing your own ideals onto Stella?"

I scoff. "How in the world did you come to that conclusion?"

One side of Taryn's lips pulls up into a sad smile. "Because Stella has a chance at something you never did. However small."

I swallow, my drink landing with a hard clang against the wood. "That's not—I'm laying out facts, not fantasy. Aesha is here. Rex will do whatever is best for his daughter, and with me out of the picture, it'll be easier for him to realize what that is—"

"Harp, Rex is not your father."

My fingers curl under Taryn's hand. "I've never once thought that."

"Stella is not you."

I pull my hand away. "Stop it. You're not making sense."

"What happened in your past is terrible. When you lost your dad in that crash, you lost your whole family. You were left adrift."

I wipe hard under my eyes at the moisture there. "You don't know *anything* about what it is to be emptied of love."

"You're right. I don't. Not in the way you were forced to experience it. But history will *not* repeat itself in this case. Rex would lay down his life for his little girl."

"Yes. I know that. I know." I scrape my palms over both my cheeks, the tears traveling down.

"Rex is a man, one you've fallen for, who is bull-headed and frustrating and makes mistakes. But he needs to make them himself. You can't force Rex to choose what might not be right for him and Stella in the first place because of your fear that Stella will become you, and Rex will turn into Nick Mei."

"When I first met Rex, that's exactly who I saw," I whisper. "My dad. He was so cold, so aloof, so *scheduled* with his daughter. I thought, oh God, it's going to happen to another little girl."

"But it didn't, did it?"

After a moment of thought, I shake my head. "It took a while, but I began to understand Rex, and he has something my dad still doesn't quite possess. It's buried under a lot of anger, but it's there. A heart."

Taryn leans forward and squeezes my arm. "Whether or not you quit, Rex will come to his own decision about Aesha. Don't suffer, Harper. If you want Rex as more than a boss, *tell* him."

"And what? Be rejected? Have Stella hate me for trying to replace her mom?"

"It's love, isn't it?" Taryn sits back and crosses her legs. "It's worth the risk."

I stand and shove my phone into my purse, lying in a nearby chair. "Risking it all for love may have worked for you and Easton, but I don't have time to dream about happy endings. I need to find a new job, pay my rent, and try not to fall apart every time I think about them. So please, Taryn, don't give me hope."

Taryn stands with me. "I'm not—"

"You are. But this isn't my destiny, okay? Like you said, Rex and Stella won't fix my past. I have to move on."

After a beat, Taryn sighs. "Okay."

I pull her in for a hug. "Thank you."

"I'm always here."

"It's time for me to go home, lay out a plan of some sort." I adjust my purse strap on my shoulder. "Be a big girl."

"Maybe after you get some sleep." Taryn smiles as I stumble from lack of balance. "I'll call you a car."

CHAPTER 45

Rex

THIS WEEK SUCKED.

The last thing I wanted to do amid the shitstorm that is my life was find a new nanny, so I took on the task of getting Stella ready for school, dropping her off, and picking her up. With the help of June, the kid continued to eat well—otherwise she would've been getting a lot of PB&J sandwiches.

I gave up texting Harper around Wednesday.

I emailed Aesha, who was back in California awaiting my word, on Thursday.

On the surface, it seemed like I was handling my female situation with maturity, aplomb, and organization, like all things in my life.

On the inside, I'm melting down.

It's now Friday night, and after juggling an afternoon at the studio with Stella in tow, since I still have no babysitter and June needs to be with her family, I'm nursing my third whiskey, sitting near my office window and staring out at nothing. My hair's a mess from Stella pulling at it while giving her a bath and her demands I become King Triton while she plays Ariel, and my white muscle tee is stained for the same reasons.

Like I give a shit.

Mumbling a bunch of nothing, I throw back another glass.

The doorbell rings and the security monitor by my door lights up. Mumbling some more, I come to slow stand and stride over until I can peer at the screen.

I press the call button. "The fuck you doing here, Mase?"

The black-and-white image of my bandmate holds up a bag. "I come in peace, bearing libations."

"What kind?"

"Your only kind. Macallan."

"Mmf."

"Is that a 'come on in'?"

I press the button to open the main entrance. "I guess."

The allure to slump back into my leather office chair is strong, but I have to let Mason into my penthouse suite, so I clomp down the stairs in preparation for his arrival. He doesn't waste time and knocks by the time I make it through the foyer.

Once the door opens, Mason inhales through his nose. "Why did I bring the expensive shit when you already smell like an ale house?"

"Stella's asleep."

"Okay. Good." Mason steps in, glancing around. "Let's sit."

"What do you want?"

"Can't I visit a friend for no reason?"

"No."

I lead him into the main room, where I take a seat in one chair. He chooses the couch and leans back, tossing the bag beside him and spreading his legs wide on a sigh.

"Fine," he says. "The studio session today could've been better, we need to talk as a unit, but I thought it was crucial to chat with you one-on-one, first. This 'break' we've been talking 'bout with the band, it's growing legs. I'm here to make sure you understand that."

I shrug and scratch at my two-day-old scruff. "Maybe it's a good thing. We all have stuff to figure out."

"You sure as shit do." Mase props his elbows on his thighs. "You've made no mention of Aesha. Or Harper. Where'd she go? Why was Stella sitting in our ratty red leather studio couch today?"

I itch for another drink and make a hand motion for Mase to toss me the bottle he brought. "If it helps, it's all related."

"Mm." Mase throws the scotch, which I catch with ease. "Let me see if I get this right. Aesha comes back into the picture, Harper freaks out because you've been sleeping with her, then quits when she realizes Aesha isn't a gold digger but is attempting to pursue a relationship with her daughter, and she doesn't want to impede that. Do I have that right?"

I twist off the cap and take a long swig. "You win. Do you accept check or cash?"

"You don't have to be so cavalier with me, man."

I pause halfway through another swig. "How'd you know all that? I didn't tell you half that shit and I *know* you're not that perceptive."

Mason motions for the scotch, and I screw the cap back on and chuck it over. "Easy. Taryn and Easton told me. They were my first stop before this."

I mull this over. "Well, shit. Was Harper there?"

Mason's gaze slides away from mine. My back goes up.

"Mase." I say his name with zero inflection. Zero slur. "What aren't you telling me?"

After a gulp of scotch, Mase throws his hands up. "Nothing. Harper got a new job, is all."

"Oh." The disappointment is slick and heavy. "I get it. The girl knows how to hustle."

"Yeah, so, I guess everyone's moving on." Mason swallows. "Right?"

"Sure." But I'm still studying my friend. "What else are you hiding, Mase?"

"I'm not—"

"I'm drunk, not stupid. Tell me."

Mase curses under his breath. "All right. Jeez. Harper's new job is in Sydney. Australia."

Every bone in my face fuses into thick concrete. "Come again?"

"She interviewed this family on FaceTime or some shit, they loved her and want to fly her down. I don't know how it works, exactly, but Harper assured T and East that it was safe and something a lot of American nannies do."

"No. Not possible."

"Rex, man…"

"She's not—Harper's not going to *fucking* Australia." I stand, rubbing the back of my neck. "That's fucking insane. I knew she'd run, but not that fucking far. All because of her fear of fucking family."

"Hang on." Mason remains seated, but he has on his Thinking Man face. "I'm trying to sort through all your f-bombs to find meaning in your sentence."

I wave him off. "Harper has this conception that family is the foundation for everything in someone's life. Maybe she's right about that part, but she's convinced you can't control who those people are. That you're stuck with what you got, and you become who you're meant to be because of it. It's ridiculous. She doesn't understand that you can *choose*." I pace around the expansive room. "I can be a father to Stella. I can choose for Aesha to be a mother to Stella, but not be romantically linked with her myself. Aesha and I don't have to love each other, we just have to get along. And Harper—that stubborn, annoying, *frustrating* girl is choosing to escape what we have because she's afraid. She's got no idea that I fucking choose *her*." I halt in the middle of the room.

"Holy shit," Mase says. Instead of elaborating, he tosses me the bottle, now one-third empty. "Pretty sure you're gonna need this."

"No." But I catch it, anyway. "No, I didn't—don't—mean that."

"You're saying you don't want her? Harper?"

"I'm saying—ah, fuck." I rub my face, then peer at Mase through my fingers. "Am I saying that?"

"Dude. You are."

"Motherfucker," I mumble, then tip the bottle back. Far down my throat.

"Uh … on second thought, maybe slow down the liquor train, buddy."

"Why? Our band is going to shit, my girl is moving across the world, and I've pissed all over any shot this week of finding Stella a new nanny."

"Then stop her."

I drop the bottle to my side. "Who? Harper?"

"Yes, you fucking moron. Your misery all stems from your refusal to admit your feelings for her. You're gonna let her leave tomorrow because you're too thick-brained to show some weakness and open up to her. You're going to lose her, Rex. And you just finished telling me all the reasons why you and Stella shouldn't let her go."

I latch on to a key fact in Mase's ramblings. "Tomorrow?"

Mason sighs. "Yes. Harper's leaving tomorrow morning. Early, at like 5 a.m. from JFK airport." Mase points at the half-empty bottle at my hip. "I'm thinking you should sleep some of that juice off, then get your girl."

We stare at each other in silence.

Then: "I'm gonna get my fucking girl."

DESPITE IT BEING the ass-crack of dawn, the airport is as crowded as rush hour traffic on a weeknight.

I wait in the security line, reading a book on my phone and pretending my heart doesn't ache from saying goodbye to Easton, Taryn and Jamie as they dropped me off twenty minutes ago. I don't think on the faces that weren't there, and how Stella must've taken the news this week that I was no longer her nanny.

The person in front of me shuffles forward, and I follow suit, dragging my suitcase behind me as we slowly wind through the accordion line to the TSA check. I didn't bring much, just enough to last me a few weeks, since I figured I could shop while in Sydney for six months, especially since I subletted my New York apartment within forty-eight hours of listing it.

I can do this, I think as my attention stays on my phone's screen but don't read the words. Rex's face casts its imaginary reflection instead, then Stella's, and I catch my lower lip to stop it from shaking. *I'm doing the right thing.*

I'm so focused on my mantra that I don't register the surrounding gasps. Or the whispers. I definitely don't hear the mumbled words of "omigod," and "it can't be," and "seriously, did my phone have to die *right fucking now?*"

There is only a singular name that bursts through my clouded thoughts, and it's said by multiple people surrounding me.

"Rex. That's Rex Sloane."

My head jerks up and I glance around. Surely, I'm imagining the change in atmosphere. The parting of the blustering airport crowd. The softening shimmies of bodies as everyone stands still to look.

But I can't mistake his sandy blonde head. Or those broad shoulders coming towards me. Nor can I disregard the muscles of his bare arms, the length of cords and tendons under their skin as he strums an acoustic guitar, walking toward me.

The beginning notes of 'Forbidden Cherry' fill the crowded space. Rex opens his mouth and sings.

"I'm not supposed to like you,
I can't need you,
Yet my everything wants you."

Rex sings softly, yet the entire terminal, as big as and vast as an air hangar, can hear him. He doesn't look to anyone else but me as he moves forward, his fingers curling against the strings, his Adam's apple bobbing, and his lips moving sensuously over the words.

Through a thicket of tears, I see him belt out:

"You're forbidden to me,
You're next to me,
You hold my baby's hand,
And I'm doing the best I can."

I'm frozen as he sings, the airline passengers surrounding me drifting away the closer Rex comes. My hand slips from my suitcase and it goes toppling forward, onto my feet, but I don't feel it.

Rex stops within a foot of me, nothing but a thin blue strap sorting the lines separating us. His chin dips low and there's not a break in the music, but I'm feeling the snaps of those strings close to my heart.

Rex finishes: "*And leave the marks of my lips ... on you.*"

The impromptu audience bursts into applause. The silence that overtook us fast succumbs to shouts, flashes, requests for him to turn around and take a selfie.

But Rex doesn't change his stance.

He spins the guitar so it lays against his back, but he maintains our closeness, won't raise his head, and studies me.

"Rex..." I say, and it comes out tremulous.

"I made a mistake," he says.

CHAPTER 47

Harper

"You didn't make a mistake," I say. "You have to choose Aesha. For Stella."

"That's where you're wrong. I'm not sure that I do," Rex replies. His chin is dipped so low, we stand almost nose-to-nose. Only I can hear him. "You're right about one thing, though. Aesha may have changed, despite Patrice's efforts to blow this family apart. And, for Stella's sake, I have to see if that's true. I just have to be very careful."

"I'm glad," I say, and mean it.

"But there is one woman who's stable in Stella's life right now. A woman who's making her happy. Not only that, this woman is making her no-good, undeserving, grumpy father feel pretty good, too."

"Me?" I ask.

Rex smiles, exasperated, breaking our intense stare-down. "Yes, you. The too-young, too-vulnerable, too-wise-for-her-years nanny that showed up soaking wet on my doorstep asking for a job she didn't deserve. I thought you so irresponsible. So spontaneous and ill-suited for my daughter. So *wrong*, on every level."

I lift my brows. "Thank you for those compliments. Can I include you in my reference sheet?"

"You proved me wrong, Miss Mei. Every negative I saw was a positive for Stella. And every time you moved, my eye was drawn to you. My lyrics called for you. My life needed you. No, not only me—*we* needed you."

I rub at my eyes, suspiciously damp. "I think I needed you, too. That kid of yours, God, that Stella. She's opened up spaces in me I didn't know I had. Which is why I'm so scared, Rex. Because you can take that away. Maybe it needs to happen, before this goes too far. There's a little girl involved and I don't want to hurt her." My expression wrenches. "To be the source of hurt to Stella, I couldn't—"

Something casts over Rex's face. A pained realization. He says, "I don't want to have that kind of power over you."

"And I can't believe I was stupid enough to give it over. I shouldn't have slept with you. We should've kept this professional."

"Do you think we could have?" Rex cups my cheek. The crowd whistles. I think I hear a TSA agent yell to keep the line moving, but I'm frozen by Rex's words. "Do you think, if we hit rewind we could've gone on with our roles without glancing at each other too long, risking touches, gaining knowledge of our histories, adding hope to each other's lives? We both came into this lonely, Harper. And we're both coming out of it a little more whole."

"I won't be whole, not if it's without you."

I clamp my mouth shut after a sharp inhale when I say that. I didn't mean to. It's his eyes. The cold depths of them, where I've witnessed the hidden warmth.

He strokes my cheekbone with his thumb. "See, that's where our paradox lies. I don't believe Stella can get through her next days without you, either."

I break our gaze, disappointment coating my vision. "Rex, I've resigned. I'm in line at the airport because I've accepted a new job."

"Harper, I know."

I drift out of the palm of his hand. "I can FaceTime Stella, if that'll make it easier for her. But I can't come back as her nanny."

He says. "I know that, too."

My gaze skates back to his, and I hope I squelch my desolate shock in time. "Consider us professionally severed, then."

"Harper," he says, with an irritating, chastising tone. "You can't be my nanny anymore. We've established that."

I nod. I rub at my face, hiding any trembling twitches that warn of an impending sob.

"Harper, look at me."

"I'm looking."

"No, you're not. You're hiding behind your fingers."

"Because ... because allergies." I sniff. I refuse to let him see me cry.

Rex exhales. "Fine. I'll say this to the back of your hands. I don't *want* you as my nanny anymore. I'm not here to hire you back."

"Yes, you've made that clear."

"But I want you to continue being a part of my life." His voice goes deeper, floats closer, so near that he's almost whispering against the nape of my neck. "An important part."

"GET OUT OF THE LINE IF YOU'RE NOT MOVING, MA'AM."

The TSA agent's screech breaks through all of us, including the surrounding crowd, and I rush to step under the accordion banner and out of her target zone. Yet, the line doesn't shuffle forward. Everyone's immobile, staring at us.

Rex tucks a strand of hair behind my ear, shivers spiraling down my shoulder and spearing in places they shouldn't. Namely, a place with a steady, throbbing beat. "I want you to be an everlasting part of my life."

"You..." At last, I drag my fingers down my face, exposing my scarlet blush. "You do?"

He nods. "I've been fighting it every step of the way. Thinking that falling for you is nothing but a bad decision. But you know what? Bad decisions and stress follow me every day. The band, Patrice, Aesha. It took me a while to see, but the only thing that's brought any light on those topics is *you*. I had to read my own lyrics to understand it. Can you believe that? A singer not understanding the meaning of his songs. Of 'Forbidden Cherry.'" He scrapes his fingers through his hair. "Fuck, it took facing down my biggest demon, Aesha's reappearance, to understand that I *am* a good father. I *can be* a good man. And I can be a good man to you."

My mouth opens and closes. The words are there, the sincerity complete, but the fear won't go away.

"Rex," I say. "I can't expect you to change the man you are. You're growing, I see it, but I can't help but think I'm nothing but an outlet—"

"You're not."

"I'm young. Inexperienced, like you said—"

Rex cups my cheeks again. "You're mine. I'm growing with you. We're evolving together."

"I—" My lips tremble. "I don't know if I deserve a family."

Rex bends so his nose touches mine. "I choose you."

"People leave," I whisper. "We both know that too well. How do I know how to stick around, when I've never been taught?"

Rex finds my hand, holds it against his heart. "We'll learn together. Harper, I ain't perfect. We're going to fuck-up, I'm sure of it. But I want to wake up to you. Talk to you. Make love to you. I *want* you in my life. And if we grow as a family? So be it. But I'm not putting that kind of pressure on you right now. I just want you to stay. Can you do that?"

Rex is warm. Warmer than he's ever been, inside and out. And I can't help but rise to the hope. "I can try."

"Call us forbidden. Call us a mistake, but to everyone else, I'll call it fate that you came into my and Stella's life when you did. I ... fuck, I'm falling for you, Harper."

My lips part on a silent gasp, at the same time hope swells and fills my heart so much I don't think I can breathe. "Holy crap, me too, Rex."

His face breaks into a true, beguiling smile. "Finally, something I've been looking forward to hearing all day."

I lift my hands, holding his face, ensuring he searches every aspect of my eyes, every second of seriousness I want to impart on this man. "This is something I've been looking forward to hearing my whole life."

Rex lowers his head for a kiss.

The entire room bursts into applause and cheers. There are a few female *boo's*, but I ignore them, so immersed in the man in front of me.

When we break apart, it's with reluctance, but there remains a solemn vow in both our stares.

"We should tell Stella," he says. "Right now. Let's go save her from Mason. I want us out in the open."

I nod. "She may throw her tiaras at me for leaving her for a week."

Rex rolls his eyes. "She's not going to—wait, you're still allowing her to play with those?"

"Is now not the time to tell you about the stash under her bed?"

"I forbade—" Rex catches himself. "You're no longer her nanny, so I won't lecture. But—"

"I want to show you something."

Rex watches me pull my phone out of my pocket and scroll through my pictures until I find what I need. Flipping the screen around, I show him.

"This is Stella at *Swan Lake*," I say. "Do you see that smile? I haven't seen it since. Not that bright, anyway. She's enraptured."

Rex's expression is blank as he studies the photo, one I took of Stella in the darkness of the theater when she wasn't paying attention. It's her profile, but the white of her teeth can clearly be seen, and the crinkle of her eye, so much like her father's when either of them deign to smile.

"I think dance will help bring her out of her shell," I add.

Rex, please say something.

"And I know," I continue, "I *know* you're worried about injury and Aesha and all the badness that brings, but history doesn't always repeat itself, and Stella's blooming. Blossoming. I think we can help her thrive."

When Rex says nothing, I think I've gone too far, and probably I have. But I can't help but remember the expression on Rex's face when he described watching Aesha dance. He could have that with his daughter.

I squeeze his hand. "Stella has an instinct for it. And maybe you'll love to watch her dance one day. I won't push it anymore, but—"

"Right. You. Not push."

"Fine," I relent. "Let's start with telling Stella the truth about us, then we'll deal with dance recital rebellion."

His lips grow stern. I'm readying for the lecture he promised he wouldn't give, but he mumbles, "Send me that picture," then takes my hand and begins pulling my suitcase with the other.

I smile, then stifle it as soon as he glances down at me.

"I want to be in your and Stella's life," I say as we walk out of the airport. Calls and shouts follow us and a few stragglers attempting pictures on their phone. We ignore them. "To be here for it all. Whether Aesha becomes permanent, whether Stella can dance, whether or not you write more songs about me ... I'm here, Rex."

He pulls me close and kisses the top of my head. We stroll toward the waiting car, hands clasped together.

"You're here," he repeats, and a small smile plays across his lips.

Epilogue

"I'M NERVOUS."

"Don't be." Rex comes up behind me, lifting my hair and assisting in clasping the necklace. He lowers his head, kissing the back of my neck before he releases my dark strands.

"Beautiful," he murmurs.

We stare at each other in the mirror, Rex's hands placed possessively on my shoulders. I don't mind it. I'm too busy wondering if the butterflies in his stomach are as active and flitty as mine become when we lock eyes.

He towers over my smaller form so completely that I could lean back and be absorbed by his muscular chest, barely contained by his tight maroon tee.

Rex's nipples stand at attention just above my head. It's no secret between us that I can turn around and bite them with ease, before climbing this man and tearing his clothes off while we fall back on the bed...

"Not now," Rex growls, his clear eyes turning cloudy with lust.

"But it's the perfect way to release some of my nervous energy."

The passion dissipates and humor takes its place as he laughs. "You act like you're about to face a Drill Sergeant."

"I *am*." I spin to face him and cross my arms, drumming up

authority. "Should it matter that this military leader is three feet tall with adorable curls? I think not. Stella can still fell me with a single look."

"A look she's perfected from you." Rex grins, then puts his finger under my chin. "She'll be over the moon that I found you at the airport and brought you back. I swear. Now." He bends closer. "Let me grab a taste of those forbidden cherry lips so I can collect some sweet courage."

"I knew it!" I bop him on the arm. "You're nervous, too!"

But I give him what he asks for, because I want it, too.

Our lips come together in a perfect clash, hard to my soft, salt to my sugar, rough and inviting and all-consuming.

My heart leaps at how familiar he tastes, that this is a craving I'll never have to try to forget. Rex is mine now. And even better, he wants me to be a part of his family.

I have a family.

Bravery comes with the bloom of a rose inside my chest, and I reluctantly break away from him and take his hand, ensuring we walk out of the room together.

Stella waits patiently on the couch, her eyes glued to her tablet as she plays *Minecraft* and builds all kinds of heavily pixelated houses. She doesn't glance up as we wander in hand-in-hand, but I know this child. I can tell a stifled grin on that cherub face a mile away.

"Stel? Can you turn off your tablet for a moment?"

Rex requests it innocently, but it's the type of ask that doesn't bear repeating. Stella listens to her father and slides it off her lap, blinking at us expectantly.

I shuffle in place like I'm undergoing another interview, except this time in front of the pint-sized Sloane. It reminds me of the last time I was scrutinized, so closely it was like my bones and muscles were on display along with my desperation. "We, um, we have some news."

"Yes?" Stella cocks her head.

I see. I'll be the one doing the talking, then. "Your dad and I..." I glance up at him, and I'm momentarily startled by how gently he's regarding me, with an encouraging, patient smile. Rex isn't known for patience, yet here he is, basking in the moment his daughter and his love introduce themselves to each other as family.

A smear of faint red gloss sparkles at the corner of his mouth. I resist the urge to thumb it off and feel the reassurance of his stubble.

"My daddy and you are getting married." Stella nods sagely.

"What? No!" I blubber, then raise my hands in defense, while my head ping-pongs between them in panic. "Not married, Stella, but we are together. I mean, I already live here, as you of course know, but now we're, now Rex—your Dad and I are—"

Rex quells my nervous vibration by palming my shoulder and squeezing. "We'll only get married if it's okay with you, Stel."

The ping-ponging stops on Rex, my mouth falling open. "We will?"

"Absolutely. As my Stella knows, I don't date just anyone, and I certainly don't introduce women to my girl unless she's important. And Harper Mei is extremely important. To me, she is the warmth of this house, and special to this little girl."

Aw, crap. Tears pour into my eyeballs.

"Daddy, you're making her cry!" Stella pops off the couch.

"Then you better hug her so you can catch all those happy tears," he says, chuckling. He hasn't removed his hand, and it's the grounding anchor that I need, because this is just too much of a dream come true. It can't be real.

But it truly is when Stella bounces up to me and wraps her arms around my waist. She buries her face in my stomach and embraces me hard.

My arms come around her tiny shoulders and I bow forward and try to surround her with the kind of belonging she's gifted to me. It only makes me sob harder. She lifts her head up to catch my eye.

"I like hugging people this size. It means I get to stick my face in a soft, gooshy stomach and not hard hairy legs like Daddy."

That does it. I laugh through the tears. Enough to even ignore the *soft gooshy stomach* part.

"My girls fit perfectly together," Rex husks out beside us. "I couldn't wish for more."

"Well, I'm wishing you'd get in here, too." I lift one hand to bring him in. "We simply aren't complete without embracing hard hairy legs."

Stella giggles. I keep laughing. Rex's chest rumbles with amusement and he drops a kiss on top of my head before pressing me against him.

I did it. I'm home.

Stella's voice comes up between us. "Harper, can you still be my nanny?"

"Oh! I almost forgot." I wipe the rest of the tears off my face, tuck my hand into my pack pocket to grab the gift, then bend to her level. "I brought you this."

It's the other half to the necklace Rex just finished putting on my neck. A half heart that fits flawlessly to mine. We walked by it in the airport, after the adoration and attention died down, and I couldn't resist. I've never loved a child so much that I felt like I was carrying my heart outside my body, but here she is. And now she has mine.

Stella lifts it with awe, the piece glinting in the light. "It's so amazing!"

"And it's yours." With my actual heart swelling, I spin her around and rest the necklace against her neck. "To answer your question, sweetie, I'm going to be better than a nanny."

"My new mommy?" Stella looks over her shoulder, her brows furrowed in consternation.

"No," I say, firmly and gently. "I'll never try and take your mom's place. Consider me a bonus, or an extra person who loves you to the moon and back. Someone who wants to hang out with you forever."

When the necklace is clasped, Stella turns to face me, her hand already fidgeting with the half-heart. "Someone like that gets the name Mommy. Right, Daddy?"

Rex clears his throat in raspy confirmation, too overcome to speak.

"You deserve to be a mommy, Harper, and I'd like you to be mine. My friend Brittany has two mommies and no one gets confused why, so why should anyone be confused that *I* have two mommies, too?"

Laughing, I ruffle her hair, those soft curls running through my fingers like silk. "I'm honored. Thank you, Stella, for accepting me so completely."

Stella, sensing the soberness of the moment, folds her hands in front of her and says, "Thank you for letting me eat ice cream at night."

"Speaking of which, let's go get some," Rex says, in total odds to his usual cranky *no sugar at bedtime* retort.

Maybe my presence is causing changes in his heart, too.

Moment lightened, we get our coats and head outside, all three of us making a paper people chain, holding on to each other the entire trip.

We stuff our faces with a banana split and stumble home whence we came, full of chocolate and thrumming with sugar.

Taryn, after reading through my multiple text messages updating her on Rex and my decision to stay, immediately offered to take Stella for the night so Rex and I could "catch up."

Her words.

We drop Stella off with Taryn where Easton takes her under his wing by asking multiple *Minecraft* questions that put him in her good books. She follows him without a backwards glance and I'm happy to see Stella trustingly look forward, like with my assurance that I'm not going anywhere, she feels safer leaving the shadow of her father.

On the trip home, Rex asks if I want to stop for dinner and I can't hold it in anymore. I look over at him hungrily.

My expression is the answer he needs, so he gives a single nod. "Yep. Me, too. Definitely, absolutely, one-hundred-fucking-percent, me too."

Grinning like fools, we practically fall into the elevator to his penthouse. We're well aware that the security officer on the bottom floor and the blinking red light in the corner above us are connected, but that doesn't stop Rex from casually grazing my denim-clad ass, then squeezing, then drawing a distinct line between my cheeks, from the small of my back to—

"*Rex,*" I hiss, clenching and squirming against the damp need fast collecting in my underwear.

"I'm trying, really attempting to control myself here, but all I want to do is toss you up on my shoulders and eat you out."

It's enough of a shock for me to jerk toward him and say honestly, "I'd like that."

"Start unbuttoning your pants." His teeth flash white. The elevator doors slide open, and he takes a commanding step forward.

I follow, giddily unbuttoning my jeans while shimmying down the hallway and into his—my?—home.

Rex swings around me and shuts the door, primal heat wafting out from his pores as he corners me, his half-lidded eyes watching me slide my jeans down and off.

I kick them away like they're on fire and move to the hem of my shirt. Having Rex observe my strip-down is satisfying and filled with power. He's not on his knees, but I feel like I'm making him want to fall to them with my slow, languid movements.

"That's it." He can't take anymore. He prowls forward and lifts me while my shirt is halfway over my head, shifting until my legs are over his shoulders and my pussy in his face before I can so much as squeak.

"Oh my—Rex, holy shit. Holy omigod *shit!*" I cry through the shirt's fabric before untangling myself and finding balance by gripping his head.

His tongue drives into me with the power of a cock except a lot more dextrous. He laps, nips, and sucks my folds, then spreads them with a long, lazy circle of his tongue, and I melt like butter on a hot pan.

Rex walks blind through the entryway, his fingers digging into my ass cheeks and pressing me so hard against his face, even his nose is buried in my scent.

His voice vibrates from his throat, to his mouth, and into me. Sex Toy Rex continues getting me off, stopping only to allow me to convulse with my first orgasm.

Thank god the ceilings are so high, because I rear back, riding his head like I'm on a bull and hanging onto his hair, yanking hard, until the electric ripples inside me dissipate to a normal level.

Rex somehow guided us into his bedroom and he lowers me with ease. His cheeks are flushed, lips wet, and stubble shining with my want for him. I resist the urge to rise up and lick it off him only because he says, "I love making you come. The sounds you make are better than any instrument and I'm damned determined to have you making music all night."

My thighs clench in anticipation.

"I want to be on top of you," I say.

I'm testing the boldness of my desire on my tongue, feeling out the ability to tell him what I want without being laughed at or regarded as innocent and insecure. Rex would never, but these are my insecurities that refuse to die. And being so exposed and naked in front of a guy like him, I mean come on, who wouldn't want to both jump the hell out of him and crawl into a hole and die of embarrassment when your body is pitted against his?

Rex reads something on my face. He tucks a strand of hair behind my ear. "You can be on top, in reverse, upside-down, fucking spread-eagle before me and I don't think I'll ever come close to discovering all there is you have to offer."

I shake my head, bashful, but he cups my cheek, stalling it. "You're glorious, Harper. That's the best word I can find at the moment and even that's not enough. The thought of you riding my dick, with your tits bouncing and those cherry lips opened wide, I'm about to blow up right now and die a happy man."

I smile against his calloused palm. "Then let me kill you while I'm coming. It's only fair."

Pushing at his shoulders, I get him to lay down, tossing his pants, shirt, and briefs. I'm naked, dripping, and ready for him, and by the time I'm mid-swing, his sturdy cock is pressing into my entrance.

I slide down it with a moan. The rumors are true—a large man has a large dick, and it fills me to an almost painful extent. But it's a painful delight, and when he grabs my hips, I bounce the way he huskily said he wanted, my breasts, small but mighty, bouncing in tandem to my quickened pace.

My breaths get shorter. My thighs burn. My head falls back on a glorious curse.

Rex's abdomen flexes with his efforts to take me and hold himself back. His biceps bulge as he grips onto me and lifts his head, a sheen of sweat along his forehead.

"That's it, baby. Take my cock," he says, holding steady with my gaze. "Come. Come for me, Harper. Come so hard I want you dripping down my balls so you can lap it up after."

The dirty talk does what it's supposed to. An orgasm barrels through me, somehow stronger and better than the first one. Our skin slaps with my frantic beats as I try to ride the orgasm as long as I can, and when it abates, I fold over, ready to burrow into his chest and maybe play idly with one of his nipples.

He stops me mid-flop, his dick still nestled inside. "You're not done yet."

I ask him through bleary vision, "Huh?"

"Has anyone given you more than one orgasm at a time?"

The odd question draws my head up.

"No?" he surmises. "I thought so. I'm determined to make your memories of those *boys* of your past obsolete, unnecessary, maybe pitiful thoughts. Allow me to be the man who gives you multiple orgasms without giving myself one first." He lifts his upper body until we're face-to-face. Not easy, considering our height difference.

He finishes by saying, "That's how a real man pleasures his woman."

All I can do is nod. My pussy gives away all my thoughts, anyway, swelling and becoming slick around his still-hard cock.

"Good girl. Now turn around and fuck me while I watch your ass in the air."

"Yes, Mr. Sloane, " I breathe out, sliding off him. I reverse my position, my hands on his firm, powerful thighs.

Without waiting for any further sign, Rex lines himself up with my entrance and guides me down.

"Ride me, cowgirl," he says.

Biting my lip, I do, starting off tentative and somewhat sore. Soon, pleasure overtakes the ache of an overused pussy and I'm bouncing as hard as I was initially, my eyes rolling back in my head at the curious, wonderful mixture the ache and the pleasure create.

Rex shocks a squeal out of me when he thumbs my asshole and presses inside.

The sharp pain is immediate. I freeze, not sure what to do.

Then, he stretches it out using a massage method I'd never

knew existed before this moment. Saying nothing, he continues to gently prod, stroke, and push, stretching me with more fingers, his body thrumming with his approval.

"Oh my god," I whisper as my eyes fall closed. "I never knew ... never thought..."

"I'm honored to be the first to hit your g-spot. Keep going, Harper. I want all your holes, and I want them all tonight."

"Yes," I say, then louder, "*Yes.*"

Rex keeps his thumb in me as I resume chasing another orgasm, sliding up his dick but too desperate to linger and slamming right back down. His hips thrust, beginning to meet me halfway and making the movements shorter, brutal, and pointed. Rex controls when I'll break, and for him, I want to shatter into a thousand pieces if it means he'll always be there to put me back together.

I can't see his face, but his grunts tell the story of his determination to hold back, his jaw probably jutting out and locked down, the tendons in his neck bulging under his flushed, reddened skin.

When I come, it's with starry eyes, utter lightness exploding through the center of my body and splaying out my arms. I orgasm like I'm the center of the show and I've come to the big finale.

It's so fantastic that I arch my back and scream, so completely happy and full that I could have Rex inside me all night.

"That's it," he croons as my movements slow. Both of us are covered in sweat. "That's exactly the song I want you to sing."

I start to relax on top of him, but that's when he grabs me by the waist and flips me onto my back, covering my body wholly with his.

"You're not done yet." Rex glances down at me with a wicked grin. "My turn."

Do you want more lover moments with Rex? Maybe sweet instead of filthy (though we love filthy).

Sign up as a VIP and get exclusive access to a bonus epilogue of Harper and Rex's wedding! You don't want to miss Rex's sweetest moment yet.

keep reading for a sneak peek of Trust, Locke and Carter's book.

IT TOOK ME DAYS, *weeks*, to muster up the courage to get on a plane and confront Paige's baby daddy, Lachlan Hayes.

I thought of ignoring it. It was so tempting to dismiss this guy and let the courts handle him. Child Services could inform Lachlan of his DNA match in the form of a baby. He means nothing to me—not one iota after I finished my research on him before booking my flight.

Especially after looking him up on the internet.

"Ugh," I mumbled while reading.

This king of his college days, man of the football field, running back of record-breaking NFL dreams, is still an ass almost two years later. Every social media pic I spotted of him on my computer, he had his arm draped over a girl, and always a different one. Seemed he didn't have a preference. Blonde, brunette, pink, rainbow...as long as they were hot, he'd bare his chest for them.

"God, Paige, what did you see in this jerk?"

Yet, I couldn't look away. My finger just kept scrolling and scrolling, my eyes eating up all the words and pictures, the girls and tailored suits, until the last article I came across, referring to some kind of injury. My finger hovered over the mouse as I read.

Lachlan was hit hard, the wrong way, his knee blown out, during his very first game in professional football.

There was a link under the article that read **CLICK HERE FOR GRAPHIC DETAIL**. And like the bait it was meant to be, I clicked.

It was a video, with close to a million views. I turned the volume up and bent closer to the screen. The thunderous white noise from the crowd sounded first, then the official announcer, discussing the set-up for the next play. Lachlan was number 18 according to the article. I tried to find him on the field. I thought he was the player running back and forth behind the line of large, padded men readying for the quarterback to hoist the ball.

That's the extent I can talk about football. Paige and I attended many college games, yet I couldn't tell you the plays, the yards, the positions. I *could* tell you when a touchdown happened since that's when the stadium went wild and a ton of beer spilled on me.

"We've got a rookie on the field, Lachlan Hayes, who comes with plenty of pressure on his shoulders," the announcer said through my computer's speakers. *"Heisman Trophy winner, captain of his alma mater, he's got plenty of stats to his name, too. We're looking forward... Plenty of fans are eager to see what he can do, especially after his magic on the field during pregame season..."*

While the announcer's jabbering, the QB punts the ball between his legs, immediately redirecting the announcer's chatter. There's a scramble, some confusion, then—there—Lachlan had the ball. He was running close to the sideline, ball tucked under his arm, gaining yards, leaving the opposing team behind, when—BOOM—out of left field, *literally.*

He...he's...

Oh, God.

I thought only dolls could bend sideways like that.

And break.

The viral video had me cringing. Lachlan's writhing in the field, the cameraman unable to pan out or focus anywhere else.

He, like the rest of us, was plenty human and wanted to see it all, regardless of how grotesque it might be.

I tilted my head, following the new angle of Lachlan's leg. *God,* that was some career-ending shit.

I'd've felt sorry for the guy if the pictures of him and various women had also stopped. But, of course, they grew in proportion the day after it was announced he couldn't play football anymore. In these recent pics, his eyes were more hooded, his shirts not buttoned properly—if they were at all—his drinks frozen in mid-slosh as he posed, mouth mawing open like he's one second away from insulting the person behind the camera phone.

Drunk.

"A drunk, dastardly bastard. And you slept with him, Paige." I shook my head, my finger tapping against the mouse.

No wonder Paige never mentioned who Lily's father was.

To be fair, online accounts alone weren't enough to put him into asshole territory. At first glance, anybody would think he engaged in pretty typical college-guy, then pro-athlete, debauchery. It was also the *remembrance* of him that gave him the dick flag. The fact that it was almost two years after college and he's still babooning through life the same way he did during our senior year when Paige and I first had the chance of meeting college royalty.

Oh, did I *ever* remember Lachlan Hayes. Got to witness first-hand how he captured that dick flag and kept it close. I just didn't know Paige *slept* with the guy that same night.

We'd always talked about how hot he was, laughing as we took cringing sips of Fireball and munching on M&Ms and Skittles on our dorm room bed. But that's all Lachlan Hayes was in our conversations—gorgeous, unobtainable, a guy who absolutely, one hundred percent, ran with a different crowd. It was no secret most co-eds crushed on him, and he knew it.

What Paige didn't know was, I crushed on him, too.

Stupidly. I tell myself now it was more in a celebrity way, with no chance in hell of ever finding out if he and I could work. I mean, the chances of meeting the guy were slim, never mind engaging in conversation with him or—gasp—*dating* him.

So, imagine my surprise when the last college party we went to, he was there. Lachlan Hayes, in all his glory, with all his buddies, drunk and twisted on championship fame.

He'd seen me that night. Our eyes clashed and held—mine widening the longer I realized he was staring. Then, like a lizard unable to blend into its surroundings, I scurried away, too scared to do anything about Lachlan's clear and sudden interest.

Little did I know, Paige was able to conquer that same fear.

Realizing this makes me feel like I never truly knew her. Not in the way I thought.

So, when I got off the plane to New York City, when I stepped up to Lachlan's door this morning, finger trembling as I buzzed, fist shaking when I took the stairs to his apartment door and knocked, I didn't think he'd recall who I was.

Now here we are, sitting awkwardly in Lachlan's living room. Old, stinky clothes are flung over the upholstery; single socks discarded on the floors like they were forced to search on their own for their mate since their owner gave up on them. And... do I see? Yes, I see. A woman's lace thong hanging over the kitchen faucet.

"Um," Lachlan says, redirecting my attention.

He leans forward in a wooden kitchen chair he dragged over from a table two feet away, facing me on a sofa that I hope, hope, *hope*, did not feature in his sexcapades last night. It smells like it might've.

"Can I get you a drink?" he asks.

"Sure," I say. "Coke, if you have it."

He lights up. "I do."

Lachlan practically leaps out of his seat, and I notice the slight, almost indiscernible limp in his left leg as he strides six feet into a small kitchenette. Bottles rattle as he opens the fridge.

I should take this time to further survey this apartment, a

second-floor walk-up in Williamsburg, Brooklyn, but I don't need to. It all adds up—the smells, the tangled clothes belonging to both sexes, the mussed-up hair, the face of Lachlan Hayes. I know enough.

He returns, cracking open the can of Coke and leaving the tab up as he passes it to me.

"So..." Lachlan sits back down, rubbing his palms against his knees.

He's dressed in black-and-red athletic shorts and a vintage Van Halen tee. I'm trying to reconcile the college eye candy he was to the man who's in front of me, with one eye half-closed like he's attempting to reconcile this day with real life.

There were two ways this could've gone. Lachlan's instant denial coupled with a good few seconds of blubbering. Maybe the paleness of shock capped off by cracking his head on the pavement when he passes out. Or, Lachlan could be stunned senseless, stupefied by the fact that of the many, *many* women he slept with, he shockingly happened to knock one up.

"Do you want to know her name?" I ask.

"I want to know...everything." Lachlan shakes his head, dislodging some stupor. "So, it's a girl? I have a girl baby?"

I angle my chin in an attempt to soften my scorn. I must remember, this guy has no clue. He didn't expect me to come into his home and scope out his place like he was a father needing to take care of a kid. He didn't know when he woke up this morning there would be a baby somewhere that needs him.

"Yes," I say. "Her name is Lily. Lily James Tobias."

"Cool." Lachlan nods. "That's a cool name."

"It is." I scold myself to cut back on the sarcasm.

"So, um..." Lachlan licks his lips, and I almost want to pass him my Coke so he can take a drink and collect himself.

"I'm sorry to show up and drop a bomb on you like this," I say. "If it could've been any other way...I mean, had I known earlier, maybe I could've prepared you somehow..."

"You?" Lachlan sits back, his legs splayed out in a wide V. "But didn't you say it was another girl whose baby this is? You're not—"

"No. Definitely not." I set the can down on the scuffed glass coffee table. "My best friend, Paige, is Lily's mother. You heard right."

"Okay, so, why are you here instead of her? Why are you telling me this? Is she afraid to confront me or something?"

I've been dreading this part. "Paige is dead."

His hands fall right off his thighs, hanging loose as if without bone. "I'm sorry, what?"

"She—"

"Dead?"

"Cancer," I say quickly, so I don't have to sink into the memories for too long. "She was diagnosed soon after she had Lily. She lived about nine months after that."

"Holy shit."

"I know." Despite my attempts, I tear up anyway and use the cuff of my denim jacket to swipe them away. It only manages to smear streaks across my cheeks.

"That fucking sucks," he says.

"More than you could ever know." I dig my nails into the denim. Then I clear my throat. "Paige's parents are both dead. Same with her grandparents. She was an only child. Her parents had no family. You see where I'm going here."

"Uh, yeah." Lachlan blinks. "But what about you? You're here."

I nod. Can't help but picture Lily holding her hands out to me so she can be picked up. Squishing her cheeks with my kisses. Squeezing her chunky, adorable thighs and letting her rip out of my hold so she could crawl to her mother, little legs and hands smacking across the floorboards.

"I'm not family according to the courts," I say. "The law says you're the next of kin. Of course, a DNA test will have to be done to prove you're the father, since Paige never put you on the birth certificate and there wasn't time to deal with government bullshit while she was so sick, but—"

"Wait. Hold up. Stop right there." Lachlan spears out a hand, palm out like he could physically keep me from saying anything more. "I'm not...no way. I can't *have* her. You can't bring her here." His voice is getting higher the longer he talks. "I'm no father."

"Lachlan," I say quietly. "You're all she has."

"Locke, call me Locke."

I shake my head. "Fine. Locke. You're all she has."

"No, I'm not. There's you. Let me sign whatever I need to sign, and I'll hand her over to you. You can be her new mom."

I am zero-point-two seconds away from flinging myself into his face, claws out, maybe using my teeth to chew off his nose. I expected Locke to be shocked and upset. I didn't think he'd be so cavalier as to dismiss Lily's mom and want to *hand* Lily over to someone else like she was a trophy he didn't want, then go on about his day.

"Hey—*ow!*"

I throw the half empty can of soda at him instead.

"You haven't even met Lily, never mind *seen* her," I say, coming to a stand. "You have no clue what a wonderful, vivacious, incredibly gorgeous baby you made, and I was willing to give you credit for that. How could you know when Paige never clued you in? But here? Now? Lily is with a foster family. Strangers who didn't raise her, people who the state employs to take care of a baby until a family member can get her. And believe me when I say I *wish*, with everything I have left in me, that I could be the one to take her. That it could be me to hold her, tell her everything's okay." My voice cracks. "But I can't. Some judge in Gainesville tells me I can't because of a dying letter my best friend wrote naming you as the legal guardian. So here I am, trying to find Lily a person who wants her as badly as I do."

Suddenly, a cool, collected calm falls across my shoulders, and I level Locke with a look. "You know what? You're right. You don't deserve her."

His brows jump like I'd tossed so many words at him and he was still collecting the meanings.

"You want to sign away your parental rights, fine. But here." I fumble in my back pocket, pulling out my phone and angrily tapping until I find what I need. "This is her."

Lily was almost six months old on her playroom floor in the picture, stubby legs splayed out in a V, her favorite toy bunny in her hands, gumming it up for the camera with a toothless smile. Her blonde ringlets were just coming in, little curlicues around her ears. Her eyes, a stunning blue, were no less bright even while crinkled with a grin.

"I..." Locke lifts his hand for the phone as if programmed on automatic. "Oh, my God."

"*This* is who you want to pass off to strangers. This little girl who has done nothing but bring light into our lives, who did nothing to deserve losing her mom. All she asks is to be loved." I smack my chest. "And I *love* her. Which is why I'm here, before CPS comes, before you're given some official document instead of Lily's face to decide whether you want her, to tell you that Lily..." I glance around Locke's space, cringing outwardly and deep down in my soul. *I can't give her up like this.*

"You're terrible for her," I admit.

Locke peels his eyes away from my phone's screen. "Huh?"

"You're a bad idea." I nod, cross my arms, swallow, and pretend not to notice how his expression has softened, how he strokes the screen like he's bringing Lily to life. "But you're her father. And Lily doesn't need a new family. She needs her father."

"I can't..." He blacks out the screen and gives it back to me, but is still bemused. "This is a lot to take in, you understand. I need time to figure this out. You have to give me the decency of a minute."

I release a breath, sails billowing closed. "You're right. Of course. Coming at you like this, throwing a baby in your face." I rub my face, tangle my fingers in my hair as I hold it at the back of my neck and look at the ceiling for answers. "I'm scared, Locke. That's why I'm here, why I'm yelling at you. I'm so scared for that baby."

"Hey." Locke reaches out, strokes my arm. Then, as if afraid I'd bite it off, quickly draws it back. "It's a lot for both of us. But...you said Gainesville. Florida. So how long are you here?" He audibly gulps. "How long do I have? To decide?"

"I'm here for another twenty-four hours." I throw my hands out. "But I can be a tourist in New York City for a few days while you figure stuff out."

"Okay. Good." He pulls out his phone from his shorts. "Give me your number. I'll call you."

I do as he asks, but my stomach plummets over the idea that Lily's life will be decided when this guy calls me. A man who probably says those exact words to a hundred women, less than a third of whom he follows through with. A booty call. A sext. A *sorry-not-sorry* excuse.

"As soon as you can," I say to Locke, and make sure he's looking into my eyes, that I'm drilling in the consequences of his decision into Lily's mirror blues.

"Yep," he replies.

I'm ushered out the door, his large palm hovering near my back. He's tall, tanned, with a full head of sand-brown hair that would appear mussed with sex even if he were a virgin. True masculine beauty, but he's not enough for my Lil.

I pray he can be enough.

read this found family romance now

all in kindle unlimited

If you like your grump to be a single dad (or a dad-to-be), read:

Trust

Rock

Play

If you like your men to fall in love in a small town, read:

Lover

If you like your playboys with a dash of suspense, read:

Dare

If you like your tattooed bad boys and morally gray heroes, read:

Rebel

Crave

If you like thriller with your romance, read:

To Have and to Hold

From This Day Forward

If you want enemies to lovers with a side of secret societies and gothic academies, read:

Briarcliff Academy Series

Rival

Virtue

Fiend

Reign

Thorne of Winthorpe Series

Thorne

Crush

Liar

If you like dark romance and mafia men, read

Titan Falls Standalone

Cruel Promise

Corrupt Empire Duet

Underground Prince

Jaded Princess

About the Author

Ketley Allison has always been a romantic at heart and loves writing over-the-top, plot-twisty romance and characters. Ketley was born in Canada, moved to Australia, then to California, and finally to New York City to attend law school, but most of that time was spent in coffee shops thinking about her next book.

Her other passions include her two daughters, wine, coffee, Big Macs, her cat, and her husband, possibly in that order.

Visit Ketley's Website:

facebook.com/ketleyallison

tiktok.com/ketleyallison

instagram.com/ketleyallison